# Love in TIME

# Love in TIME

PENNY ZELLER

*Dedicated to all of those who have tasted the goodness of God's grace, mercy, and faithfulness.*

*And we know that all things work together for good to them that love God, to them who are called according to his purpose.* ~
Romans 8:28

# CHAPTER ONE
## MISSOULA, MONTANA, 1913

HAD SHE HEARD HIM correctly? He wished to dine with her for the noonday meal at the Bellerose Hotel and Restaurant?

Wayne Lingis was awaiting her answer, and she was sitting there in her dumbfounded state. Her gaze met his, and he smiled. That dapper smile she'd been fond of all these years. Her heart pounded in her chest, and she felt the blush creep up the back of her neck and onto her face. Did Wayne notice?

Arrosa Chapman took a deep breath. How not to sound overly thrilled even though she was—that was the question. "Yes, Wayne. That sounds lovely."

"Perfect. I'll meet you at the Bellerose Restaurant in two hours. At least it's not far to walk."

Her smile was one of hesitancy. It may not be far for him or even far for her were it not for her current circumstances. But as such, she'd need to give herself plenty of time to traverse the gift shop, walk through the hotel's main foyer, and then proceed to the restaurant on the other side.

"I look forward to it. Good to see you again, Arrosa."

She watched him leave with his purchase, his confident swagger one she'd memorized from all those years ago when she was secretly fond of him during their school years and beyond.

How was she supposed to wait calmly for the next two hours? Especially if the number of customers was lacking? The time would undoubtedly crawl by. They had much to converse about, and she wanted to hear all about his time at dental school in Chicago.

A thought popped into her mind unannounced. But what of Father's incarceration for embezzlement? Did Wayne know? If he didn't and he found out, would that affect his desire to partake in a noonday meal with her? To have anything to do with her at all? Arrosa worried her bottom lip. When their family fell upon hard times, Father made an unfortunate choice—a choice for which he ultimately was caught, and the Chapmans lost everything. During that time, Arrosa became ill with rheumatic fever, and now, all this time later, Father remained in jail in Bleakney, a town not far from Missoula. And Mother and Arrosa, with her sister, McKenna's help, started over with nothing but a few clothes and a drafty and dilapidated apartment in a neglected and poverty-stricken part of town.

But God had been faithful. Mother would mention that day after day, while Arrosa lay in bed with pain and fatigue so horrible she couldn't move. And it was true. While Arrosa had never given much thought to the Lord before all of this transpired, she was beginning to understand just *how* faithful He was. And who He was. And what He'd done for her.

Two customers entered, perused the tiny shop, then left. Arrosa peered at the clock on the shelf. An hour left. She'd be sure to start her journey to the restaurant beforehand because it took her a significant amount of time to hobble along, and she'd be exhausted when she reached the table. No sense in Wayne seeing her huffing and puffing to catch her breath.

What should she say if he asked about Father? Should she volunteer the information? The Lingis family was affluent and would likely never allow their son to associate with the likes of her after Father's transgression. If only Wayne had taken an interest in her years ago. After all, she'd fancied him and had admired him from afar. Well, mostly from afar. She could count on one hand the number of times they'd carried on a substantial conversation.

Today was one of those times, and she wanted nothing to hinder their time together. What if someday he sought to court her?

Clearly, she was swooning. While she'd dreamed of Wayne Lingis *noticing* her, it was unlikely he'd ask for her hand in courtship anytime soon. If he discovered Father's crime, maybe never.

Her twenty-fourth birthday came and went last month, and she was surely considered a spinster. Wayne was a year her senior. It was never too late for true love. Or so the novels said.

But Arrosa wasn't in a novel. This was real life, and she needed to quit swooning.

Finally, at a quarter to noon, Arrosa reached for her cane, closed the gift shop, locked the door, and tottered to the restaurant. The aroma of sirloin beef and baking bread infiltrated the air, and she inhaled deeply. When was the last time she'd eaten at a restaurant? Had eaten anything but crusts of bread, scrambled eggs, and beans?

Not that there was anything wrong with bread, eggs, and beans, for there wasn't. She'd been grateful for her mother's and sister's sacrifices that allowed them to have any food at all. And thankful for the donations Pastor Shay delivered monthly.

But, oh, to partake in a scrumptious meal once again! Perhaps even some sponge cake or blueberry pie. Her stomach rumbled in response as she followed the waitress to a table in the corner. She sat and tucked her cane beneath the table and against the wall so no one would trip were they to walk by.

Not five minutes later, she spied Wayne enter the restaurant, and she waved at him before pressing any wrinkles from the same skirt she wore every day to the gift shop. Did her hair look a fright? She should have checked it in the ornate mirror for sale at the store.

Wayne reached for her hand, and thankfully, she didn't have to stand, as that would have taken some time and caution not to bump the table. He kissed the back of her hand, his lips lingering for a brief moment—or at least she imagined they did—before he gently released her and took a seat. "I never knew you were working in the gift shop," he said, reaching for a menu.

"Yes, just three weeks ago."

He grinned, and her heart turned over. Goodness, but he was such a dapper man with his perfectly oiled brown hair, manicured mustache, and expensive suit. "It suits you."

"Thank you." It really *didn't* suit her since she was shy, and working in a retail position demanded she engage in conversation, but she wouldn't say as much. Instead, she would bask in the glow of time spent with Wayne. "So, you mentioned you were going to open a dental practice here in Missoula."

"Yes. I attended dental school in Chicago, and learned the most fascinating things." He flashed her a dazzling smile with his perfectly straight, white teeth, then proceeded to tell her all about his education.

The waitress arrived and took their orders, and after she left, Wayne asked, "How is your family?"

Should Arrosa mention Father? "Doing well." That was true. Never had she been happier than she had been the day she could walk more than just around the apartment. The day when the pain lessened, and her joints were no longer as swollen or achy. "McKenna is married and living in Hollow Creek."

"Hollow Creek? I've never heard of it."

"It's a small town beyond Bleakney."

"Ah, I see. I never figured McKenna to be happy in a village."

From the description McKenna had given of the town, Arrosa wouldn't consider Hollow Creek a village, but perhaps to someone so well-traveled as Wayne—especially having spent time in Chicago—Hollow Creek might seem like a meager hamlet.

"And your mother and father?"

Arrosa shifted in her chair. Fortunately, the waitress stopped to refill their lemonades and interrupted the moment, giving her more time to ponder how to best answer Wayne's question honestly. "Mother is doing well." That was true. Mother much preferred the hotel job over cleaning houses. Arrosa had begged her to consider working in the gift shop, but Mother said that it was better suited for Arrosa. In hindsight, Arrosa knew it was because her mother worried about the melancholy that settled in after so many months of being ill. Arrosa needed to get out of the apartment and commence living her life. So Mother had taken the hotel maid job. Tears burned her throat. Mother had sacrificed so much.

"And your father? How is he after…" Wayne cleared his throat.

Wayne knew? "He's doing better."

"Is he at Deer Lodge?"

"No, thankfully, he's still in Bleakney. They were able to allow him to remain there."

"Ah. Well, that's good news." Wayne placed his napkin in his lap just as the waitress arrived with their orders.

What a blessing Wayne seemed not to care about Father's crime. That meant there might be hope for the two of them, should he ever see her as more than a friend or acquaintance, or whatever he thought of her. She unfolded her own napkin and clasped her hands, readying herself to say grace.

Wayne was staring at her. "Shall we eat?"

"Oh, yes, it looks scrumptious. I was just going to pray first."

He arched one of his dark eyebrows at her. "Oh, all right. Proceed."

Praying before meals was a relatively new occurrence, but one Arrosa would not neglect. After all, she knew what it was like to be hungry, and any meal, no matter how small or how unsubstantial, was a gift from the Lord. A God who had most certainly provided in her family's darkest days. She bowed her head, offered her prayer of gratitude, then lifted her fork.

They continued in pleasant conversation with Wayne never again broaching the topic of Father's crime. The blueberry pie arrived, and although Arrosa could scarcely eat another bite, she'd not allow the delicacy to go to waste. She cut the pie in half and savored each bite before pushing the plate aside. "For later," she said. Oh, but wouldn't Mother enjoy the delectable treat? Arrosa would ask the waitress if she might borrow the plate and return it tomorrow. Once Wayne had left, of course.

"Perhaps we ought to do this again," Wayne said.

"Oh, yes! I mean, oh, yes, we should." She gathered her wits about her and added, "I have always loved eating at this restaurant and could never tire of it."

The fact was, she hadn't eaten at the Bellerose for at least a year until today.

Wayne chuckled. "I always did appreciate your charming wit."

He did? Heat infused her face. "Well, thank you."

"Certainly. And I daresay I insist we meet again for the noonday meal at some juncture in the future."

It was difficult not to allow her enthusiasm to show, but Arrosa tamped it down. "Yes, we shall." What a blessing that he wanted to spend more time with her. And what a blessing Wayne didn't care about Father's embezzlement.

"May I walk you back to the gift shop?"

"I'm fine. I'll go in a moment, but thank you all the same."

"I insist. My mother raised me to be a gentleman, after all. I'll even carry what's left of the blueberry pie."

"Oh. All right." It would be easier not to have to manage the cane *and* the plate of pie, especially with her unsteady gait.

Wayne walked around and pulled out her chair, and just as if they were courting, reached for her hand. "Just a moment," she squeaked. Clearly, Wayne's close proximity caused her to have a case of the nerves. She leaned down and retrieved her cane. "All right." She reached her hand to his, and it was then she noticed a peculiar expression on his face.

His eyebrows dipped. "Why do you have a cane?"

"Oh, I just—well, I just need it—for now." She'd refrain from saying she'd likely need it forever.

Wayne said nothing but continued to assist her from the chair. She wobbled on shaky legs and nearly toppled. Such happened on numerous occasions when her weak legs decided they didn't much care to stand after a lengthy time of sitting. The swollen and painful knee didn't help matters.

He steadied her as any gentleman would, but his demeanor had changed. Arrosa grasped the cane. "Thank you."

"You're welcome. Look, Arrosa, I just remembered I needed to meet with some colleagues posthaste." He peered at his timepiece. "I regret I won't be able to accompany you back to the gift shop after all."

"Oh." She attempted to hide her disappointment. "That's fine."

"Yes, well, I'll take my leave then."

"I look forward to our next noonday meal."

Wayne averted his gaze. "I'm sorry, Arrosa. I think it best we don't meet for another noonday meal."

Tears fogged her vision, and with effort, she attempted to keep her voice from wavering. "Is it because of Father? Because he's a good man, and while he shouldn't have done..."

"No, it's uh..." Wayne rubbed the back of his neck. "It's not your father. I know he was a respected member of the community and has paid his debt to society."

"Oh, well, thank you. Yes, he has. But then, why?" But she already knew the answer even before Wayne's gaze flitted from the cane to the door of the restaurant.

"I had no idea you were—I didn't realize you were crippled."

*Crippled.* The word stung her, even though it was true.

"I wish you well," he said, then turned on his heel to leave.

Pain so deep lodged in her throat, making it difficult to breathe.

# CHAPTER TWO

ARROSA HAD NO IDEA how she made it through the next three hours. Thankfully, only one customer visited the gift shop, and she was a woman of few words. The tears were so close to the surface that Arrosa wasn't sure she could keep her emotions in check if the slightest bit of overt kindness was shown.

Finally, at five o'clock, Mother arrived with the wheelchair someone at church had loaned them. "I thought you would enjoy this," Arrosa said, pointing at the piece of blueberry pie.

"Thank you!"

Arrosa knew Mother was doing her best to eat the pie in a ladylike fashion, but she also knew her mother was likely hungry after a day of grueling cleaning. If only Arrosa could have saved some of her other food as well.

"How was your day?"

Arrosa blinked. This wasn't the place to share the disappointment and hurt that Wayne caused. "Fine."

Mother tilted her head, concern in her weary countenance. She knew something was amiss, but Arrosa would wait until they were home before sharing. She limped to the wheelchair and took a seat. Mother pushed her out of the gift shop.

Random raindrops pelted them as Mother hastily pushed her down the boardwalk past the numerous businesses. A gust of wind caused Arrosa to shiver, and lightning flashed across the sky. Thunder roared, and people rushed to and fro to their destinations. The rain grew heavier, and Mother attempted to duck beneath the canopies of several of the storefronts as she quickened her pace. The wheelchair bumbled along, its wheels nearly getting stuck several times. "If this continues tomorrow, we'll have to take the streetcar." Mother's muffled voice competed with the storm's cacophony.

Arrosa ducked her head. Why couldn't the nasty weather have waited until they were safely in their apartment?

Tears fell then, competing with the raindrops. If she weren't so weak, and if her wrists, ankles, and especially her right knee weren't still swollen, she could walk with Mother.

If she weren't sickly and feeble and "crippled", as Wayne had so eloquently stated, then she would be working longer hours and making better wages. Such would enable them to take the streetcar each day, rather than battle the fickle early-spring weather.

If only...

A squelched sob burst from her mouth, and she hastily refrained from allowing her emotions to get the best of her. Mother needn't have to stop and console her while battling a rainstorm and sidestepping puddles.

The wind blew forcefully and slapped hard raindrops against Arrosa's cheeks. She closed her eyes and gripped her cane in one hand and the wheelchair's armrest with the other. Why did the journey to the apartment seem lengthier than usual?

An automobile passed and splashed them with dirty street water. Arrosa swiped at her hair as she gasped for breath. They had no business being out on such a frigid and abysmal evening. But what choice did they have?

A memory flashed through her mind of Father's 1912 Packard with its comfortable leather seats. They would be home in a jiffy if they still had the beautiful blue automobile.

Home.

Their 7,000-square-foot stately home, with its Doric columns and Honduran mahogany throughout, was the envy of many in their social circles. At one time, they'd hosted over five hundred guests. The Chapman home with its accompanying carriage house, acreage, and well-maintained gardens, was one of the most glamorous homes in Missoula.

Now lived in by someone else.

Arrosa strained her eyes to see the blurred street sign. Heersink Avenue. Almost there.

What she wouldn't give to trade Mother places. That she would be the one to push another in a wheelchair down the city streets. A drunkard staggered by mumbling something indiscernible. The storm clouds blocked any remaining sunlight, and Arrosa shivered almost as much from the dreary surroundings as from the cold. Finally, they reached Thorburn Street. McKenna mentioned many times that the area reminded her of photographs of the tenements in New York with the clothesline strung across nearly dilapidated apartment buildings. Arrosa agreed.

The timeworn, run-down, orange brick building announcing to all that they had entered an area of squalor stood before them. She was grateful to have a roof over their heads, but there were so many times when she wondered just how safe they were staying here. Mother would remind her that the Lord would keep them safe, that they ought not fret.

Easy to say, difficult to put into practice. But the more Arrosa learned about her Heavenly Father, the more she came to trust him. Especially since he had brought her through her horrible rheumatic fever. Some weren't as fortunate.

Mother stopped the wheelchair and assisted Arrosa from it. She teetered precariously on her cane as she and Mother traversed up the crumbling front porch stairs. At least Mother had been able to secure a room on the bottom floor to replace their former one on the top floor. This one was much the same as the other one. Even though Mother and Arrosa did their best to keep them clean, no amount of scrubbing removed years of filth on the dirt-crusted, stained floors. A musty smell lingered in the room, despite Mother opening the windows whenever the weather allowed, and their makeshift table and two chairs, one with a broken leg, remained in the center of the bleak room. Fortunately, there was electricity and running water. If Arrosa had to skedaddle outside every time she needed to use the privy, she didn't know how she would have managed, especially in her condition.

She may have resorted to a chamber pot.

Her breath came in gasps, and she took a seat in one of the chairs. Her heart ached when she saw Mother with her mud-splattered skirt and exhaustion in her countenance. "Thank you," she whispered.

Mother took a seat and reached across the table to take Arrosa's cold hands in her own. "We made it through another day. Praise the Lord for His providence. Now, tell me about your day. About your noonday meal with the handsome Wayne Lingis."

The emotion that had built throughout the day rose to the surface and fogged her vision. She proceeded to tell Mother about what Wayne had said, and about the hurt that settled so deeply into her heart. She wished she were strong and hardy like McKenna. But she wasn't. She had always been more delicate and fragile in body and emotions, even before the illness.

"I am so sorry, Arrosa." You didn't deserve that. Mother scooted her chair closer, and Arrosa rested her head on Mother's shoulder. Mother patted her hair. "People can be so cruel." Mother consoled her as the minutes ticked by.

Someday, they would move on from the apartment and hopefully join McKenna in Hollow Creek. Her sister still sent money when she could, and Father's jail sentence grew shorter by the day. Oh, but for all of them to be together again.

The following day, Arrosa was busily organizing some items on the shelf in the gift shop when two ladies entered. They paid her nary a mind and proceeded to the farthest corner to a display of the latest shipment of knickknacks. Before long, they had amassed an armload of items and marched to the counter. Arrosa turned and smiled. "Good afternoon."

She hadn't recognized them until now—two high society women Mother's age.

"Do excuse us a moment," said Mrs. Wargo, a redhead with an exaggerated sense of self.

"Isn't that Egbert Chapman's daughter?" asked the other, a curly-haired brunette named Mrs. Benchouk.

If they were attempting to speak in hushed tones, they were failing miserably.

"Indeed."

"Ugh. What a travesty to see her here."

"I'm surprised they allow her to be in the employ of the Bellerose. She could be a chip off the old block, as the saying goes."

"Indisputably."

They both returned to the counter where Arrosa was adding the totals of the items.

"We won't be needing those." Mrs. Wargo sneered.

"We can't and won't purchase anything from the likes of someone whose father embezzled from the bank," declared Mrs. Benchouk.

"I can't believe one would do such a thing, and to think we entertained your family in our homes. Suppose during one of those visits, our silver had gone missing." She pointed her nose in the air. "If it had, we would, for certain, know who to blame."

"Utterly distasteful individual if you ask me. But thankfully, Egbert is in prison in Deer Lodge now, and our hard-earned money is safe at last."

Arrosa wouldn't correct Mrs. Benchouk and tell her that Father was instead in the Bleakney jail. She trembled as she removed the porcelain figurines from the brown paper and prepared to return them to the farthest corner shelf. She'd wait until after the women left. No sense in giving them more fodder when they saw her need for a cane.

That evening, after she and Mother returned home, the mailman delivered a letter from McKenna. They sat in their chairs at the table, and Mother opened the envelope and withdrew the missive from inside. McKenna's flowing handwriting leapt from the page.

*Dearest Mother and Arrosa,*

*I hope this finds you doing well. I miss you both so very much. I have enclosed some funds. I know it's not much, but I am hopeful it will help with necessities.*

*How are you both faring? I am doing well. It seems like so long that I must wait for this little one to be born, and I can say that I am rather impatient.*

*Arrosa, I have stupendous news for you. Mrs. Emilie Evanson, a dear friend of mine, is in need of a nanny. She is pregnant and bedridden. Her four children are a handful, but they are such dears, and I do believe you would be perfect for the position. I mentioned your name the other day when I paid her a visit to deliver some items from the boutique.*

*Might you be interested? If so, the job would start immediately. She would pay for your train ticket to Hollow Creek, and you would receive room and board as well as a stipend.*

*Mother, I do hope you will join us in Hollow Creek as well. I am only working at the boutique three days a week, but Aunt Julia Mathilda has mentioned she would like to hire a full-time employee so that it might be open all five days. Would you be willing to consider it? I know in the past it has caused you some apprehension, but I have no doubt you would do a fine job.*

*Clayton and I were able to visit Father recently. What a marvelous day it will be when he is released. He was doing well and asked that I tell you both hello.*

*Please do write and tell me how you fare. Arrosa, let me know posthaste if you are interested in the nanny position. Emilie is a kind and godly woman, and I am confident you will enjoy being in her employ.*

*With Love,*
*McKenna*


"Arrosa, this is such marvelous news!"

Arrosa was still attempting to recover from the shock. Mother handed her the letter, and with a trembling hand, she re-read McKenna's words.

A nanny position? In Hollow Creek? She loved children and hoped to have a passel of them herself someday. Or rather, *had* hoped. With a diagnosis consisting of long-lasting fatigue, joint pain, and the potential for heart issues, she wasn't so sure such a dream was now possible.

But she could care for another's children.

Mother draped an arm around her shoulders. "This is the perfect opportunity. What do you think?"

"I have always loved children."

"And you are good with them. I recall that from when we would have our society meetings, and the children were drawn to you." Mother smiled. "And it would be a way for you to relocate from Missoula to Hollow Creek."

Arrosa stared into Mother's lovely but weary face. More wrinkles fanned her eyes in recent days, and a random assortment of gray hairs framed the area around her ears and forehead. Some of that stress was due to Mother caring for Arrosa, and the guilt weaseled its way into Arrosa's heart. Her chest tightened. She couldn't, wouldn't, just leave Mother here in Missoula, no matter how promising the position sounded. "I can't leave you here, Mother."

"Pshaw. You can and you should. While the choice is ultimately up to you, I would highly recommend it. Where else would you be able to work and live in a fine home?" Mother gestured toward the decrepit room. "You would no longer have to live here, you would always have enough to eat, and you would be doing something that you enjoy. I daresay prayer is in order, but it is clearly an opportunity not to be missed, especially since McKenna has vouched for Mrs. Evanson."

"Even if it paid a hundred dollars a day and I had a room like the one I had in our former home, I'd scarcely say yes. Not with leaving you here to work as a maid at the hotel."

Something flickered in Mother's eyes. "I appreciate your loyalty, Arrosa. As for working as a maid at the hotel—"

"I didn't mean to make it sound as though it is a disparaging position, I just—" Emotion burned her throat. Mother couldn't help that that was the only job available. Not even Aunt Julia Mathilda had been able to hire her.

Mother drew Arrosa closer. "I did not take it as such. No one in our social standing would have ever imagined that I would work as a maid in the Bellerose Hotel, especially not myself. I've never been overly fond of cleaning, and making beds and ensuring clean linens is not on my list of most desirable tasks. However, do you remember the day when I was searching for a job?"

Arrosa did recall that day. She'd been so sick that she could barely lift her arms. The weakness had taken over her entire body. She'd suffered from involuntary twitches, and the chest pain was nearly her undoing. But that day, Mother had been searching for a job all throughout Missoula. A city of that size surely would have offered more opportunities. Yet the only prospects for a woman lacking work experience were as a maid. So Mother first started cleaning in the homes of a few former friends from their high society circle. She would walk to and from the mansions that she'd formerly visited for parties, balls, and charitable meetings, and would instead tend to laundry duties and cleaning. Recently, she was able to secure a job at the Bellerose Hotel for slightly better pay, shorter hours, and more respect. "Yes, I do remember."

"It was not a pleasant time in my life. What if I were unable to locate employment? What would happen to my daughters, especially the one who was bedridden?"

"I'm so sorry, Mother."

"I don't tell you this to shame you or to place undue guilt on you. Rather, I tell you this so that you can witness for yourself God's fingerprints all over every part of our lives."

"Even over Father's embezzling and putting us into this predicament?" But even as she said it, she regretted the words. Father had embezzled to pay the debt that they'd accumulated by being extravagant, yes, but also to pay for treatments for Arrosa.

Expensive treatments that never worked.

Her eyes misted. "I should not have said that."

Mother reached for her hand. "What Father did was a crime. Well, yes, we had begun to live above our means, and that was entirely our fault, but he wanted so desperately for you to be healed."

"I know that, and I know how much he loves me."

"Very much so, yes. He always talked of his girls and how much he cared about them, even when long hours at the bank commanded his time. We can always look back and see things that we would like to have changed. Would he have wanted to go about paying off our debt and securing treatments for you in a more honest way? Of course. But what was done has been done, he is paying his debt to society by serving his time, and he has been ordered to pay back some of the funds not covered by the sale of our possessions. I daresay your father is a changed man after being convicted. God can take something so utterly awful and turn it to good. Yes, your father is still in jail, but not in Deer Lodge. That is a blessing."

Mother took a sip of the water from the stained, used teacup someone had donated. While her life had changed dramatically, Mother would always be a lady and always exhibit proper etiquette. "Before this all happened, your father had no time for the Lord. And neither did I. But now, we have both surrendered our lives to the Savior we never gave an ounce of our time to in the past. The Savior who still loved us even when we would attend church only during Christmas and Easter, and only for show."

Arrosa nodded. "Yes, that is a blessing."

"Indeed. An eternal blessing. Especially since both of our daughters are also walking in faith. So the day that I started searching for employment working for some of our former friends, it was distressing at times, to say the least. I won't go into details, but I was relieved of both of those positions due to no fault of my own. At that point, I wondered how I would be able to provide for us. Thankfully, McKenna was working so very hard in Hollow Creek and sending us money, and the church was helping us. Both of those blessings I attribute to God's mercy. As I also do for the position at the Bellerose Hotel. It may not be my dream job, but it is honest work nonetheless, and I am extremely grateful for it."

"I just…it was at one time beneath us."

"Yes, it was. But, honestly, no job should be beneath us. We are not so good that we should elevate ourselves above certain duties. I realize that now. In my snobbery, I thought myself better than others. Now, I see things differently. I have been humbled. I have repented, and in my repentance, the Lord has blessed us richly by giving me the job at the hotel."

"I just want us all to be together again."

"As do I."

"Would you consider moving to Hollow Creek and working at the boutique?"

"Very much so, yes. But I gave my boss my word that I will stay at the hotel for at least another month. I will not go back on that."

"But your boss might allow you to leave sooner."

"Doubtful as we are approaching our busy season, but I have been in prayer about moving to Hollow Creek as well. Especially since once your father is released, it would do us good to start over in another location. We'll pray for the Lord's guidance about you accepting the nanny position and me moving there after I have fulfilled my promise."

Arrosa bit her lip. "Yes, I agree. And yes, I would like to be a nanny."

"You would make a fine one. Now, then, shall we see what we can find in the cupboards for supper?"

With effort, Arrosa stood to assist Mother with preparations. There was no one she respected more than the woman who had sacrificed so much. As Mother hummed while setting a pan on the stove, Arrosa realized there was something about her day that she'd not share.

She'd not divulge to Mother about the two women who'd entered the hotel gift shop and spewed hateful words and refused to make a purchase, for it would only discourage her mother. But Arrosa would pray that the Lord would help her to forgive Mrs. Wargo and Mrs. Benchouk.

And that He would make it clear whether or not she should accept the nanny position at the Evanson Ranch.

# CHAPTER THREE

MALACHI CALLAHAN WIPED HIS hands on his jeans and walked up the steps of the Evanson home after being summoned because Mrs. Evanson needed to speak with him. Sienna, one of the maids, led him to where his employer sat surrounded by a pile of pillows and a bright quilt.

"Ma'am? Is everything all right? Do you need me to fetch Doc?" He took his responsibilities very seriously.

Mrs. Evanson smiled at him, but he could see from her pale face and the dark circles beneath her eyes that she wasn't feeling well due to her pregnancy. "No, but thank you. I was hoping you could drive into town and retrieve Arrosa Chapman from the train depot. Thad and Pete are in Helena, and Vera and Morris are minding the children."

"Arrosa Chapman?"

"Yes, she's McKenna Beringer's sister. McKenna and Clayton are out of town as well."

"Reckon I can do that, ma'am."

Mrs. Evanson smiled. "Thank you so much. I can't imagine how she would feel with no one to retrieve her, let alone greet her, when she arrives in an unfamiliar town. She boarded the three o'clock train."

"Yes, ma'am. And how will I know who she is?" While Malachi hadn't yet ridden this particular train, he *had* seen the vast number of folks disembark while he'd been seeing to errands in town.

"She is about your age with auburn hair. Perhaps the best plan would be to make a sign with her name for her to see when she steps off the train."

He could do that.

"And feel free to take one of the two automobiles."

He couldn't do that. "If it's all the same to you, I'd prefer to drive the wagon."

Mrs. Evanson's brows dipped. "All right. That's fine. Thank you, Malachi."

"You're welcome, ma'am." Malachi left, and several minutes later, he prepared to leave the house when he nearly ran into little Ephraim Evanson, who was bounding down the hall, followed by his sister, Adelia, and behind her, his other sister, Mamie, wheeling as fast as she could in her wheelchair.

Ephraim stopped and huffed and puffed and gulped for air, attempting to catch his breath. "Hey, there, Uncle Malachi. Do you want to play tag with us?"

Somehow, between the time Malachi was hired as a ranch hand last year and now, the children had all resorted to calling him "Uncle", even though he wasn't related and had never—and would likely never—be an uncle because he had no relatives, except…

Vera, with her unkempt appearance, rumpled skirt, and baby Thad Junior in her arms, tossed Malachi a flustered look before addressing the children. "But goodness, I'm far too old for such shenanigans."

"Come on, Grandma Vera! We can't play tag in here." Adelia reversed course and took Vera, an elderly Evanson Ranch employee, by the hand.

"Sure you don't want to play tag, Malachi?" Vera asked.

He chuckled and shook his head. "No, thank you, Grandma Vera."

She removed her hand from Adelia's just briefly enough to swat Malachi on the arm. "All right then, Uncle Malachi."

They shared a laugh before Vera was tugged away, down the porch steps, and outside into the lush front yard.

"Mamie, do you need help?" he asked the tiny girl in the wheelchair.

"No, Uncle. I'm fine. Daddy made the ramp, so now I can get off the porch much easier." With amazing proficiency, she veered around him and through the open front door.

Malachi marveled at how far she had come in the time since the Evansons adopted her. It just went to prove what a difference a good home could make in a child's life.

Not that he would know anything about that, because he didn't.

Adelia, too. The limp she'd been born with had become less obvious in recent months. Probably all the running and playing she did. That and having to keep up with the rambunctious Ephraim.

Malachi finished some chores, then hitched the horses to the wagon and drove to town to meet Miss Chapman. While he'd like to someday drive an automobile, he had no training, and the last thing he wanted to do was crash and ruin something owned by his employers. He liked this job. Needed this job. And would do whatever it took to keep *this* job.

He whistled as he steered the wagon into town, down Main Street, and to the train station. Hollow Creek had grown just in the time he'd lived here, which hadn't been long. A new hotel—the only one in town—was being built on the corner of Main and Sixth, and a drug store moved into the vacant building beside the mercantile. A new dentist moved in last year, by the name of Dr. Molar, as well as the opening of a new shop called Miss Julia Mathilda's Fine Dresses. More automobiles drove the streets, and someone talked of opening a library.

Town growth was fine with him as long as it didn't bring in more riffraff. One sort of riffraff in particular.

Malachi pulled the wagon to the side and parked. In the distance, the train whistle and the accompanying roar of the wheels on the tracks indicated the train was preparing to enter town. He disembarked, grabbed the paper sign, and strode toward the depot.

The train came to a stop, and within several minutes, the doors opened, and passengers flooded the boardwalk. Malachi inched closer and held up the sign. Maybe Miss Chapman had been delayed. Or decided not to arrive in Hollow Creek today. He scanned the crowd for an auburn-haired woman of about his age, as Mrs. Evanson mentioned. A few seconds later, he caught the gaze of a young woman with a cane. She must have noticed his sign because she ambled toward him with a serious demeanor.

"Miss Arrosa Chapman?"

"Yes."

He took a step and put the sign down at his side. "I'm Malachi Callahan. Mrs. Evanson asked if I could fetch you from the train station and deliver you to the Evanson Ranch."

"Oh?" She angled her head and peered around him. Was she hoping someone else had arrived to retrieve her?

"Mrs. Evanson regrets that she was unable to retrieve you, but she is bedridden. Mr. Evanson is currently on a trip."

Her dark eyebrows knitted, but she said nothing.

"Well, I-uh-I'm parked over here." He gestured in the direction of the wagon. "I can take that for you." He reached for the carpetbag, which she gladly relinquished. "Do you have a suitcase or a trunk?" From her appearance, she was an elegant woman, and he figured she had three or four trunks for him to haul to the wagon.

"Just one suitcase. It's over there." She angled herself somewhat unsteadily and nodded to a line of suitcases and trunks the porter unloaded onto the boardwalk. "It's the brown one."

"No offense, ma'am, but several of them are brown."

"Oh, yes. That is true. Well, mine is the tattered one." She started to walk with him to the line of suitcases and trunks.

"Miss Chapman, if it's all the same to you, I can easily fetch it and meet you back here."

She blinked. "All right."

He hoped he hadn't upset her, but there really was no sense in her struggling through the thick crowd of people when he could grab the suitcase and be back in a jiffy.

Miss Chapman was correct about the tattered suitcase. He'd never seen such a dilapidated piece of luggage. Faded, worn, and scratched, it appeared to have been through a few wars, or at least skirmishes. He clasped the handle and strode back to the woman. Shuffling the carpetbag, suitcase, and sign to one hand, he offered his arm. "I'll assist you to the wagon," he said.

"Thank you kindly." She placed a hand through the crook of his elbow.

Now he wished he'd parked closer. Malachi walked slowly, ensuring he didn't cause her any more distress than she already faced. Should he move the wagon closer? But if so, where would he park? The congested area left no other alternative. He was about to ask her if she needed to rest a minute, but a glance at her proud profile told him she'd not take kindly to any insinuation that she was anything but capable of walking the entire distance.

So instead, he asked, "Do you mind if we stop a minute? I need to adjust the luggage."

"Certainly."

He stopped and took his time shuffling the carpetbag and luggage in his left hand. "Sure is a nice day."

"Indeed."

"Have you ever been to Hollow Creek before?"

"No, I haven't. Sadly, I missed my sister's wedding."

He caught the pain in her eyes before she focused her attention on passersby. "I'm sorry to hear that, ma'am."

"Thank you. But I do look forward to visiting with her now that I'm here." Her sorrow was quickly replaced with a smile. "Do you know my sister and her husband?"

"I do know the sheriff, yes, and have spoken to your sister a handful of times."

"She works at Miss Julia Mathida's Dress Shop, which is owned by our aunt in Missoula. I trust you haven't been to the boutique?"

The slight lilt in her voice convinced him she wasn't serious. He laughed. "No. Can't say as I have. Now, if it were the livery, hardware store, or mercantile, then yes."

Miss Chapman didn't resemble her sister. While McKenna Beringer had blonde hair and blue eyes, Miss Chapman had auburn-colored hair and hazel eyes. They both, however, did have a dimple in their chins, although Miss Chapman's was more pronounced. She also had a delicate beauty about her. Lest she think he was staring, he hastily averted his gaze and cleared his throat. "Well, reckon we should continue on."

He exchanged greetings with the passersby. It had taken some time for him to become accepted in this town, by his way of thinking, anyhow. But now, between spending time in town conducting errands for the ranch and attending church faithfully, he'd come to know a good lot of the folks who called Hollow Creek and the surrounding area home.

"This seems like a friendly town."

Miss Chapman's voice brought him back to the present. "Most folks here are friendly, yes."

Finally, after one more block, they reached their destination. "Here it is."

Miss Chapman turned her head to the right, then to the left. "There?" she asked, pointing to a Studebaker.

"No, sorry, ma'am. It's the wagon."

"The wagon?"

"Yes."

Her eyes widened as her shoulders slumped slightly. "Oh. I see."

"Sorry, but while Mrs. Evanson suggested I take one of the automobiles, I figured the wagon would be better." A second after the words left his mouth, he regretted them. How could a wagon be better for someone who needed the assistance of a cane? The motorcar would have allowed Miss Chapman easier access and would have been a smoother, quicker ride to the ranch. If only he'd decided on it instead. Even though he'd never driven one and could end up in a ravine like it was reported Tippi Harkins—now Tippi Toolin—had done, it would have made transport easier for Miss Chapman.

Malachi regarded her. Was it his imagination, or were her eyes glistening? Was she about to cry? If so, he had no idea how to deal with that type of emotion. Or any emotion, really. He'd stuffed his own emotions away—carefully hidden, where no one would see them. "I-uh-please don't fret, Miss Chapman. I'll lift you into the wagon straightaway."

"Oh, yes, I would appreciate that." Her gaze traveled to her cane.

And he did his best to act nonchalant. No sense in embarrassing her. "Have you ever ridden in a wagon?"

"No, I have not. A buggy, yes, but never a wagon."

"Well, you're in for an adventure."

That brought a smile to her face, and he breathed a sigh of relief. "I'll put your bag, suitcase, and cane in the back and then assist you into the wagon." Malachi carefully did so, then lifted her onto the buckboard. She gripped his shoulders, and for a minute, he wasn't sure she would release him.

"Is my cane in the wagon?"

"It is."

That seemed to settle her slightly, but she proceeded to clutch the side of the wagon as if in fear for her life.

"There are some ruts from recent rains, but we'll drive slowly," he said, climbing up beside her.

She worried her lip. "I know I sound like a ninny, but I've never ridden in such a contraption before."

"It's not so bad. Automobiles are smoother and quicker, but this'll get us where we need to go." He flicked the reins and gingerly pulled out of his parking spot. He'd drive as slowly as necessary to calm her fears. "So, what brings you to the ranch?"

"I'll be working for Mrs. Evanson, tending to the children."

"Ah, well, Vera will appreciate that. Poor woman was a bit haggard when I left earlier."

"Oh?"

Malachi chuckled. "Vera is the hired help, but more like a grandma to those children, well, one of their grandmas anyway. Mrs. Evanson's parents visit from time to time. But Vera's getting up there in years, so I'm sure she'll be happy to pass the children to you."

"Are they rambunctious children?"

"Somewhat, I reckon, but I don't really know a lot about children. They love to play tag and are a happy lot. I think you'll like them."

"Oh, I'm sure I will." She bobbed her head quickly, and for a minute, he thought she'd relaxed her hold on the wagon seat slightly.

That was until they inadvertently hit a bump. Her free hand flung toward him and gripped his arm. "But goodness. Is it possible for someone to bounce plumb out of a wagon?"

He stopped just to ensure she was all right. "Yes, ma'am, that could happen, but I won't let you bounce out of the wagon."

Miss Chapman maintained her grip on his arm, and he was beginning to lose feeling in his fingers. His eyes darted to her hand.

"Oh, dear. I do apologize."

"Not a concern, Miss Chapman. You just hang on to my arm for as long as you need to." He flicked the reins again, and she, indeed, held on to his arm for several more minutes. Finally, when the Evanson Ranch was in sight, she released her hold.

Malachi covertly opened and shut his hand and wiggled his fingers to get the feeling back in them.

When she whipped her head back around after taking in the view, her attention settled on his open and closing hand, an unspoken question on her face.

"Ever since last winter, when my hands froze because I'd forgotten to put on my gloves and thought it would be fine to walk outside for a few minutes and unhitch the horses, this hand has been a little stiff."

It was true. He had forgotten to put his gloves on, and it was also true that from time to time, the fingers on his right hand stiffened, so he wasn't telling an untruth. But he hoped his words would alleviate any disquietude she may have from clutching his arm. He didn't know Miss Chapman, but he did want her to feel comfortable and accepted at the ranch.

"I am so sorry to hear that."

He removed his hat, wiped the sweat off his brow from the hotter-than-usual spring day, then slapped it back on his head. "Thank you. Much obliged for that. You're from Missoula, correct?" While he didn't want to make a nuisance of himself with so many questions, he was genuinely interested and wanted to put her at ease.

"I am, yes."

"Ever been to a small town?"

"In our travels, yes, but only passing through."

"This must be quite different from what you're accustomed to, then."

"Indeed. I've only ever lived in the city. At any moment, I expect to see tall buildings, multiple automobiles, and streetcars, and to hear the sounds of the city."

All of those things would be enough to drive a man crazy. Malachi always relished the quiet and solitude of the ranch. "I've never lived in a city. Sounds chaotic."

"I wouldn't say chaotic, at least not in my opinion. Sometimes the bustling of the city is exciting."

He regarded her. "Reckon I wouldn't do well in the city. I like to have plenty of room to stretch my legs."

"While I love the city, there are some things that aren't so pleasant."

An indiscernible shadow crossed her face, and he waited for her to continue. When she didn't, he nodded to the expansive white house surrounded by manicured gardens and more acres of ranchland than he could count. The majestic snow-tipped mountains in the background provided the perfect backdrop. To wake up every day to that sight had been a pure blessing from God. Barnabas's dream had become Malachi's, and he thanked the Good Lord often for leading him to the town of Hollow Creek. Thankfully, the Lord hadn't seen fit to plop him in the desert. He much preferred the mountainous pines to cacti. He didn't mind the spikey sagebrush in some areas, but for him, the ruggedness of the high-reaching mountain tops was like none other. "There it is, just up ahead."

"What a lovely setting," she breathed.

"I think so too. Some places you just know the Lord spent extra time on. You should see the mountains in the wintertime. Still lots of snow at the higher elevations, but after that first dusting, when the white mixes with the blue-green of the pines, and then a blue sky overhead? It's almost too beautiful to look at."

"Sometimes, on a perfectly clear day, I could see the mountains from our veranda. You're correct in that it was almost too beautiful to behold."

A thought entered his mind. The woman beside him didn't appear to be wealthy, and especially not with her one tattered suitcase. However, she spoke as someone of higher society, and he'd never known anyone with a veranda besides the Evansons and a former boss at a previous ranch.

"You'll like Mrs. Evanson. She and Thad are nice folks." He should know. The Evansons had altered the course of Malachi's life when Thad had offered him a job last year. Malachi situated the wagon as close to the house as possible and set the brake.

"What a lovely home." Wistfulness flashed across her face, and she nibbled on her bottom lip. Was she worried she couldn't ascend the stairs? How had she come to need a cane?

"Mamie, the youngest daughter, is in a wheelchair. But Mr. Evanson built a ramp to make it easier for her to enter and exit the porch."

"A little girl in a wheelchair? The poor dear."

"Yes, but Mamie doesn't let anything stop her. She's headstrong and capable, that one." He thought, as he did on occasion, how the Evansons had adopted all three of their older children from the orphanage and had given them a forever home.

A forever home with loving parents.

A weight settled in his chest. If only every child could be so fortunate.

"Mr. Callahan?"

"What? Pardon?" Her words drew him from his thoughts.

"I do appreciate you retrieving me, Mr. Callahan."

Lest she think he needed a hearing trumpet, he'd better explain himself. "I apologize, Miss Chapman. I was just beholding those amazing mountains. And you can call me Malachi. I don't know who you're talking to when you say Mr. Callahan. Most folks call me Malachi, anyhow. You'll find it's informal here on the Evanson Ranch."

"And you may call me Arrosa."

"Arrosa it is."

"Mr. Callahan likely makes you think one is speaking to your father." A rosy blush covered her face.

"My father?"

"Yes, the other Mr. Callahan."

He cleared his throat. "Sure." He'd not let anyone know that he'd changed his name for the very purpose of not being confused with his father.

# CHAPTER FOUR

SHE'D KNOWN MCKENNA WOULDN'T be able to retrieve her from the train depot since she and Clayton were out of town, but she hadn't anticipated one of Emilie Evanson's employees doing so.

Malachi Callahan seemed to be a pleasant fellow and, for certain, a gentlemanly one. She appreciated that he drove slower than he could have due to her obvious apprehension by clutching his arm and the side of the wagon.

Hollow Creek was different in many ways from what she expected. While McKenna had described it in her letters, and Mother had given her some insight since both she and Father had attended McKenna's wedding, still, she had not realized it would be so small. There was no streetcar, no tall buildings, only one main street, and the distance from town to the Evanson Ranch, while likely not far to those who traveled it often, seemed a lengthy distance to Arrosa.

She'd wanted to attend her sister's wedding, but she'd been too ill at the time; however, she had met Clayton, McKenna's husband, and approved of him, much to McKenna's delight. She and McKenna had always been close, so she was grateful that Clayton appeared to be a godly and protective husband. Hopefully, they would return to Hollow Creek soon from their trip. Arrosa couldn't wait to see her sister.

They entered the house, and Malachi set her suitcase down just inside the door. At that moment, a harried older woman with a baby boy in her arms pootled after two children excitedly dashing to the front door, followed by a girl in a wheelchair. He introduced her to Vera. "A pleasure to meet you. Those young ones who just breezed past are your charges. It's their first day playing outside after several days of rain, so they're overly enthusiastic. We came in to eat, and it was all they could do to take a second to consume some sustenance before dashing back outside."

"It's nice to meet you, Vera."

"Grandma Vera, are you coming?" The little girl in the wheelchair remained on the porch.

"I'm coming, dear." She smiled at Arrosa. "I best be on my way. We're glad you're here."

A moment of despair entered Arrosa's mind. Would she be able to care for the energetic Evanson children in her condition?

"I'll introduce you to the maids, Sienna and Roxanne, and Cook," Malachi was saying.

"I am a stickler when it comes to the times I serve food," said Cook, a round woman with an expansive girth and curly gray hair. "If you wish to eat at unconventional times, I will need to know in advance. Otherwise, please adhere to the breakfast, noonday, and supper timeframes. Right, Malachi?"

"Yes, ma'am." Malachi rubbed his jaw. "Cook doesn't appreciate having to warm a meal again after supper."

Cook swatted Malachi on the arm. "This young man knows full well the appropriate times for supper, yet he insists on lollygagging outside tending to cattle rather than eating. Of course, I always suggest that he can eat in the bunkhouse as an alternative."

Malachi straightened his posture and sweetened the tone of his voice. "My dear Cook, bread crusts and a can of fruit are far less appealing than your delicious, scrumptious, decadent meals."

"Delicious, scrumptious, and decadent. This one here is a charming one." She smiled and focused her attention on Arrosa. "Welcome to the Evanson Ranch, Arrosa. I know I speak for everyone here when I say we're glad to have you."

"Thank you."

"You're welcome. Sienna just delivered some tea to Emilie, so I know she's awake. Her room is up the stairs and to the right."

Up the stairs? Of course, a home of this size had a second, and possibly a third, level. She'd seen stairs when she'd entered before fixing her attention on the children and Vera. Arrosa couldn't very well delay meeting her employer, but the thought of a staircase sent shivers of anxiety through her.

They exited the kitchen, and Malachi left her side to speak with a lanky young man who'd entered through the front door.

Arrosa stood just at the bottom of the steps, fixating on the daunting staircase, which consisted of one set of stairs, a landing, and a second set of stairs. Her stomach clenched into tight coils. There was no way she could scale them. She gripped her cane so tightly that the muscles from her fingers to her forearm and all the way to her neck tensed. She never should have thought she could manage such a feat, given her current circumstances. Why had she thought that one of the most well-known and respected ranches in Montana would have a house with only one level?

Footsteps behind her drew her from her predicament. Malachi strode to the hall tree near the front door, removed his hat, and hung it on a hook. He ran a hand through his wavy blond hair and started in her direction.

She returned her attention to the stairs. She'd never been one to give up. To admit defeat.

Yet she might as well climb a mountain as struggle up the steep wooden stairs.

"I can help you."

Malachi was now standing beside her, a broad smile on his face.

"I don't want to take you from your work." Her voice quivered, and she regretted the tears that squeezed from the corners of her eyes.

He shrugged. "I have a task awaiting me outside that I'm not eagerly anticipating, so I'd be happy to assist you."

She vacillated between allowing his assistance and asking him to deliver a message to Mrs. Evanson, indicating she'd changed her mind about being a nanny. She swallowed the lump that had formed in her throat.

"Besides Mr. and Mrs. Evanson's room, there is only one other room upstairs of concern for caring for the children, and that's the playroom." Kindness shone in his blue eyes. "And from what I've seen in my time here, they most often prefer being outside."

Even if she didn't have to navigate the stairs often, she would *still* have to navigate them.

"When they do play upstairs, someone has to carry Mamie as she's in a wheelchair. No one minds, as everyone is happy to help." His eyebrows edged up, and he inclined his head toward her in an unspoken question before adding, "I'd be happy to assist you."

"It's just that..." A myriad of emotions settled in her chest. Fear of failing. Fear of falling. Regret that she thought she could undertake such a position. Exhaustion from the lengthy train ride.

Malachi offered his elbow. "I'll take your cane, and you can grip the railing with one hand and hold on to me with the other."

"And if I fall?"

"I'll be here to catch you."

A man with broad shoulders and strong arms such as himself could no doubt uphold that promise. "But I'm so unsteady."

"Yes, and it is a climb, but the steps are somewhat wide, and with the carpet runner, it makes one less likely to slip. What do you say?" A glint shown in his eyes.

Should she take the chance? Part of her wanted to admit defeat before even trying. But another part—a much larger part—wanted to prove she could succeed. "All right." Arrosa handed him her cane and clutched his muscular arm. She gingerly stepped up the first step, brought her other leg to rest there too, and stood as the seconds ticked by and she once again found her resolve. "I apologize that this will be a laborious and prolonged event."

"Fine by me. As I mentioned before, I'm in no hurry to tackle the chore outside."

She took the next step, her weak legs wobbling and her knee throbbing. If it was this distressing on the second step, how would she be able to manage—she counted the remainder of the stairs—ten more? "Is there only one more set after this one?"

"Only one more set. And then when you come down, you're welcome to slide down the banister."

A bubbling giggle rose in Arrosa's throat, replacing the fear. Of course, he was joshing her. "Yes, but are you sure that's all right with Mr. and Mrs. Evanson?"

"Perfectly all right. I do it myself all the time."

At the landing, Arrosa stopped to catch her breath. A window offered a view unlike any other of the expansive ranchland dotted with cattle and the rising mountains in the background. She gasped.

"The view is remarkable. Some places on the property allow for a gander even more astonishing than this."

"Really?"

He nodded. "God knew what He was doing when He created such a beautiful place. There's nowhere I'd rather be."

"Not even the Sahara Desert?"

Malachi chuckled. "As tempting as it sounds, I'll have to decline." He peered to the right. "Down that hall is Mr. and Mrs. Evanson's room. Up the stairs is the playroom."

"So only one set of stairs for now."

"Only one set of stairs. Good job on accomplishing that undertaking."

A lightness settled in her chest, and she craned her neck to see from whence she'd come, a prayer of gratitude on her lips. She gripped Malachi's arm even tighter in her excitement. "Yes, I did it." And she couldn't have done it without Malachi's benevolence. Arrosa peered up at him. Perhaps they would become grand friends.

A person could never have too many friends.

"I'll deliver you to Mrs. Evanson's room, and then I'll return for you in a while to help you back down the stairs. That is, unless you do want to slide down the banister."

"Perhaps on my first day, I ought to refrain from such childish schemes."

He laughed again, not seeming to mind that she was likely prohibiting the blood flow in his arm. She loosened her hold, and they walked down a hall with numerous photographs on the walls and to an open-doored room.

The stroll was invigorating, but also tiring, and once again, she struggled to catch her breath. Her shoulders heaved. Finally, she straightened her posture and took a step forward.

Malachi gestured for her to go ahead into the room.

"Thank you, Malachi, for retrieving Miss Chapman."

"You're welcome, ma'am." He caught Arrosa's eye and nodded, their unspoken agreement offering Arrosa some comfort.

"Welcome to Hollow Creek and the Evanson Ranch." Mrs. Evanson was propped against a pile of pillows. Her amber eyes sparkled, and her smile lit her entire face. "We are so glad to have you here. Please do come in and have a seat." She gestured to a pink paisley cloth-covered Queen Anne chair with ornate armrests and a matching ottoman.

"Thank you for the warm welcome." Arrosa doddered to the chair when a pain cramping her knee nearly caused her leg to buckle. She reached out to the back of the chair to steady herself, her cane clunking against Mrs. Evanson's bed before coming to rest on the floor. Heat flushed her cheeks as a sense of dread filled her. Her legs threatened to bow from beneath her, and she closed her eyes, willing that she wouldn't take an unladylike tumble and land in a heap on the ornamental carpet.

*Lord, please steady me.*

Her eyes fluttered open, and she noticed Mrs. Evanson leaning forward, gaping. "Are you all right?" The woman's gaze veered toward Arrosa's cane, still on the floor.

Was she all right?

No. Not at all. Besides her wounded pride, all of her hopes and dreams had just been dashed. Her right leg continued to wobble as she grasped the edge of the chair. She needed to fetch her cane, but stooping to that position on the floor demanded a slow and deliberate process.

Seconds ticked by.

Would Mrs. Evanson dismiss her before Arrosa had even started?

Arrosa's heartbeat pounded so loudly in her ears, she doubted she would hear anything Mrs. Evanson said over the deafening roar.

"Are you all right, Miss Chapman?" Mrs. Evanson asked again.

Arrosa edged her way around the side of the chair and plopped into it. Mrs. Evanson's brow furrowed, but she said nothing.

Finally summoning the courage and her breath steadying, Arrosa wrested whatever pride she still had left. "Yes, I promise you I am fine."

Relief flooded Mrs. Evanson's countenance. "You had me worried for a moment. Unfortunately, I'm not much help in my condition."

"Please. I know I have a cane, but I can do this job, I know I can." Her words tumbled from her mouth and sounded desperate and frantic in her own ears. What must Mrs. Evanson think of her clumsy ways? Would she declare her an unfit choice? After all, how could a woman with a cane supervise three energetic children and a baby?

The weight of the burden pressed upon her shoulders. Never had she felt more inadequate. *Lord, help me muster courage.* Arrosa squared her shoulders. "I know I can tend to the children. Please give me a chance." Although she'd hoped to sound competent, she feared her words sounded more like apprehensive drivel.

"Miss Chapman, please don't worry. I know you are fully capable. You come highly recommended." Mrs. Evanson punctuated her words with another smile. "I have but one concern, and that is the stairs. Although that's not too much of a concern, as the only rooms you'll need to visit are mine and the playroom."

This wasn't the time to admit that the staircase might be a struggle, so Arrosa merely nodded. "I'm grateful that I'll be spending most of the time on the lower level."

"And outside. The children would play outdoors all year if we didn't receive such frigid temperatures in the winter. Even Mamie. Thad designed some runners for her wheelchair so that someone can walk behind her and push her in the snow."

What a thoughtful father Mr. Evanson must be. While she hadn't yet met him, he sounded much like her own father in wanting to help his daughter however he could.

Arrosa attempted to tamp down her nervousness. She wanted to do all she could to secure this position. "You have a lovely home."

"Thank you. Now, Miss Chapman, do tell me a bit about yourself."

It was a question she hadn't anticipated. Mrs. Evanson inquiring about her prior work with children, perhaps, or even previous employment, but not about something so personal. She searched for the words. "Well, I was born and raised in Missoula, and as you know, I have a sister named McKenna. My mother still resides in Missoula, and my father—." How could she share truthfully with Mrs. Evanson without divulging Father's whereabouts?

"McKenna has shared with me about your father. Please accept my condolences. I know it's been a difficult time for your family as of late."

"Thank you."

"Now, I must insist you call me Emilie. We are extremely informal at the ranch. May I call you Arrosa?"

"Yes." A bit of the trepidation left her. She could succeed at this. With the Lord's help, of course.

"I wanted to outline a few of the responsibilities you will be expected to undertake. Thad and I have four children, not counting our baby, who is about to be born soon." She rubbed her stomach. "Unfortunately, I haven't handled this pregnancy well, and due to—" a shadow of sadness temporarily darkened her countenance. She recovered and continued. "Doc has put me on bed rest, and as such, I am unable to care for the children at this time, besides reading in the evenings or snuggling our youngest, Thad Junior—whom we refer to as Junior—when he is not wiggling about and attempting to satisfy his curiosity. He's an active little boy, but a sweet one." She laughed. "I can only wonder how lively he'll be once he can walk. Ephraim is our eldest. He has an abundance of energy, but you won't find a kinder boy. Adelia, our eldest daughter, is a delightful child and so smart. I'm not sure if McKenna told you or not, but we adopted our three oldest children from the orphanage. Adelia came to us with a limp, but you wouldn't know it unless you were paying the utmost attention. She can nearly keep up with Ephraim, and that is no easy feat. We also have our spirited and kind-hearted Mamie. Although she's confined to her wheelchair, she doesn't think of herself as any different and strives to keep up with Ephraim and Adelia."

Emilie took a sip of the water from the teacup on the nightstand. "You will have a room on the main floor between Mamie's room and the parlor. It's a cozy but lovely room, and I hope you'll find it satisfactory."

Arrosa would find any room in this elegant home satisfactory, especially one on the main floor. "Thank you."

"Junior's room is beside ours, and Ephraim's and Adelia's rooms are on the other side. Up the second set of stairs is the playroom, and on the very top level are the maids' rooms. Also on the second level is Vera and Morris's room. They are, I suppose you could say, hired help. However, they are much more like family, and as you will note, our children tend to attach familial names to those they are closest to. For example, Grandma Vera and Grandpa Morris." A sadness befell her face. "I assume it's because they came from an orphanage where everything was so temporary. It's been a change for them to have a permanent home, and I believe they attach themselves deeply to those they ascertain as ones who care about them."

Poor, sweet children. Arrosa had always been loved and cherished by her parents and had never known a day when she had to worry about being cast aside or placed in an orphanage. "What a blessing for them to have a secure home."

"A blessing for them, yes, but also for Thad and me. God is so very good. Now, as I'm sure McKenna mentioned to you, you'll receive room and board along with a stipend. You will be expected to teach the children, as we've found it's much easier to do so here than to drive them into town each day. Once they finish their schoolwork, they may play outside or in the playroom to their heart's content until it's time for chores, supper, our Bible reading, and bedtime. You will have Sundays off and some Saturdays as well, although on Sundays, if Thad is out of town, we kindly ask that you assist Vera and Morris with transporting the children and tending to them during church services when needed. Also, if you require time off for any other reasons, please don't hesitate to let me know." Emilie smiled. "Do you have any questions?"

"I don't think so. I really do appreciate you giving me this opportunity."

"You are most welcome. It is you who is doing us a favor. I can't wait to meet this baby, but I daresay this pregnancy has been arduous. Vera can show you to your room, and if you need anything at all, please let either of us know."

They chatted for several minutes longer before Malachi emerged in the doorway to aid Arrosa to the bottom level. And for the first time since arriving, peace enveloped her.

Malachi hadn't been sure Arrosa could manage the stairs, even with his help. He could see the mix of embarrassment, determination, and fear in her eyes. But she'd succeeded, and he admired her all the more for it.

"Are you ready for the banister?" he asked, once again extending his elbow.

"If you go first."

He chuckled. It was doubtful the Evansons would appreciate the hired help sliding down the banister, but it had been amusing to discuss as much with Arrosa.

"Did the meeting go well?" he asked once they'd left Mr. and Mrs. Evanson's room.

"It did. At first, I wasn't sure."

"You weren't sure?"

"I wasn't sure that I would be the right one for the position."

"Why not?"

"I nearly took a fall when I entered her room."

"I'm sorry to hear that."

"It's just...I'm not accustomed to stairs. In our new home, we were on the main floor."

He again took her cane, and she held onto him with one hand and the railing with the other. "You'll like working here, and I'm sure you'll do fine."

"Thank you, Malachi. I appreciate your assistance more than you know."

The way she smiled at him did something peculiar to his insides. It was good to be needed.

# CHAPTER FIVE

FOR SOME TIME, THE nightmares had eased, but tonight, they were back.

This time, he was aboard a ship on the ocean—even though in reality, he'd never even been to the ocean. Never had been anywhere even close.

Lightning flashed across the vast sky, and thunder roared. As he gripped the railing on the deck, the ship rocked to and fro, causing his stomach to lurch. Several other passengers stood at one end, including mean Mr. Redding, who laughed when Malachi's feet slid across the wet floor of the ship, and he nearly lost his balance. While the others were sheltered, rain pelted Malachi, the sting of the downpour biting into his face and bare arms.

*"It's time,"* said Mr. Redding.

Suddenly, Boyd was on the deck too, and they, along with some others Malachi recognized, prepared to lower the dinghy into the ocean. *"Get in, boy,"* growled Mr. Redding.

*"I'd rather stay here,"* he shouted over the sound of rushing waves and another clap of thunder.

*"Ain't your choice to make,"* yelled Boyd. He gripped Malachi's arms and, together with Mr. Redding, hoisted Malachi into the dinghy before lowering it completely into the raging ocean. Only when the lightning lit the sky could Malachi see those still

on the ship as he floated further and further away from them. The boat bobbed and dipped, and waves crashed over the top, drenching Malachi with water.

*"Help!"* he yelled. But no one heard him. Instead, the ship proceeded in the opposite direction.

*"Help!"* he screamed again, just before the boat flipped over and dumped him into the unforgiving ocean.

Malachi awoke, sweat soaking him. His breath came in gasps, and his entire body shook. Where was he? Was he still in the ocean?

But no, it had been another nightmare.

He swung his legs over the side of the bunk and sat up. Thankfully, he was the only resident of the bunkhouse, or else he would have for certain awakened his roommates. *Lord, please calm me.* Yet his heart still pounded in his ears, and his legs trembled. Sweat still slicked his forehead and the creases of his elbows. *Lord, please calm me*, he repeated. His chest rose and fell with rapid breaths. He knew from experience that God's peace always came, but it wasn't always immediate. *"It increases our faith when we await his peace and realize it's Him and only Him that we can rely on. Him and only Him who can calm our panic and cover us fully in His peace. Real peace,"* Reverend Arkley once told him when they'd discussed prayer. Malachi had shared some with the Hollow Creek pastor, but not much, for he hadn't told anyone about his nightmares and kept secret the life he'd lived before arriving in Hollow Creek.

Finally, it was as though the Lord's arms enveloped him. Peace flooded his troubled mind, and Malachi whispered a prayer of gratitude.

Several minutes later, he climbed from bed and padded along the wood floor to the pitcher on the table. He poured himself a glass of water and peered out the window. No ship. No ocean.

No Boyd Goshorn and no Mr. Redding. No others standing by watching him struggle.

He turned on the new light powered by electricity, and willed himself to settle. The small wooden box tucked beneath his bed beckoned him.

Not the most opportune time to rehash something from the past, but looking back through the items gave him a peculiar sense of calm about how far he'd come.

Only by God's grace.

Malachi kneeled on the hard floor and pulled the worn box toward him. He opened the rusted latch and retrieved first the newspaper article published last year in the *Hollow Creek Times.* It told of the capture of Pietro Salazar, a wanted outlaw, and Malachi's assistance with the stolen horses being returned. Never before had his reputation improved so rapidly as it had that day. He could count on one hand the folks who knew him in Hollow Creek until he stumbled upon the horses at a deserted barn. One of those horses was Thad Evanson's. A pricey stallion that he was grateful to have back.

Passersby nodded and told him what a fine job he'd done, and for the first time, Malachi felt accepted. He re-read the short article again and stared at the clear photograph of himself, his only time having ever had his picture taken. He hadn't changed much over the years, and by his way of thinking, strongly resembled his ma, or what he remembered of her, anyhow. Information at the bottom of the page indicated the outlaw hadn't survived the gunshot wound he sustained during a crime.

Malachi returned the paper to the box and pulled out the next one in the stack.

The wanted poster.

He unfolded it, pressed the wrinkles from the piece of paper he'd, on numerous times crumpled, the image and words memorized.

*WANTED DEAD OR ALIVE*
*Reward $1,000*
*Boyd "Bad Dog" Goshorn*
*Height: 6'2"*
*Weight: 250*
*Build: large*
*Brown hair, gray eyes, a full mustache and beard.*
*Criminal occupation: murderer, train and bank robber, and cattle thief.*
*At least six times a killer.*
*Do not apprehend. Go to the nearest sheriff's office or contact a marshal.*

Boyd's hardened eyes stared up at him. Had he ever been caught? Was he still alive? Would Malachi someday become like him despite his best efforts to live a law-abiding life?

He hoped not. Prayed not. Tried to do everything right so he wouldn't succumb to the lot in life that would surely be his.

Malachi had even changed his last name. He was now Malachi Callahan. Had been for the past while. No one ever need know the truth about him or his father.

He folded the paper into fours and placed it back into the box, and next retrieved the picture he'd kept in pristine condition.

The drawing of Ma.

Over time, the memory of her had faded, and this haphazard sketch, drawn by a boy of eight—himself no less—was all he had. But it reminded him that Ma had curly blonde hair and a smile, and blue eyes and a round face that he'd inherited. But why hadn't she taken him with her when she left?

He was transported back to the day he asked the kindly preacher and his wife that very question. They hadn't had an answer for him, but reassured him that his mother loved him. He attempted to recall the night his father, whom Malachi now called by his given name, nearly took her life. Ma had reached for his hand, but Boyd hadn't allowed it. Boyd yelled something, and Ma stumbled from the house. She'd tried thrice more to snatch Malachi, but Boyd had stood guard at the door.

Or something akin to that.

The memories were fuzzy, and he struggled to recollect exactly what happened.

Malachi folded that paper too, and lastly withdrew the tattered nametag with the name "Victor" on it. That very nametag allowed him to escape the life he lived—into another dismal one—but that ultimately led him here.

The events flashed through his mind of the orphan train and subsequent homes as he journeyed along the rough road of rejection and pain. He released a strangled breath, shoved the box back beneath his bed, and stood.

No one would ever know the life he'd lived before becoming Malachi Callahan of Hollow Creek, Montana. He'd hold every memory, every heartache, and every pain-ridden moment behind a well-made façade.

Arrosa assigned the children their schoolwork, then withdrew a piece of stationery and began penning a missive.

*Dearest Mother,*

*How are you? I miss you so much and can't wait for you to move to Hollow Creek. I've been counting down the days.*

*McKenna should be back soon. It will be a delight to prattle on with her once again. It seems we have much to catch up on.*

*Being a nanny is all that I had hoped it would be and more. The children are a delight. A lively group, but delightful nonetheless. The Evanson home reminds me so much of ours in Missoula, not so much in appearance, but in the elegant décor. The view is nothing short of magnificent, and while at first I wasn't so sure I'd cotton to a small town lacking all that Missoula has to offer, after a week, I find that I could live here permanently.*

*I attended church for the first time this past Sunday. Reverend Arkley delivered a timely sermon with solid doctrine. I also met several townsfolk and have found everyone here to be welcoming. I daresay both you and Father will enjoy residing here.*

*Please do write soon and tell me how you fare.*
*With Much Love,*
*Arrosa*


A knock at the door sounded, and one of the maids answered it. "Hello, Mrs. Beringer."

"Sienna, hello. I'm in search of my sister."

"McKenna?" Arrosa grabbed her cane and rose to her feet as her sister strode toward her. They embraced, and tears filled Arrosa's eyes. "I was just writing to Mother and telling her how much I missed you and how I couldn't wait for you to return."

"We arrived just an hour ago. Oh, Arrosa, it's so good to see you."

Mckenna greeted the children and sat beside Arrosa at the table. They talked nearly nonstop for the next several minutes, catching up on all the topics of discussion they'd missed in recent days. The conversation then turned to Mother.

"I have the best news. Whenever Mother is ready to move to Hollow Creek, a job awaits her at the boutique. I finalized matters with Aunt Julia Mathilda. Mother can reside upstairs in the apartment, or she can come live with Clayton and me. Either way, we must get her here posthaste."

"I agree. The only problem is that she has promised her boss that she would stay until the fifteenth of next month."

"That's less than three weeks away."

"Indeed."

Mckenna tapped her chin. "I think that would be the perfect amount of time to get everything settled. Of course, the matter is entirely up to Mother, but I do think relocating to Hollow Creek would do her good. No more working at the hotel, and she would be able to get settled before Father is released. Now, do tell me how it's going with you here."

"I love this job. Thank you for speaking to Emilie about it for me."

"No problem at all. I knew you'd be just the one for it. Have you made many friends in Hollow Creek?"

Arrosa had always been the shyer one, while McKenna made friends much more easily. "I have. You would be surprised to know that I spoke to several of the townsfolk at church on Sunday, as well as making friends here at the ranch."

"Aren't Vera and Morris such dears?"

"Indeed, they are, and Malachi has been so helpful."

A suspicious glint shone in McKenna's eyes. "Oh, yes, Malachi. He is a fine gentleman."

"He retrieved me from the depot when I arrived and has aided me with traveling up and down the stairs, which has been no easy task."

"Clayton speaks highly of him. I'm glad you two have become friends."

"Yes, he's much more gentlemanly than Wayne Lingis."

McKenna looked taken aback. "Wayne Lingis? Now that is a name I haven't heard  in ages."

"He came into the gift shop while I was there and took me to the Bellerose Restaurant for the noonday meal."

"Really? I remember when you fancied him. Is he still just as dapper?

"He may be dapper, but he is also an insolent cad."

"An insolent cad? Whatever did he do?"

Arrosa proceeded to tell her sister about that day and how Wayne referred to her as a cripple. McKenna reached for her hand. "I'm so, so sorry, Arrosa. You didn't deserve that."

"All of that wasted time I spent in silly daydreams, being so daft and entertaining the notion that he might someday ask me to court him. I've been so foolish."

"Wayne Lingis doesn't deserve someone like you, Arrosa."

"I see him now for who he truly is, but it was such a painful experience."

"I'd like to see him again and give him a piece of my mind." McKenna glowered. "How dare he be so impudent to my sister?"

Mckenna had always defended Arrosa if the need demanded it. She couldn't ask for a more steadfast, loyal, and devoted older sister. "Thank you. It won't be necessary, but I do appreciate the suggestion."

"Now, then, we won't give Wayne Lingis another thought. Were you able to see Father on your way to Missoula?"

"Regrettably, there wasn't enough time to alight from the train, hobble to the jail, and board once again before it departed for Hollow Creek. I miss him terribly."

"I do as well. Fortunately, he is nearing the end of his sentence, and while he has lost some weight, he is very much the same father we have always known and loved."

And if they could persuade Mother and Father to move to Hollow Creek, and Father found employment, they could both begin anew.

Just like the new chapter the Lord had led Arrosa to in her life.

# CHAPTER SIX

RIDING THE RANGE GAVE Malachi plenty of time to think, sometimes to his detriment. The other hands rode on ahead, laughing and joking. At least on the Evanson Ranch, Malachi felt like he belonged. Such hadn't been the case on some of the other ranches he'd worked.

After a time on the orphan train, Malachi was offered a home with the abhorrent Mr. and Mrs. Redding and their equally abhorrent children. After being rescued from that home, a kindly couple named the Kerrs then took him in, but unfortunately died soon after. Malachi was then sent to an orphanage in a nearby town. Malachi's first thought was that he would run away. He got as far as the neighboring farm when his stomach grumbled. He reversed course, returned to the orphanage, and found that once he settled in, he realized the place wasn't so bad after all. There wasn't much love shown, and he credited that to the fact that the workers were overly busy. Or at least that's what he tried to tell himself. That there was a reason they couldn't provide the tender care a mother would. Not when there were so many children of various ages.

By that time, Malachi had reverted to his real first name. Victor hadn't suited him much, and it was doubtful Boyd Goshorn, the man who'd fathered him, and the man he now simply referred to as Boyd, would find him in a rural eastern Nebraska farming community, so far from his original Indiana home.

The "orphanage children", as they were derogatorily termed by the local schoolteacher, were allowed to attend the school in town. Each morning, an orphanage worker delivered them to the school, and each morning, Miss Becht, the spiteful and uncharitable teacher, would rap her ruler on the corner of each child's desk and sometimes on a child's fingers or shoulder, should they fail to do what was commanded. She was especially impatient with the "orphanage children", and in Malachi's way of thinking, immediately determined her disdain for him. *"You resemble my wayward cousin who landed himself in prison after robbing a stagecoach,"* she'd told him that first day.

He couldn't help who he looked like. He was just grateful he didn't resemble his pa.

Miss Becht had shown him no mercy when he'd swiped a pencil after his own had been taken. He was eager to learn and had always enjoyed school. But as he sat at his desk and attempted to work the arduous arithmetic problem, Miss Becht strolled to his desk and glared down at him. When he looked up, he noticed her angular face, overly prominent cheekbones, and deep-set, close-together eyes that barely allowed a nose in between. She glowered at him, unblinking. If he were creative and could write stories, which he wasn't and couldn't, he could have made her an evil character. The thought brought a wry grin to his mouth.

*"You, Malachi Goshorn, are an insolent and unlovable child."*

He hadn't cared about the word insolent. But the term unlovable stuck with him even now. So unlovable his ma hadn't taken him with her. So unlovable that his pa neglected and abused him. So unlovable that he still didn't have a permanent home.

Yes, maybe Miss Becht was correct.

Malachi hadn't argued with her when she punished him for stealing the pencil. *"You continue on this path of being a criminal, and you will find yourself in the harshest of prisons someday."*

He couldn't stop thinking about her words. He didn't want to be anything like Boyd Goshorn. He didn't want to find himself in the harshest of prisons someday. After that public discipline, most children at the orphanage didn't speak to him much. Already at school, he was somewhat ostracized for being one of the "orphanage children".

But loneliness could have its advantages. He threw himself into his schoolwork. He enjoyed reading, although there weren't many books that he hadn't already read several times over. And he especially appreciated arithmetic. Writing was something he struggled with. The forming of paragraphs didn't come naturally.

Three separate families arrived at the orphanage over the course of time, each convinced they wanted to adopt Malachi. And each one, in the end, returned him to the orphanage for one reason or another. He tried his hardest, did what he was told, attempted not to eat too much, and rarely backtalked. But no one wanted him.

Because, as Miss Becht mentioned, he was unlovable.

At sixteen, Malachi left the orphanage for good. At first, he stayed in the small Nebraska town and worked odd jobs. One day while in town, a discarded newspaper on the mercantile counter caught his eye. Thumbing through it while waiting for the clerk to ring up his items, Malachi came across an advertisement for cowhands in southern Montana. He'd never worked on a ranch before, but he had plenty of experience on farms. Besides, nothing in eastern Nebraska was keeping him there. So, the next day, he packed his belongings, said farewell to the boardinghouse owner, and rode his horse the endless distance to Montana. Boyd would never think to look for him there—if Boyd even cared to try to find Malachi. Which Malachi hoped he never would. He clenched his jaw at the thought. Some children at the orphanage had been adopted by loving families, but that had not been his experience. At this late stage in life, hopes of having a real family seemed unlikely.

He moved on rather quickly from the first two ranches. The third ranch, the Hoyer Ranch, a sizable one at 650,000 acres, included 12,000 head of cattle and 200,000 head of sheep. On his first day, he settled into one of the bunkhouses with four other men. It took him a while to fit in, especially since Munch, a tall, thin, brown-haired man in his thirties, with uneven, beady brown eyes, did all he could to get Malachi dismissed from his job.

But if Malachi hadn't crossed paths with Munch, his life wouldn't have been altered by Barnabas Callahan.

Munch, a self-appointed supervisor, gave Malachi the worst jobs, attempted to start arguments, and constantly mocked him. It wasn't new to Malachi. He'd met people like Munch before. All he wanted was to keep to himself, earn an honest paycheck, and learn the ranching trade.

Things came to a head when Malachi, Munch, and a grizzled old cowboy named Barnabas Callahan headed into town for supplies. A woman Munch cottoned to smiled at Malachi, and Munch flew into a rage. His fist had connected with Malachi's face, and Malachi quickly returned the favor.

He'd not start a fight, but he would finish it if necessary.

Soon, it was an all-out brawl. Munch pulled his gun from its holster. *"How about a duel, Goshorn?"*

Fighting with his fists was one thing. A duel with pistols was another. Not that Malachi had any family to miss him if he lost, but he wasn't ready to enter the afterlife, whatever that entailed. As such, he wouldn't do anything impetuous.

*"Come on, Goshorn. What are you? A spineless coward?"*

He'd about had enough of Munch's derision. *"I'm not interested in a duel, Munch."*

*"'Course you ain't. You'd lose anyway."* Munch, who'd stopped by the saloon for one too many drinks, tottered on wobbling legs. *"Come on. Let's see what you got, or ain't you never shot a gun before?"*

He'd practiced plenty of shooting at tin cans and hunting for food while on his own. But Malachi wouldn't delve into the possibility of shooting a man unless it was in self-defense. *"Put the matter to rest, Munch. You're making an ignominy of yourself."*

*"Well, ain't that special? Goshorn here knows such big words. What are you, a teacher?"*

*"No, just well-read."*

Munch took a step forward and bunched Malachi's collar in his fist. *"I should shoot you for smiling at my woman."* He hit Malachi square in the nose.

Barnabas sidled up to Munch, who was reeling from Malachi's perfectly placed punch to the ribs. *"You got what you deserved, Munch, now take a step back and leave Goshorn alone."*

*"Ain't none of this any business of yours, Callahan."*

*"Oh, but it is. Ain't gonna stand here and watch you two continue your skirmish."*

Munch scrunched up his big nose and inclined toward Barnabas Callahan, but thankfully didn't hurt the man. If he had attempted to, Malachi would have been there to defend the elderly soul who'd always been kind to him.

*"Come on, Goshorn."* Munch bounced around on unsteady legs, one hand on his pistol and one hand flailing in the air.

*"Now just a bitty minute here, Munch,"* said Barnabas. *"All you do is try to cause trouble and make a nuisance of yourself. Goshorn here never done nothing wrong."*

*"Like I done told you, this ain't any business of yours, Callahan."*

*"You continue on, and you'll be seeking other employment."*

*"You'd rat me out, Callahan?"*

*"I would."*

On that day, Malachi found a friend in Barnabas. But even more than that, He found a mentor. Barnabas taught him about the things of the Lord, things Malachi had never even heard before.

*"I know you ain't had a good earthly pa, son, but you got a Heavenly Father who loves you and gave His life for you. In the midst of sorrow, thinking about Boyd Goshorn and all he done, don't stop thinkin' about the Good Lord and all* He *done."*

Barnabas's words impacted Malachi's life dramatically, and he made a decision to follow Jesus one day while sitting around the campfire with Barnabas. While his new friend didn't have answers to all of Malachi's questions, he knew where to find them. He assured Malachi that God heard all prayers, big and small. *"And someday, when I'm no longer here, I want you to have my Bible and my pocket watch. Ain't never had me a son, so you could be the son I never had. If that's all right with you."*

*It was more than all right for Malachi. "It would be an honor to be your son, sir."*

*"Consider it done."* Barnabas reached an arthritic hand toward Malachi, and they shook on it to make it authentic.

But something about Barnabas wanting to give him his only possessions bothered Malachi. *"I appreciate your generosity, but you'll be here for many more years."*

*"I'll be here as long as the good Lord sees fit. But someday when I ain't here, I don't want you to mourn for me. I'll be in Heaven with my Savior."*

The hunched-over cowboy with a long, graying beard that made up for the lack of hair on his head, then immediately changed the subject and discussed his plans to someday work a ranch near the Bitterroot Mountains. *"That's always been my dream."* He'd even pinned down the town—a small one called Hollow Creek. But Barnabas passed away before he ever had the chance to realize his dream.

When the only other person besides maybe his ma who had loved him passed, Malachi knelt at Barnabas's grave. Tears, so foreign to him, filled his eyes. He'd missed the man who'd come alongside him. Who'd defended him and mentored him in ranching, but more importantly, in the ways of the Lord.

Malachi left three days later with the four things Barnabas had given him. The seeds he'd planted in Malachi's heart for Jesus, a Bible, a pocket watch, and a new last name.

Even now, Malachi realized what a blessing it had been to travel to the place Barnabas had always wanted to see. He rolled his shoulders and shifted in the saddle. He'd missed Barnabas more than he ever realized was possible, even though he'd only known the man a handful of years. And he'd had no problem finding Hollow Creek, Montana, near the Bitterroot Mountains. He'd staked his claim as a ranch hand for Thad Evanson, and every time he looked at those mountains, he thought of Barnabas and the impact he'd had on Malachi's life. Because God had placed the kindly senescent man in his path, Malachi was a changed man.

# CHAPTER SEVEN

MALACHI WATCHED AS ARROSA, Adelia, Ephraim, and Junior made their way down the brick pathway to an area on the side of the house where several toys littered the lawn. Even from his location on the porch, he could hear the excitement and the laughing as if this was the first time they'd been outside all year. When, in actuality, they had been outside more often than not.

Arrosa had stopped and was peering behind her, presumably to ensure Mamie joined them. But the petite girl sat in her wheelchair at the top of the porch, hanging her head and her arms folded across her chest. "Mamie, what's wrong?" Malachi asked.

She shrugged her thin shoulders, and he knelt beside her.

"What's wrong?" he asked again. "Do you need me to push you to the play yard?"

"No," she squeaked.

"Then what is it?"

Mamie swiped at a tear. "Ephraim said they're going on a hunt next week to show Aunt Arrosa where to find treasures. I can't go where they find treasures. Not in my wheelchair."

Her words hit him squarely in the gut. He knew what it was like to be excluded. Had dealt with it much of his life. Were the children *really* going to go on a treasure hunt in the woods, or was Ephraim spinning tales? Malachi cleared his throat. "Don't fret, Mamie."

She peered up at him, tears hovering in her large brown eyes. "Why not?"

"Are you sure they're really going on a hunt? Maybe Ephraim was mistaken."

Mamie shook her head so quickly her brown curls swung. "He's not mistaken. They really are."

"Still, I wouldn't worry."

"But I *am* worried."

"I know. But I reckon we can fix that problem quite easily."

But could they? And would his plan work?

"How?"

"Well, I once saw a toy wagon for kids to be pulled in. It has four wheels so it can go places your wheelchair can't."

At this, Mamie's eyes widened. "A wagon? With horses? Like a covered wagon? Like the pioneers rode in?"

"No, a person pulls it by a handle." Would it be possible to purchase such a contraption from the mercantile or hardware store in time for next week? If it had to be ordered, it wouldn't arrive for weeks. Malachi instantly regretted mentioning it because he didn't want to get her hopes up.

"A person pulls it? And I ride in it?"

"Yes. It's not very big, just a rectangle, but you'd fit just fine."

Mamie's tears disappeared, and a smile replaced her frown. "I've never seen one in all my years."

All of her years, meaning five of them. Malachi chuckled. "Well, I hope we can find one in town. If not, we may have to ask Ephraim and Adelia if we can postpone the hunt until it arrives by train."

She patted him on the arm. "Thank you, Uncle Malachi. I won't worry about it anymore."

"I'm glad to hear that. Now, how about I help you catch up with the rest of your family?"

"All right."

Malachi gripped the wheelchair handles and steered it gently down the gradual ramp Thad had built, which made descending and ascending possible for Mamie.

Arrosa's appreciative gaze warmed his insides. It again felt good to be needed.

To be wanted.

Malachi finished the errands for the ranch and then strolled into the mercantile. He'd battled the driving rain on the way to town, but the foul weather didn't bother him much. Not when he had an important objective in mind.

Hopefully, they would have the item he sought.

"Callahan, what can I do for you?" Mr. Dell greeted him the second he entered.

"I'm looking for a children's wagon."

Dell nodded. "Ah, yes. The Lightning Express wagons are quite popular, especially around Christmastime."

"How much do they cost?"

"One dollar and twenty-five cents."

Malachi had fifty cents to his name until payday. He already had an account at Dell's Mercantile—an account he'd be paying on for the foreseeable future since he'd needed new boots, jeans, and a coat. Still, there had to be a way to help Mamie be able to accompany the rest of the children on the treasure hunt.

"I only have one right now," Dell was saying, and he gestured for Malachi to follow him to the back room where a red wooden wagon was plopped against the far wall. "A customer ordered one, but when it arrived, the brace was bent."

Malachi lifted the wagon and turned it over.

"Could be that it's available for a special sale."

That piqued his interest. "A special sale?"

Dell stroked his beard. "Do you think you could fix it?"

"Yes, I do."

"How about you help me unload some freight, and I'll pay you with the wagon."

Malachi tamped down his excitement. "Sir, I think you have yourself a deal."

An hour later, Malachi loaded the toy into the back of the wagon with the other supplies he'd retrieved for the ranch and headed home.

Home.

That was not a word he thought he would ever use. As he steered the wagon down the road and waved at an oncoming automobile, he looked at the dense fog shielding the usual rise of the Bitterroot Mountains in the distance. The way was clear in the valley, although raindrops pelted him and dripped off the brim of his hat.

No matter the weather, be it a hot summer, a warm spring, a crisp fall, or a glacial winter with abundant snow, he loved Montana. Loved Hollow Creek. Loved the opportunity to work hard and earn a decent wage. But there was something he'd love even more.

A home of his own.

A place to bed down at night.

But it was more than that. He rested his head each night on the firm mattress in the bunkhouse, but that didn't make the bunkhouse his home. Maybe what he really sought was a place to belong. A place where those around him accepted him. Even cared about him.

He lifted his eyes heavenward. God's fingerprints had been on every detail of his life, even before Malachi surrendered his life to Christ. Although there had been many, many times when Malachi figured he was alone, he never truly had been.

And who was he to complain that he didn't have the acceptance he sought? Or a cabin to call his own? Or more than the clothes on his back? No, he had more than he'd ever thought possible, and in that, he would continue to find contentment. Because, if Malachi was honest, the only thing that truly mattered besides attempting to—with the Lord's help—live out his favorite scripture verse, was that Boyd hadn't found him and never would.

As he'd entered the Evanson property, he realized that he *had* been accepted. Thad and Mrs. Evanson, Vera and Morris, Pete and Jep, Reverend Arkley, and numerous others in town—and now Arrosa—accepted him. The Evansons treated him better than any real family ever had, save the Kerrs, whom he'd known for such a short time. And Barnabas, whom Malachi would always consider his father rather than Boyd.

His adoptive father that the Lord had blessed Malachi with, even though it was short-lived.

Malachi unloaded the ranch items, then carried the wagon to the bunkhouse. He'd fix it later after his chores were finished. Shouldn't take long to remove the brace, straighten it, and attach it again. He'd test it too, to make sure it was sturdy, although Mamie was so petite she likely didn't weigh much.

Tonight, he would eat supper in the main house, which was always an option for the hired hands. The Evansons were generous folks, and after pleasing the Lord, Malachi wanted nothing he did to displease the ones who'd taken a chance on him.

Even after his short stint in jail.

An hour later, the maids bustled about setting the table, and Cook brought out a pot of potatoes. Malachi's stomach growled at the savory aroma of the steaks she carried out next. He'd been hungry too many times to count in his life. During those times, he'd—with effort—squelched the hunger pangs by distracting himself or guzzling as much water as he could. Even now, out of habit, he found himself looking for a way to avert his attention from the sliced bread Cook brought out next.

His stomach grumbled in defiance.

"How are you today, Malachi?" Morris patted him on the back.

"I'm fine, sir."

"Say, I think I might have heard the train a bitty second ago."

"The train?" The Evansons lived far enough from town that they should rarely hear such commotion.

The elderly man's eyes twinkled. "Wasn't that a train roar I heard?"

Malachi laughed. "You mean my grumbling stomach."

"Was that what that was?" He attempted to feign innocence, but Malachi knew better. Morris's thoughts were always well-written on his wrinkled face. Likely, he rarely got away with anything he attempted to hide from his wife.

"Can't help it with this food," Malachi said.

"Oh, yes. That is true. Glad you could join us."

Morris's words caused emotion to build in Malachi's chest. Never had he been more welcomed than at the Evanson Ranch.

Now to maintain that welcome and not bungle it.

Arrosa entered the room behind Ephraim and Adelia, Junior in one arm, and the cane in her other hand. She'd only been here a short while, but already everyone in the household adored her.

He strode toward her. "Can I help?"

"Thank you." She handed Junior to him and assisted Mamie from the wheelchair to her special chair at the table. The baby snuggled against him before reaching for Malachi's ear.

"Ky."

Malachi chuckled at the baby's name for him. Junior twisted and pointed at the table. "Cookie," he said.

"He thinks everything is a cookie," said Arrosa.

"Do you want me to put him in his high chair?"

"Yes, thank you." She turned the chair sideways and removed the tray.

How she did as much as she did with having to use a cane drew his profound respect for her. He appreciated their new friendship. Good friends for him had always been few and far between, and a man could never have enough friends. Not that he knew what it was to have true and abiding friendships, for he didn't.

Not until he'd arrived in Hollow Creek, anyhow. Now he considered the Evansons, Vera, Morris, the other ranch hands, and Sheriff Beringer to be his friends. And Arrosa. She was staring at him, awaiting his assistance with the high chair, while he stood there musing about friendships.

Malachi put Junior into his place. "Cookie?" the baby asked.

Arrosa slid in beside the high chair, and Malachi took his place beside her. Funny how that happened. One minute, it was the only seat left, and the next, it became *his* seat when eating supper with the Evansons.

Thad and Mrs. Evanson's chairs remained vacant due to Thad still being gone and Mrs. Evanson taking supper in her room. "Malachi, would you care to say grace?" Morris asked.

"Sure." When he first started praying aloud, Malachi had stumbled all over himself. But now, with Morris regularly asking him to say the blessing, it came as a second nature of sorts. "Dear

Lord, we thank You for this food, for the hands that secured it, the hands that prepared it, and the hands that served it. Please let it nourish and strengthen us. We pray for Mrs. Evanson and the baby and for Thad's safe return. In Jesus' name, amen."

When he finished, he noticed Arrosa gaping at him, her eyes wide.

"How did you learn to pray like that?"

"Over time," he said, placing the napkin in his lap. "Wasn't easy at first for me to pray out loud, but now…" he shrugged.

"One thing I've noticed about Malachi's prayers is that they are always so heartfelt," said Vera as she passed the plate of sliced bread to Ephraim, who started to take three pieces, then thought better of it.

"That's true," agreed Morris. "We take turns praying, and Malachi has done a right fine job from the start."

"Sometimes it's my turn," squeaked Adelia.

"And mine too," added Mamie.

"Cookie?" asked Junior.

Ephraim laughed and handed Junior a green bean. "Yum, cookie," the baby said.

# CHAPTER EIGHT

MALACHI CARRIED THE LIGHTNING Express children's wagon to the barn for the treasure hunt in the morning. He'd been able to fix the brace and couldn't wait to see Mamie's face when she realized she would now be joining the rest of the children on the treasure hunt.

There was just one problem. He needed to ask Thad if he could take a few hours tomorrow to accompany Arrosa and the children. There was no way she would be able to manage pulling the wagon, and while Ephraim would valiantly attempt to do so, he wouldn't be strong enough.

Malachi noticed Thad walking up the stairs of the porch. "Thad?"

His boss pivoted to look at him. "Hello, Malachi."

Malachi knew that at this time every evening, Thad, who'd recently returned from his trip, would gather his children around Mrs. Evanson, and they would talk about their day, read the Bible, and say their good nights before Thad would tuck them into bed. He admired Thad Evanson and how he continually put his family first.

The opposite of what Boyd had done.

"Could I speak with you in the barn?"

Thad entered the barn, and Malachi led him to the wagon. "This is for Mamie tomorrow for the treasure hunt."

"For Mamie?"

"Yes, she was upset that she wouldn't be able to join the other children, and of course, they wouldn't be going without her, so this solves the problem altogether."

"I really appreciate you thinking of her. How much do I owe you for the wagon?"

Malachi brushed his question aside. "You don't owe me anything, sir. I worked in return for it. But would you be agreeable to my joining Arrosa and the children for a few hours tomorrow afternoon to take them on a treasure hunt? I won't be gone for long."

"Yes, absolutely."

"Thank you."

"Malachi, I can't tell you how much I appreciate this."

He shrugged. "I just didn't want her to be left out. Although I know they would alter their plans and take a different route so she could maneuver it with her wheelchair, this makes it possible for us to follow that pathway that leads over by the creek."

"Sounds good. Take your time and enjoy the treasure hunt."

They spoke a few minutes longer before Thad again made his way to the porch and Malachi trotted down the road to the bunkhouse.

In the morning over breakfast, Arrosa leaned over and whispered. "Is everything set to go?"

"It is."

She smiled at him, and for a minute, he forgot the bite of scrambled eggs resting midair on his fork.

"Mamie will be thrilled."

"Mamie? Oh, yes, Mamie. Yes, I hope so." What was wrong with him? He and Arrosa shared a close friendship that had grown in the past few weeks. Why then the doltish confusion?

Must be because he hadn't slept as well as he'd hoped that night, what with another nightmare about Boyd and Mr. Redding dropping him into the ocean to fend for himself.

She was still smiling at him, and he reluctantly tore his eyes away and focused on the scrambled egg that had nearly met its demise on his now half-tilted utensil.

The children finished their schoolwork in record time, and Malachi met Arrosa on the porch.

"We're just going to stay where my wheelchair can go, right, Aunt Arrosa?" asked Mamie, her dark eyebrows pinching.

"Don't you worry about a thing, sweetie. Oh, look, here comes Ephraim with the basket Cook has packed for us."

"Ooh, a picnic lunch. Do you suppose she packed us some cupcakes?" Adelia licked her lips. Those are my favorite."

"Yes, there are cupcakes in here," Ephraim assured her. Malachi noticed some crumbs and what appeared to be some frosting on Ephraim's upper lip. Had he sampled the cupcakes Cook had packed for their picnic lunch?

"Before we go, Uncle Malachi has something to show you."

Malachi nodded. "Mamie, close your eyes and keep them closed."

Mamie did as he directed, and he raced to the barn for the children's wagon.

"She's peeking," tattled Adelia.

"No peeking, Mamie. It's a surprise," Arrosa reminded her.

Malachi pulled the handle, and the wagon bumped along the dirt road. He parked it in front of Mamie. "You can open your eyes."

Mamie clapped her hands. "Is that the wagon you were telling me about? The one for me to ride in?"

"It is."

"I can't believe it. All my life I've wanted one of these."

"Have you even seen one of these before?" asked Ephraim.

"No, but I'm just so 'cited!"

Arrosa inclined her head near Mamie's. "Are you ready to hunt for treasures?"

"Oh, yes. Yes, yes, yes!" Mamie squealed and leaned forward in her wheelchair. "May we go right now?"

Malachi lifted Mamie and set her in the wagon. "You're the bestest uncle," she said, beaming.

And something in Malachi shattered. He was no one's uncle. Not really. Yet, the Evanson children had accepted him as a part of their family. He cleared his throat. "Are we ready for a treasure hunt?"

"Yes, we are," chorused Ephraim and Adelia.

"But I am sad about one thing," said Mamie. "I won't be able to hunt down the treasures."

"No, but you have a very important job." Arrosa handed her a notebook. "You'll be the scribe."

Mamie's eyes enlarged. "The scribe?"

"Yes. Your job will be to circle each item that we locate."

"I can do that, Aunt Arrosa. I can." She bobbed her head. "Good thing Junior isn't with us today. He'd be curious about the notebook." She pointed at each word. "I can't read yet since I'm just a little girl. What word is this?"

"Ephraim, would you please read each word to Mamie so she knows which one to circle when we locate the treasure?"

"Yes, ma'am." Ephraim stooped down beside Mamie and read the words: *pine cones, smooth rock, feather, purple flower, bird nest, butterfly, robin.*

"The robin will be easy," noted Adelia. "There are millions of them on the ranch."

Before long, they slowly moseyed through the back hill and toward the creek with Ephraim leading the way, followed by

Adelia and Arrosa. "Uncle Malachi?" asked Adelia. "Do you have any brothers and sisters?"

"No, just me." He wouldn't consider the Redding children or the ones at the orphanage his siblings.

"That's sad," said Mamie. "I use to not have brothers and sisters either until Mother and Daddy 'dopted me."

"I'm so glad they did," added Adelia.

"Me, too. Hey, look, there's a bird nest!" Ephraim pointed high up in a poplar tree.

"Very observant, Ephraim. Do you all see the mother robin? She's sitting on some eggs that will hatch soon," Arrosa explained.

"That means I get to circle both the bird nest and the robin in the notebook," said Mamie, pencil poised.

Malachi listened as Arrosa patiently explained about the baby birds that would soon hatch. He admired how gentle and dedicated she was in teaching the children. He'd had a teacher like her once at the orphanage. Miss Grigsby took time with him, even when he struggled with stringing sentences together, and encouraged him to read all he could.

After reaching the creek and eating some lunch, the children played beneath an ash tree, and Malachi seated himself on a log beside Arrosa.

"I think Ephraim had one too many cupcakes," she said.

"I noticed that. I don't think Mamie was far behind."

"I love how they are so gentle with her and make sure to include her."

Malachi had lifted Mamie from the wagon, and she sat on the quilt beside her siblings. They played a silly game of *sleuth*, where they took turns finding something to stare at while the others had to guess what that was just from descriptions. Their contagious giggles sounded through the crisp spring air. What would it have been like to have siblings? To have brothers and sisters to play with? To have someone go through the rough times with you? What if children at the Redding home had been accepting and kind rather than hateful and treating him as though he were their servant?

"Did you ever play games like that when you were a child?"

Arrosa's cheerful inquiry interrupted the questions Malachi mulled over in his mind. "No, I can't say as I did." He shifted his long legs out in front of him and crossed them at the ankles. "What about you?"

"We did. Although McKenna was adept at vagueness. For instance, we had these colorful ornamental flowering shrubs in the gardens, and she would describe them with such obscurity, I never did guess. That or she would find a specific purple hydrangea to describe when there were at least two dozen of the same color. She always did win that game, although I bested her time and again when we played charades."

Malachi attempted to imagine a much younger Arrosa. Would she have been like Adelia or Mamie? She'd mentioned ornamental flowering shrubs. Had she grown up in wealth? If so, how was it that she was now a nanny? "You mentioned your family had gardens. Was your house similar to the Evanson home?"

"It was, in many ways, as far as the interior, although dissimilar architecture." She stared out over the meadow as if contemplating her home.

"Do your parents still reside there?"

"They do not."

Would Arrosa elaborate? From the way her face had taken on a melancholy expression, it likely wasn't something she wanted to discuss. Had they lost it somehow? Maybe in a fire?

"We don't live there anymore, but I do miss the home. So many fond memories there."

"I'm sorry."

"Thank you. What about you? I heard you tell the children you were an only child, but where did you spend your growing-up years?"

"Indiana." That was a safe answer and the truth. He'd forgo mentioning Nebraska to avoid having to explain.

"Indiana? Suffice it to say, I have never been to that state, although my family traveled frequently to many destinations."

Good. A chance to again divert the topic of conversation to her. "You traveled frequently?"

The smile returned. "We did. Some of my favorite places were the Atlantic coast in South Carolina and Niagara Falls. Europe was worthwhile to visit, but the time on the ocean was rather lengthy, and let's just say my constitution wasn't always up for the challenge."

"You traveled abroad?"

"We did."

"Does your family still travel?"

The melancholy expression returned, and her shoulders drooped. "Unfortunately, no. You're probably wondering why a woman whose family traveled to all sorts of delightful destinations must work as a nanny."

"That did cross my mind."

She moistened her lips. "Father, unfortunately, made some business choices that were…I mean to say that my father is a good and godly man. McKenna and I are blessed to have him as our father. There have just been—there have just been some changes as of late." Arrosa opened her mouth as if she wanted to say more, but changed her mind. Seconds ticked by before she clasped her hands in her lap and turned to him. "Are your parents still in Indiana?"

Where was Ma? He'd probably never know. Should he have spent time looking for her? Returning to Indiana and asking about her? Surely someone would recall his mother, even though it was so many years ago. And Boyd was likely far from Indiana now. Wanted posters were probably exhibited in states all across the country. "No, they are not."

"Oh, no, did they pass?"

Barnabas *had* adopted him. And Malachi *was* now a Callahan. In that case, yes, his pa had passed. And there was no way he'd tell her about Boyd. What would she think of him? That he might be an outlaw as well? "Yes, my pa did pass."

"I'm so sorry. And your ma?"

"No. We just aren't close." That was true. Or at least he presumed Ma to still be alive.

She raised a hand to her lips. Likely, she couldn't fathom not being close to her kin. "I'm dreadfully sorry, Malachi. To have lost your father and to be estranged from your mother."

Malachi shrugged. What else could he do? Losing Barnabas was painful. And even though he hadn't known the man long, Barnabas had a profound—and eternal—impact on Malachi's life.

Now that he thought about it, he wasn't sure about being *estranged* from Ma. If she truly tried to take him with her, which was how he remembered it, he wouldn't be at odds with her. Just missing her. Wondering where she went. Wondering why she didn't attempt again to remove her little boy from an abusive home.

"Do you ever consider returning to Indiana?"

"No." His answer slipped from his mouth so forcefully, he felt the need to clarify. "Montana is my home."

"Mine too. Have you ever lived anywhere else?"

"Nebraska."

"And what brought you to Montana?"

"First, it was an advertisement for cowhands. Then, Barn—my pa—always wanted to move near the Bitterroot Mountains and live here in Hollow Creek. He never had that chance, but I'm glad I was given the opportunity." He'd never shared any of this with anyone before, yet he felt comfortable with Arrosa. However, not comfortable enough to share with her about Boyd and the orphanage.

"I'm sorry your father never had the chance to live in Hollow Creek. It sounds as though he would have liked it."

"He would have. Barn—my pa—was a hard worker who'd spent time on many ranches. A godly man who was always there to help anyone in need." As he spoke, Malachi figured that if he could choose any man for a pa, it would have been Barnabas. Even though he was only Malachi's pa for a short amount of time, he *had* adopted him nonetheless. In Malachi's mind, Boyd was no longer his father. He'd given up that right. And no one ever needed to know about Boyd, especially Arrosa. Malachi doubted she'd want to spend time with him if she knew his real father was an outlaw. A murderer. A thief. A man better served locked behind prison bars.

The children finished their game, and Malachi lifted Mamie back into the wagon and then walked over to assist Arrosa in standing from her place on the upturned log. She lost her footing and fell slightly into him. He righted her, but as he held her in his arms, she turned to look at him, her face mere inches from his.

His breath caught. It occurred to him, perhaps for the first time, that Arrosa Chapman was beautiful with her rosy cheeks, bright hazel eyes, full lips, and a dimple in her chin. A strand of her auburn hair had fallen against her cheek, and he tenderly reached up and tucked it behind her ear.

How had he not noticed before how lovely she was? He'd only known her for such a short time, and in that time, they had become friends, or at least by his way of thinking. How then could it be that there was this gentle nudge of feeling something more for her?

He brushed aside his ridiculous notions. He could feel something more for her, but it would never be reciprocated. How could it be? She was the daughter of high society folks, and he was the son of an outlaw and an absent mother.

Malachi finally found his voice. "Are you all right?"

"Yes. Yes, I am. Thank you."

But she didn't attempt to shift from his gentle hold on her, and he didn't so much as move a muscle. The children chatted in the background, some birds tweeted overhead, and a soft breeze blew through the nearby trees. He caught a whiff of rosewater and inhaled. "I-well-I reckon we should get back to the ranch," he muttered.

"Indeed."

He released her, assisted with loading the basket into the wagon, then pulled Mamie as they trekked back to the house, thoughts of his changing feelings for Arrosa never far from his mind.

Arrosa bid Malachi goodbye, herded the children to their rooms, and checked on Junior, who had fallen asleep on Vera's lap in the rocking chair.

"Miss Arrosa?" Morris walked through the door, waving an envelope. "This was at the post office for you." He handed her an envelope with Mother's telltale handwriting on the outside.

"Thank you, Morris. It's from my mother." She lifted the envelope's flap and read Mother's missive.

*Dearest Arrosa,*

*I hope this finds you doing well. I have stupendous news. On June fourth, I will be arriving in Hollow Creek! I can scarcely believe it. I plan to arrive on the afternoon train. I'm mailing McKenna a letter as well. Soon, we will all be together again. God is so very good.*

*Love and miss you,*

*Mother*

June fourth? That was today! She'd barely received her letter in time. Had McKenna received hers? Happiness sparkled inside Arrosa. But if she were to arrive in time for the train's arrival...she hazarded a glance at the clock on the mantle. She would need to leave posthaste.

The children had fallen asleep in their respective beds. Junior remained sleeping on Vera's lap, and Sienna promised to keep an eye on the children should they awaken before Arrosa returned.

She walked as quickly as she could, her cane tapping on the porch. She spied Malachi in the distance near the barn. "Malachi?"

He didn't hear her, so she cautiously stepped off the porch and in his direction. "Malachi?"

"Arrosa." He strode toward her.

"Yes, I was wondering if you could perhaps take me to town."

"Is everything all right?"

"Oh, yes, Mother is arriving on the afternoon train from Missoula!"

"That's good news."

"Yes, it is. Might you take me?"

"Of course."

"I know that it's late in the day, and you probably wouldn't care to drive to Hollow Creek, and you have chores to do, and you took off time to help us with the treasure hunt, but—"

Malachi chuckled. "It is late in the day, but it's no problem at all. Besides, Arrosa, if you needed me to, I would drive you all the way to Missoula to retrieve your mother."

Heat climbed her neck and face. "You would?"

"I would."

"Thank-thank you." Suddenly, she was stumbling all over herself and sputtering her words.

"You're welcome."

"And don't worry about the children. They are tuckered from the treasure hunt, and Sienna and Vera are tending to them, so they are fine."

The corner of his mouth lifted. "I wasn't worried, but glad to hear they'll be tended to in your absence."

"Yes, and I'm so thrilled about Mother. I just received the letter stating she would arrive here on June fourth, and today is June fourth." Even in her own ears, she sounded like a chattering hen. "And if need be, I'm sure McKenna and Clayton can bring me back to the ranch."

"I don't mind waiting for you and bringing you back to the ranch. I'll hitch up the horses, let Pete know, and we'll be ready to leave in just a few minutes."

She could barely wait a few minutes, but Arrosa reminded herself that patience was indeed a virtue.

A half hour later, Arrosa, McKenna, Malachi, and Clayton stood outside the depot as the train entered town.

"Mother!" She wished she could run, but instead she hobbled in the direction of Mother as she stepped from the train. McKenna clasped her arm through Arrosa's, tears in her eyes.

They were scarcely out of the way of the other passengers when they embraced. "We're so glad you're here," said McKenna.

Greetings and introductions were made, and Mother took a step back. "Let me have a gander at my beautiful daughters." A tear slipped down her cheek. "It hasn't been long, but it feels like forever since I last saw you."

"Did you discuss working at the boutique with Aunt Julia Mathilda?"

"I did. I have to admit I'm a little nervous. Even Julia Mathilda seemed a bit skeptical."

McKenna patted their mother on the arm. "You will do very well, Mother, and I will be here to help you."

"Thank you for your vote of confidence. And, Arrosa, look at you. You look so vibrant! How is the nanny position?"

"Wonderful."

"That's so good to hear."

"Mother, please do consider coming to live with Clayton and me."

"McKenna, I appreciate that so much, but I think it would be best if I resided in the apartment above the boutique, provided it is still available."

McKenna nodded. "It is still available. But do know that you are most welcome at our home."

"I do appreciate that so much. But I was praying about it and thinking about it, and have chosen to stay in the apartment. This way, when your father arrives, we'll have a home."

"You'd have a home at our home as well," countered McKenna.

Mother grasped one of each of her daughters' hands. "The apartment will be fine. I'm just so grateful to be away from the Thorburn Flats."

"You'll like it here, Mother."

"I'm sure I will, although…" Mother gazed about. "Such a small town with no tall buildings and more wagons and horses than automobiles."

"Very different from Missoula," agreed McKenna.

Arrosa offered a prayer of gratitude for the Lord seeing to it that Mother arrived safely in Hollow Creek. Now, if only Father were here, all would be perfect.

# CHAPTER NINE

THE UPSTAIRS PLAYROOM AT the Evanson home reminded Arrosa of the one she and McKenna once shared in their mansion in Missoula. Emotion built in her chest from those fond days they'd experienced so long ago.

Traversing the staircase had been no easy feat, and she was grateful Malachi had arrived when he had for breakfast and assisted her step by step, gingerly up the stairs. Vera and Morris would have gladly aided her, but there was something much more comforting about having Malachi's strong but gentle grip on her arm as she wobbled about.

Oh, but to be strong again! To be able to walk without the cane and go wherever she pleased!

Not that she would allow an ounce of complaint to take up residency in her thoughts for long. Not when the Lord had brought her so far.

"Thank you," she said when he'd delivered her to the room. Adelia opened the door and rushed inside, Ephraim on her heels. Malachi set Junior on the floor and retreated to carry Mamie up.

A four-foot gate across the doorway kept Junior contained should he decide to crawl about, and Arrosa took a seat in the rocking chair and gazed about her. Blue and white paisley wallpaper covered the walls, and toys, including a rocking horse, dolls, a toy carriage, wooden blocks, and a pretend life-sized playhouse, littered the floor in haphazard organization. A fire-place stood in the far corner, and several shelves with books beckoned a time for stories. An ornate rug covered the wood floor, and Arrosa watched as the rain pitter-pattered against the enormous window. She wagered that on a bright and sunny day, the view of the mountains was nothing short of spectacular.

Adelia and Mamie set about opening the doors of their doll-house. Ephraim took a seat on the floor to play with his toy train, and Junior climbed into Arrosa's lap.

*Lord, might it be Your will that someday I would have children of my own?* Oh, but to be a mother. It was one of the deepest desires of her heart.

An hour later, Junior had fallen asleep, and the older children played quietly. Arrosa took advantage of their well-behaved moment to open a book she had previously selected from the numerous options on the bookshelf.

They once had such a varied collection at their home in Missoula. Fiction, nonfiction, Father's financial books, and more. She never tired of settling into a chair in the parlor and reading to her heart's content.

Malachi stepped over the gate at the door. "Hello, Arrosa."

"Hello, Malachi." The dreary day was made all the better by seeing her new friend. "What brings you to the playroom?"

"I'll be going to Bleakney in a few days, and I wanted to see if there was anything you needed before I went."

"Bleakney?"

"Yes, Thad and I have a cattle sale."

"My father resides in Bleakney."

"He does? I was wondering why he didn't arrive with your ma on the train two weeks ago."

"Mother lived in Missoula. Father..." but as she said the words, she realized how peculiar it sounded that her parents did not dwell in the same town. "What I mean to say is that Father is conducting some business provisionally in Bleakney."

"Oh, I see."

She wrung her hands. Ought she ask? Would it even be possible? Would Vera be able to mind the children? "Do you think…I mean to say, would it be possible? Would it be an option—"

He waited patiently while she attempted to get her bearings about her. To be able to visit Father would be nothing short of marvelous. "Since you and Mr. Evanson are traveling to Bleakney, might it be possible for me to come along as well? I daresay I have missed Father something awful, and I would appreciate seeing him again. Provided Vera can tend to the children." She felt guilty at the thought. Arrosa wouldn't want Emilie or Vera to think she was taking advantage.

"It's fine with me, and I'll check with Thad just to be sure he's agreeable to it."

"Thank you so much! You say it's in two days?"

"Yes, on Thursday. We'll leave before sunrise to catch the train."

Then she remembered she didn't have enough funds for the fare. She picked at a loose thread on her skirt. "Do you know the cost of a ticket?"

"I'm not sure, as Thad will pay my way, seeing as how it's for the ranch."

Perhaps she ought not to get her hopes up yet until she figured out how to afford a ticket.

"I can't imagine it would be too expensive since Bleakney isn't that far."

"No, I don't imagine it would be." However, when you had little money to your name, any amount was too much. Her stipend wasn't much, and she'd assisted McKenna with purchasing some items for Mother in the apartment and had bought some incidentals at the mercantile. It hadn't left her with much until the next payday.

"I'll ask Thad and let you know."

"And we'll be back the same day?"

"The same day, yes, but it will be late evening."

"Thank you. I appreciate you asking Mr. Evanson."

Malachi left, and Arrosa pondered how she might secure the funds for train fare to Bleakney.

Arrosa gathered the coins together. Just enough to purchase a ticket. Oh, but to see Father again! She'd been unable to stop and visit him during the trip from Missoula to Hollow Creek, and the other times, she had been too sick to travel. But now, to be able to talk to him and to see for herself that he was all right was surely an answer to prayer. Emilie, always the gracious employer, encouraged her to take the day to see Father, and Vera agreed to watch the children in Arrosa's absence.

Arrosa awoke early, although she couldn't say she'd really slept at all the night before, not with the anticipation of the following day crowding her thoughts. She dressed, ate the delicious breakfast Cook provided, then met Malachi, Mr. Evanson, and Morris outside.

She and Malachi exchanged greetings, and he assisted her into the front of the white five-passenger 1912 Oldsmobile Touring car. Morris slid into the driver's side, and Malachi and Mr. Evanson climbed into the rear seat. Arrosa settled into the comfortable red leather.

The sun was just beginning to rise, casting magnificent hues over the broad sky. It took some time to make it out of the fence that surrounded the Evanson property. Arrosa had ridden in automobiles many times before, when Mother and Father owned them in days past, but never in one traveling at this lethargic pace.

As a matter of fact, if she thought that traveling to Hollow Creek and being a nanny for the Evansons was an adventure, she had no idea what an adventure truly was until being Morris's passenger. It wasn't that Morris drove fast, causing her to fear riding with him, because he didn't. As a matter of fact, he crept along the road, all the while gazing to and fro, obviously admiring the scenery. She peered at his profile, noting tufts of gray hair peeking beneath the new cowboy hat Vera purchased for him for his recent birthday. He slouched in the seat and nudged his spectacles up the bridge of his nose. "Can't be too careful about deer being out this time of day," he mused aloud.

True to his word, a mother and her two fawns clustered at the side. Morris slowed even more. "Don't even want to think about the last time I hit a deer."

"Emilie and I were just grateful you and Vera weren't injured," said Mr. Evanson.

"We appreciate that, but it sure banged up the former automobile something fierce."

Malachi leaned forward, and Arrosa inhaled the scent of fresh soap. "Was that the time you refused to stop and ask for directions?" he asked.

"Pfft. Is that the rumor Vera is spreading around hither and yon?"

Mr. Evanson chuckled. "Not sure it's a rumor, Morris."

"Well, it shore is a rumor. I love Vera more than life itself, but she was exaggerating just a slight bit when she shared that scuttlebutt." Morris took a hand off the wheel and indicated a small space between his finger and thumb. When he did so, the

Oldsmobile veered to one side, and Arrosa gasped. Any further to the right, and they'd be off the road and into the ditch.

Morris efficiently swerved and righted the motorcar.

Not many other automobiles were on the road at any given time in the small town of Hollow Creek, but especially not at this hour. Morris inclined toward the window and peered into the mirror. "Seems there's a fellow driver on the road today." He pulled to the side of the road and gestured at the wagon behind him to go past. Would Morris allow every wagon in the vicinity to pass them? If so, they'd never make the six o'clock train.

He finally edged back onto the road and dilly-dallied along. "As a matter of fact, I remember that day that Vera tattled on me for not asking for directions."

Arrosa turned to see Malachi's amused expression, and they exchanged a smile.

"It seems like just yesterday. Vera and I were going to deliver some things to the orphanage for Emilie. We were driving along on a chilly spring day. By my way of thinking, it was about ten o'clock in the morning. Vera is more fond of the automobile than I am. I'm more of a horse man myself, and if I had my druthers, Vera would have driven that day. But anyhow, we scuttled along down the road, singing like we most often do. The miles passed more quickly than usual, and before I knew it, we were lost. Appears we passed the orphanage long ago. I turned around, and we drove back the way we came. Still no sign of our destination. We came upon a town—don't recall the name of it just now—but there was a mercantile and a livery. Vera, bless her heart, can be a bossy sort at times."

Morris took a breath before he continued the story to his audience. "She told me I should ask for directions. As a man who's knowledgeable about many things, I didn't think such was necessary. That, and I do have my pride. Even though Vera got herself into a dither about it, asking for directions wasn't necessary after all. After several miles, we came to the orphanage. It was right where it's always been."

So involved in his story was he that Morris zipped right past the turnoff into town. "Uh, Morris?" said Mr. Evanson. "You might need to turn around."

A half hour later, they boarded the train. Malachi and Mr. Evanson would be gone for several hours, tending to cattle sale business. Arrosa prayed she could convince the Bleakney deputy to allow her to spend sufficient time with Father, as she wasn't sure what she would do with her time while she waited for the men.

When they arrived in Bleakney, Malachi assisted her from the train. "Would you like for me to accompany you to your father's house?"

She appreciated Malachi's chivalry, but she couldn't allow him to see the place she would visit. She politely declined, and they agreed to meet at two o'clock at the restaurant two blocks away before going their separate ways. Arrosa moseyed down the street, looking in the windows of the shops.

Bleakney was smaller than Hollow Creek, but already, folks were wandering up and down the boardwalk. She stopped into the dry goods store and asked where the jail was located. The clerk frowned, her red eyebrows knitting. "The jail?"

"Yes, please."

The woman gave her directions, and Arrosa continued on her way. She clutched the Scottish Fancies, Father's favorite cookie that she'd convinced Cook to allow her to bake last night after supper. McKenna, too, had delivered Scottish Fancies when she'd visited Father, and mentioned the joy in his countenance with the brief hiatus from jail food.

A dreary white building greeted her, and she stood in front of it for a moment, a pensive mood shadowing her thoughts. Father had committed a crime, and he had to pay his debt to society. He knew that, and his family knew that. Moreover, Arrosa was grateful it was the Lord's will that Father would remain in the Bleakney jail rather than incarcerated in Deer Lodge.

And although crime must never go unpunished, what of her formerly successful father? A man who prided himself on providing his family with the finest home, automobiles, and clothes? One who stood a head taller than most in their upper-crust society when it came to reputation, intelligence, and character?

Until… The profound guilt niggled deep inside her heart. Father had been placed in a predicament because of her. Because of her medical needs. Her illness. Her failure to recover. Because of her, they'd lost it all.

The unshed tears blurred her vision. The Chapman family had once had it all.

She steadied herself on her cane, even as her resolve faltered.

*Lord, please help me. Help me to be an encouragement to Father, even if I, myself, am feeling despondent and weighed down with guilt since I am the one who is accountable for causing Father to feel he had no other choice but to embezzle to seek medical treatment for me.*

Arrosa swiped at a tear that slid down her cheek. Emotions jumbled their way through her heart and mind. She looked over her shoulder, and that's when she noticed Malachi and Mr. Evanson across the street at the implement store. She couldn't allow them to see her entering the jail. She clutched her cane and, on unsteady legs, shuffled around the corner and stayed there for what seemed an eternity while the men conversed with two other gentlemen.

If only Malachi's back were turned. She could then proceed with her plans to see Father. She flattened herself against the building. How long would she have to wait?

Minutes ticked by. Folks passed, although most didn't notice her skulking in the alleyway. She cautiously peered around the corner.

"Arrosa?"

Malachi stood just to the left of her. When had he crossed the street? "Malachi?"

"Are you lost?"

"Lost? No. I'm just—well, I'm just visiting the dry goods store, and then I'll be on my way to Father's." She cringed as the words left her mouth. It was a half-truth if there ever was one.

Malachi inclined toward her. "But this isn't the dry goods store. That's a block in the opposite direction."

"A block in the opposite direction?" She must sound like a confused flibbertigibbet. What must he think of her hovering in the alleyway? Yet, she couldn't tell him the *real* reason. She couldn't share that her father was in jail.

He stared at her, expectation in his eyes as he waited for a feasible answer. She couldn't lie. But she couldn't tell the truth either. "I'll be on my way, then," she heard herself say.

"I don't mind accompanying you."

"Thank you. I appreciate that, but I'm fine."

"If you're sure."

"I'm sure." Malachi was such a gentleman, and she appreciated his concern. She exhaled the breath she'd been holding and watched as he again crossed the street, and he and Mr. Evanson traversed down the boardwalk. But not before Malachi turned and looked her way one last time.

When they were out of sight, Arrosa entered the jail. A man at a desk with curly gray hair and a matching mustache greeted her. "Deputy Gern. How may I help you?"

She took one more glance back just to be sure Malachi hadn't followed her into the jail. "Yes, I'm hoping to visit Egbert Chapman."

"With all respect, ma'am, visiting hours aren't for a while yet."

"If at all possible, may I visit with him now? I traveled from Hollow Creek and am only here for a few hours."

"How is it you know Mr. Chapman?"

"He's my father, sir."

Deputy Gern nodded. "Was it your sister who was married last year in Hollow Creek?"

"Yes, McKenna married Sheriff Beringer."

"Ah, yes. I think I can arrange for you to visit with your father. Please follow me."

"And might I give him these?" She set the tin of Scottish Fancies on the deputy's desk.

Deputy Gern opened the tin's lid and peered inside. The aroma of cookies filled the air. "Yes, that would be fine."

She lifted the tin and stood. Her legs threatened to once again wobble out from beneath her as she followed the deputy down a dismal and gloomy hallway where other prisoners leered at her from their temporary homes.

"Chapman, you have a visitor."

Father clutched the bars of his cell. "Arrosa?"

"Father?" Tears burned her throat.

Deputy Gern looked from Arrosa to Father. "Enjoy your visit." He smiled, nodded, and sauntered back down the hall to his desk.

Father had aged in the time since she'd seen him last. Wrinkles fanned his eyes, his face had thinned, and weariness engulfed his countenance. "Father, how are you doing?" She choked the words, knowing he couldn't be doing well if he was incarcerated.

Father reached a hand through the bars and took her cold hand in his. "While this is not the way I had anticipated spending my days, God is good."

His newfound faith continued to surprise her, although both McKenna and Mother mentioned he'd changed. "These are for you." He released her hands, and she opened the lid to the tin and passed him a Scottish Fancy.

"These are my favorite, thank you."

"McKenna mentioned they allowed you to have them, so I thought I would surprise you. I snuck into the kitchen, and with Cook's permission, mixed up a batch."

Father took a bite and closed his eyes. "These are delicious. Thank you."

"Do they taste like the ones your mother once made?"

"Even more decadent."

Arrosa wasn't sure that was the case, but she appreciated Father saying as much. "Please, have another."

"Will you have one as well?"

"I have to admit that I've already eaten several to my heart's content." She laughed as she was reminded once again how much she missed her father. Missed the way things once were. Missed her family. "How is the food they feed you?"

"Not bad. Not Cook's, but not bad. A restaurant down the street is contracted with the jail to provide two of the three meals. For breakfast, we always have slop." He chuckled. "Listen to me. Would I have ever used the word 'slop' before entering this fine establishment?" Father's eyes crinkled at the corners.

"No, likely not."

"Forgive me for referring to the runny oatmeal as such. I'm grateful for the way the Lord has provided."

Even in jail, Father was thankful. She marveled at how different he was now. In their previous lives, he never would have given credit to God for anything, let alone "slop". Suddenly, her stomach soured as the guilt settled in.

"You are here because of…because of me."

"Here because of you? No, my sweet daughter. I'm here because I made a poor choice."

"But if I hadn't fallen ill—"

"And falling ill was your choice?"

She shook her head. "No, but if I hadn't been so ill, you wouldn't have had to embezzle to pay for the treatments." Treatments that didn't work.

"I want you to listen to me, Arrosa Chapman." Father's low voice rose a notch. "You are my daughter, and you, your mother, and McKenna mean more to me than anything on this earth. As a father, I couldn't endure the thought of losing you. We fathers do all we can to protect our children. To love them the best we can. To keep them safe. To keep them from harm." His voice wavered. "I couldn't keep you from becoming ill, therefore…"

"But that wasn't your fault."

"No, it wasn't my fault, but I was powerless to find a cure for you. Someday, when you're a mother, you'll understand the lengths you'll go to help your child. For me, if it meant that if I needed to embezzle, then so be it."

"But…"

Father squeezed her hand and shook his head. "Please don't misunderstand me, Arrosa. What I did was wrong. Very wrong. How we had lived beyond our means was wrong and caused problems beyond paying for treatments for you. We would likely have found ourselves in that dire financial predicament even without the rheumatic fever. My choice to steal is my burden and my burden alone. While we may have good reasons for our choices, if those choices are unlawful, we must atone for those poor choices. For me, that is a jail sentence."

A heaviness weighed in her stomach. "I still wish you didn't have to live here. That you and Mother could live in Hollow Creek and that we could be a family again."

"Ah, we did have some wonderful times, did we not? Although I must say I have been convicted many times of the fact that I put my job before my family. What I wouldn't do to go back in time and rearrange my priorities. But alas, I must also remember that God has given me a second chance. Had it not been for my being sentenced to jail, I might never have surrendered my life to Him. That, above all other tragedies, would have been the biggest tragedy of all."

Father was right. She, Mother, and McKenna had all made Jesus their Lord and Savior through the hardships of losing everything. She bit her lip. "You're right, Father."

"Yes, and I am also grateful that the Lord has seen fit to keep me here and not at Deer Lodge. That is one place I don't ever want to live. Now, enough of that. Please tell me how you are doing. How are your mother and McKenna?"

"I'm a nanny for the Evanson family. They have four adorable children, and I enjoy being able to care for them."

"Ah, you were always so good with children. I'm proud of you, Arrosa."

The words seeped deep into her heart. "Thank you, Father."

"Practice for someday when you have your own." A grin crossed his face. "I still can't believe I'm going to be a grandpa."

"Yes, McKenna and Clayton are overjoyed about becoming parents. As for me, I'm not sure that is God's plan."

"We can't be sure what God's plans are. Could be that you are correct, or it could be that you have a passel of children someday. Either way, we know His plans are always perfect."

It was new for Arrosa to hear her father speak of the Lord. He'd never had much time for the things of God during her growing-up years. He was right…his newfound faith might never have happened had he not made the choice to embezzle. God certainly did work in mysterious ways. "The ranch is lovely. It reminds me a lot of our Missoula home, only it contains acres of ranchland and isn't in the city. The gardens, however, do bring back fond memories of Mother's carefully pruned trees and flowers."

"It was lovely there. Do you remember the time our new butler accidentally drove over your mother's latest tree? She had decided to have it planted in the driveway, and just as the butler rounded the corner, he crushed it beneath the wheels of the automobile."

"Oh, yes, I remember that. The tree was more akin to a shrub. Mother was beside herself for days."

"Until the dead tree was removed and a new one put in its place, well, not exactly in its place, but rather, safe from any veering of the automobile."

She and Father shared a laugh. "Those times seem so far in the past."

"They do. But now we'll make new memories. How has your mother taken to Hollow Creek?"

"She is getting settled, and I daresay the town is growing on her."

Father released her hands and stroked his chin. "The more I hear about Hollow Creek, the more I'd like to settle down there once I'm released. Your mother and I would be close to you and McKenna and could spend Christmases and other holidays together."

"That would be delightful." Oh, but to have her family all in one place again!

The sound of footsteps drew Arrosa's attention to the hall-way, and Deputy Gern approached them. "I regret to inform you that time is up."

Father again reached his hand through the bars and held hers. "It was good to see you, Arrosa. Please tell your mother and your sister hello for me. And thank you to you and McKenna for keeping me in Scottish Fancies."

She swallowed the lump in her throat. She would maintain a brave countenance for him. "I love you, Father."

"I love you too, my dear daughter."

Deputy Gern led her back through the jail. "How did it go?"

"It went well. Thank you for allowing me to visit him."

"You're welcome. If you see Beringer, tell him I said hello."

She cautiously peered out before stepping onto the board-walk. She had some time to spend moseying through town before meeting Malachi and Mr. Evanson at the restaurant. It would do her some good to clear her mind.

Malachi stared out the train window. The cattle sale had gone well, and he was grateful for the opportunity to accompany Thad and learn from his employer. He averted his gaze to Arrosa, who had fallen asleep, her head lolling to one side.

She was a beautiful woman. Kind, compassionate, and she loved the Lord. He was grateful for their friendship. One thing had struck him odd, however. Why had she been so evasive in Bleakney? Did her pa truly reside there? Malachi couldn't imagine being separated from his wife while he worked like Arrosa's parents with her ma in Hollow Creek and her pa temporarily in Bleakney.

And why was she lurking in the alleyway? Had she been lost, despite her words to the contrary? The most peculiar part of her statement was that she thought she was at the dry goods store when that business was a block away.

Questions without answers plagued him. When he'd turned to cross the street again, he'd noticed she was still standing there and remained for some time until he and Thad continued down the street out of sight to meet with the cattle buyer. Did she really meet with her pa? Was she somehow ashamed of him? But how could that be? She'd mentioned in one of their conversations that he'd once worked in a bank.

Malachi shrugged off the uncertainty. It wasn't his business to know the details about her visit to Bleakney.

# CHAPTER TEN

MALACHI HAD JUST FINISHED branding cattle for the day when he heard the children in the play yard. He removed his hat, reached a forearm to his forehead to swipe the sweat that had collected, and strode in that direction and found Arrosa in the play yard, sitting on a colorful quilt with Junior beside her while the rest of the children played. Malachi stopped and watched from afar. It was the perfect setting—the perfect day. The three older children were fortunate to have been adopted by the Evansons. What if someone like Thad and Mrs. Evanson had adopted him? Gave him a home? *Loved* him?

Memories flashed through his mind at a rapid pace. Of the homes he'd resided in after being sent on the orphan train, only one had the potential to change the life of a little boy for the better. By then, it was too late. They hadn't even lived long enough to make a real impact on his life.

"Malachi?"

He plopped the hat back on his head and strode toward Arrosa. Perhaps he could come up with an excuse for being in the play yard instead of moving on to the next job duty.

"Hello, Arrosa."

"Isn't it a delightful June day?"

Her smile lit her entire countenance, and for a moment, his mouth opened, but he uttered no words. Finally, he found his voice. "Reckon it is a delightful June day. Perfect day, as a matter of fact." He reluctantly averted his gaze from her face and scanned the sky above. Brilliantly blue with not a cloud to be seen. Snow still covered the tallest tips of the mountains, and the green of the pine trees at the lower elevations provided a sharp and vivid contrast to the sky. Because of the recent rains, the hillsides and the grasslands shone an even brighter hue. Before long, little sprouts that would someday be flowers would emerge.

Arrosa peered up at him. "What brings you to the play yard today?"

To the play yard? He really didn't have a reason other than he enjoyed spending time with her. "We just finished branding."

"Congratulations. I hear that is quite the undertaking."

"Yes, it was." There was something about her that drew him in. Made him want to be worthy of her.

"I'm sure the children would love to see you. They have been so diligently playing with their blocks over there in the corner by the trees. I appreciate the table that you made for Mamie."

"The table? Oh, yes, the table." Could he sound any more like a daft dodo bird? This was Arrosa. His friend. The woman he'd spent considerable time with since her arrival in Hollow Creek. And he'd built the table just last week at the perfect height so Mamie could play with her dolls and toys while sitting in her wheelchair.

"Are you feeling all right?"

Her concern warmed his heart. "Yes, just sidetracked." That was the truth. Ever since he'd started thinking of Arrosa as potentially more than a friend, he'd been more nervous around her.

Malachi stretched out beside her, and as if on cue, Junior crawled over and planted himself in Malachi's lap. "Ky?"

Malachi ruffled Junior's downy blond hair. Thad definitely couldn't deny his son. The chubby little boy looked just like his pa.

"You should have been here about a half hour ago. Ephraim was making some sort of deal with his sisters."

"Oh, really?"

"Yes. Seems they wanted to play with their new dish set, and Ephraim would hear none of it. The girls have developed a game they call *restaurant* where Mamie owns the restaurant, and Adelia is the customer. Adelia was complaining that she was always the only customer, and, of course, Mamie would not hear of switching places and allowing Adelia to be the restaurant owner. We did have a long talk about that." Arrosa's tinkling laugh rode on the slight breeze. A laugh he could never tire of.

Arrosa was so good with children. So patient with them. So loving, even though these weren't her own. Yet she cared for them better than some mothers.

Was his own ma like Arrosa? Forbearing? Kind? Devoted? He struggled to remember her, and the picture he'd drawn on the piece of paper was the only thing that filled his mind. How could he have forgotten so much about her? Yet, he could recall clearly watching her after Boyd shoved her away.

Tightness settled squarely in his chest. What he wouldn't give to know what had happened that day Ma hadn't taken him with her. She had tried, hadn't she? Or at least that's how he remembered it, but memories could be fuzzy. But he couldn't go back. Couldn't change the past. Couldn't ask his own father, a man Malachi hoped to never see again. Hopefully, Boyd Goshorn was rotting away somewhere in prison.

"The girls promised to play blocks with Ephraim if he promised to play *restaurant* with them afterward. At first, he wasn't agreeable to such a request, but after I mentioned the possibility of asking Cook for a special late afternoon treat, he readily agreed.”

Arrosa’s words brought Malachi back to the present. There was no sense dwelling on such a distressing topic as that of wondering about Ma and reminding himself of his strong dislike for his father. He glanced at the children playing in the distance and chuckled. “I’m sure that would make a difference in Ephraim’s decision.”

“Oh, it did. However, Ephraim and I did have to discuss putting others before ourselves.”

“Sounds like your parents taught you well.”

Arrosa nodded. “They did. Mother was quite busy with charities and other functions, but she never failed to take time with McKenna and me, even if it meant including us in her various social activities, fundraisers, and the like. Unfortunately, Father worked dreadful hours and traveled a lot, and we didn’t see him for stretches of time. As an important employee at the bank, he made that his priority.” She bit her lip. “He’s a different man now. Not that he wasn’t always a loving father, but now that he’s surrendered his life to Christ…” She inhaled a sharp breath. “Those days of Father working at the bank seem so long ago now.”

“I’m happy to hear about your father surrendering his life to Christ.” Would Boyd ever surrender his life to his Savior? Malachi harumphed. Boyd Goshorn would no more turn from his wicked ways than apologize to Malachi for all he’d done.

“Thank you. I’m grateful He drew my family to Him.” A tear settled just on the fringe of her long eyelashes. It seemed there was more to her story, but he didn’t want to compel her to share more than she felt comfortable. Especially since he wouldn’t be sharing many details about his parents.

Besides, what could he say? That his ma left when he was a young boy, and his father was a murderer and a thief? An image of the orphan train flashed through his mind. The pastor and his wife knew that was the only way to protect Malachi—and themselves. Gratitude overcame him as he recalled again about the choices others made on his behalf.

"Malachi?" Worry lined her face.

"I'm sorry. Did you say something?"

"Yes. I asked about any fond memories from when you were a child in Indiana. You mentioned you are estranged from your mother and that your father has passed, but what about recollections from your childhood?"

"I don't have many fond memories." He wouldn't elaborate. Wouldn't give her a chance to discover who he really was. He liked it that she considered him the kind ranch hand who helped whenever a need arose. The gentlemanly sort who'd delivered her from the train station and who drove her and some of the others to church on Sunday. The one who built a table for Mamie and found a wagon so she could join in events with the others.

Not the man he really was.

Suddenly, the air seemed thinner.

"Ky?" Junior reached up and planted a chubby hand on Malachi's face.

Why was it such a challenge to forget the past? The Lord had given him a future. Why then the constant reminders of his former life?

"Ky?" Junior repeated, this time looking up at Malachi with expectation.

Malachi ruffled his hair. "Are you being a good boy today, Junior?"

As if he understood every bit of Malachi's question, Junior nodded and smiled, revealing new teeth. If Malachi ever had a son, he'd be a good father. Or at least try to be. He wouldn't harm his wife and son.

Arrosa's brows knitted. "I'm sorry to hear about your childhood."

"Just how it is, I reckon."

"Aunt Arrosa, we're ready to play *restaurant*." Adelia parked Mamie directly in front of Malachi and Arrosa. Then she planted her hands on her hips and jutted her chin toward Ephraim. "He says he's going to go back on his promise to play *restaurant*."

Ephraim sauntered over, arms folded across his chest. "That was only five minutes of playing blocks. I'd say as sure as the sun rises and sets, that's not enough time for a trade to play *restaurant*." He scowled, and Malachi struggled not to laugh. Ephraim was a strong-willed sort, the perfect match for his sisters, even if he was outnumbered. Would Junior, with his mild-mannered personality, help balance the scales?

"It was not *only* five minutes, Ephraim Evanson. It was at least three hours."

"Three hours and five minutes," added Mamie.

"Aunt Arrosa, can you please tell Ephraim that a promise is a promise?" asked Adelia.

"Ephraim, we did discuss that you would play *restaurant* with Adelia and Mamie if they played blocks with you, and..."

"But, Aunt Arrosa..."

Arrosa held a finger to her lips. "It is disrespectful to interrupt while another is speaking."

"Yes, ma'am."

"Now, the girls did play blocks with you, and it was longer than five minutes. But because the Lord exhorts us to put others before ourselves—while it may not have been long enough and you wish they'd played blocks longer—you still have to keep your word."

"Told you so," said Adelia.

"Yes, we told you so," added Mamie.

"Now, girls, it is not kind to gloat. You two could have put Ephraim first and played blocks longer. You know how he's looked forward to this all week."

"Yes, ma'am," they chorused. Mamie's eyes darted about, and she folded her hands in her lap.

Arrosa tilted her head to one side. "What is to be the solution to this dilemma?"

"Play blocks longer?" asked Ephraim.

"All right. Since we are to put others before ourselves, we'll play blocks longer, but you have to promise us with a pinky promise that you'll play *restaurant* afterward." Adelia tilted her head toward her brother, silently daring him to disagree.

Ephraim extended his pinky. "Pinky promise. And I will play *restaurant* for a good long time."

Adelia pushed Mamie back to the blocks, and Ephraim did nothing to hide his smirk.

"You're good with children, Arrosa."

"Thank you. I've always wanted to be a mother, and while not quite the same, I have grown fond of these children in this short amount of time."

"You'll make a fine ma someday."

Her entire face lit up at his remark. "Do you think so?"

"I do. To borrow Ephraim's words, as sure as the sun rises and sets, I think you'll someday make a fine ma."

She sat up a little straighter. "Thank you, Malachi."

Junior reached for her. "Roe-Roe?"

"Come here, sweetie." She snuggled him to her, and Junior planted a slobbery kiss on her cheek.

Arrosa Chapman had no idea what a compassionate and kind woman she was.

All the more reason why someone like her was too good for someone like him.

# CHAPTER ELEVEN

DAYS PASSED, AND ARROSA found herself settling into her position at the Evanson Ranch. Her days were full—perhaps even fuller now that she was no longer administering schoolwork due to the upcoming summer. Sunny Montana days, while the children played outdoors in the yard, and Sundays, being able to see Mother and McKenna, made for a new peace that overcame the former trepidation Arrosa once had.

Mother learned the intricacies of working at the boutique, and Arrosa and McKenna were able to purchase some items for her to make the apartment feel more like home. Father remained in the Bleakney jail, and Arrosa prayed that there would be a position available in Hollow Creek once he was released.

Something had changed in Arrosa's feelings for Malachi. The more time she spent with him, the more she thought about him. And, yes, they were friends, but she'd begun to see him as more than that.

Peculiar since she'd once envisioned herself cottoning to someone like Wayne. Yet, Malachi was nothing like Wayne. As a matter of fact, his personality and appearance far surpassed Wayne's.

So did his integrity.

She saw Malachi on horseback riding toward the house, and she stood, leaned on her cane, and waved. Would he have time to stop and visit for a bit? They had started a tradition of asking each other questions, and Arrosa welcomed the challenge of coming up with another question that would help her learn more about him. He was very evasive when it came to anything about his family. She wouldn't pry, but she did want to know more about him and what made him the man he was.

Malachi returned her wave and disappeared around the corner. Within a few minutes, he was joining her in the play yard. When he walked toward her, Arrosa's heart skittered. Yes, he was by far more handsome than Wayne Lingis. He possessed a better character, too.

"Hello, Arrosa." His mouth quirked up into that dapper smile she was growing accustomed to.

"Hello, Malachi."

She handed him a sandwich from the basket Cook had packed for the children's noonday meal. He prayed, then took a bite. She waited until he'd finished chewing before speaking. "I have my question for today."

"As do I." A suspicious glint danced in his eyes. What would his question be?

"Have you always wanted to be a rancher?" she asked.

"I worked on a few farms in Nebraska, so being a rancher wasn't something I considered until working on the Hoyer Ranch in Southern Montana. It was then that I developed a preference for the cattle, sheep, the land, and riding the range."

"Not mucking stalls?"

He chuckled. "Mucking the stalls? No, that's probably my least favorite. I have a question for you now. If you could live anywhere in the world, including the places you've traveled, where would you choose?"

"Montana. There is no place I'd rather live."

"Missoula? Hollow Creek? Somewhere else in Montana?"

"I thought it was one question each."

Malachi rubbed the back of his neck. "You're right, but this is the second part of the question."

"Oh, I see. Well, in that case, Hollow Creek. I loved Missoula when we lived there and wasn't sure I would cotton to Hollow Creek due to it being so small, but I've changed my mind. I would choose this town over Missoula. And you?"

"Hollow Creek for certain."

They continued with an affable conversation. That was one of the things she especially appreciated about Malachi—how easy he was to talk to. It was as if they'd known each other for years rather than weeks.

Malachi anticipated seeing Arrosa in the play yard several times throughout the week, and today was no exception. He'd hurried to finish his morning chores, his mind constantly on the woman who was capturing his heart a little more each day.

When she'd waved at him, he couldn't tether his horse quickly enough to join her. She was thoughtful, too, always ensuring there were some leftovers for him in case he was still hungry after his noonday meal.

They talked about numerous topics, but one thing he never discussed was his days as a young'un. Nor did he mention anything about Ma or Boyd. And he never would. He hadn't even shared it all with Barnabas or in his talks with Thad and Reverend Arkley.

The oddest things could spark a memory. Malachi watched as Ephraim attempted to teach his sisters how to play the game, *Hoop and Stick.* He rolled the hoop along the ground with a wooden trundling stick, endeavoring to see how long he could keep it rolling.

"I'd rather play *Graces*," said Adelia.

"*Graces* is for girls. I don't play such things." Ephraim crossed his arms. "Don't you two want to learn how to play *Hoop and Stick*?" He cast a desperate glance at Junior, who was attempting to stack blocks. "I can't wait until Junior is older so there will be another boy."

Mamie reached a hand from her place in her wheelchair. "Don't be sad, Ephraim. We'll play *Hoop and Stick*."

"You will? Thank you, Mamie! And I have just the plan to help you play it in your wheelchair."

"And I'll play, too. That way you won't have to wait thirty years for Junior to grow older so he can play too."

"Thanks. You two are the best sisters a boy could have."

Malachi watched as Ephraim patiently taught them both how to play *Hoop and Stick*. Malachi had once longed for someone to play with. A sibling. A friend. Anyone. But after he left on the orphan train that day, things were never the same.

Fear of the unknown kept him from speaking to anyone the day he boarded the train. Several other children of various ages joined him. Some of the girls prattled on about their new homes and how they hoped to have brothers and sisters. Some of the boys talked of how their new fathers would take them fishing all the time.

Malachi had fingered the piece of paper with the name "Victor" on it. It was the name the pastor's wife had given to the orphan train agent. At first, Malachi hadn't understood. But years later, he realized it was to protect him. If anyone ever asked if a boy named Malachi Goshorn had boarded the train, the answer was an honest no. No one would think to ask about a boy named Victor.

No one would underestimate a man named Boyd Goshorn.

For a moment, Malachi was back on the train, staring out the window and wondering what lay ahead. When it passed through town that day, the pastor and his wife asked that Malachi board it and find a new family in another state. Many children were still aboard and had ridden all the way from New York City. The kindly reverend and his wife were society agents and oversaw the proceedings. They taught the children poems and songs and reminded them to always use their manners. Most of the children already knew the songs, but the reverend's wife patiently sang them over and over again so Malachi could learn them as well. His favorite was "Onward Christian Soldiers".

They traveled for what seemed like days before stopping in a town much larger than the one from which he hailed. The children were ushered to a hotel and given clean clothes. The reverend's wife pinned his name tag onto his white shirt.

The reverend cupped Malachi's shoulder and smiled. *"Now, don't you worry, young man. God has a plan for your life."*

Malachi didn't know much about God, but if He had a plan for Malachi's life, Malachi hoped it was a good plan. *"Am I getting a new ma and pa?"*

*"You are."* The reverend smiled and patted him on the head.

A man who was to adopt him checked Malachi's teeth as if he were a horse, then asked about how healthy he was. *"I'm healthy,"* Malachi assured him. He'd say just about anything to have a family who loved him.

A couple took him home that day. The reverend said they were a prominent family in the town and that Malachi would do well with them.

But it didn't take long for Malachi to realize something was amiss.

Mr. and Mrs. Redding were anything but kind. Or, rather, they were anything but kind *to him*. They had their own children, two boys and two girls. The boys were both older than Malachi by a few years, and the girls were both younger. Malachi remembered what the other orphans had discussed about having siblings.

How lucky for him that he had gained four—all in one day!

He'd never had siblings before, so he didn't know what to expect. But even at eight years old, he was fairly sure that brothers and sisters were supposed to *like* their brother.

His new brothers slept upstairs. Malachi had never seen such a big house, and especially not such a magnificent room. It boasted two beds, two dressers, a fireplace, and numerous toys. The room alone was larger than the house Malachi shared with his ma and pa.

*"Where will I be sleeping?"* He tried to figure out in his mind where a third bed would fit. He only had one change of clothes, so he didn't need a dresser.

*"You'll be sleeping in the barn."* The two boys laughed and elbowed each other.

*"The barn?*

One of them snorted. *"Well, you won't be sleeping in the house."*

*"Why can't I sleep in the house with my new family?"*

*"Because we're not your family. You're one of our hired hands."*

Malachi hadn't understood what that meant at the time, but the first night in the barn, he curled up in the hay and did his best to hold back the tears. While the family partook of fun activities, Malachi was mucking the barn, caring for the livestock, splitting and collecting firewood, and picking rock so the other hired hands could plant crops. Malachi didn't mind having chores. He knew it was important to work hard and help the family, and he'd never been a lazy sort, but he hadn't realized that chores would be all he would be doing. He was allowed to eat in the house, but not at the table with the rest of the family. On Sundays, the family went to church, but Malachi had to stay behind.

The girls called him "servant" and ordered him around, telling him to do everything from fetching them water to doing other mundane tasks. He was allowed to attend school, but his new siblings acted like they didn't even know him. If he stepped slightly out of line, Mr. Redding punished him. Mrs. Redding constantly referred to him as "that insolent child".

One time when he had dropped an enormous rock on his foot, he'd cried out in pain and had limped to Mrs. Redding. He'd told her what happened and wrapped his arms around her thick waist. She brushed him aside without so much as an ounce of compassion. Weren't mothers supposed to comfort their injured children?

Several months after he turned nine, the reverend and his wife traveled from New York for a return visit. Within ten minutes, the reverend's wife found Malachi in the barn and loaded him into the buggy they had borrowed from one of the townsfolk.

*"Where am I going?"*

*"We are taking you to another family."* The reverend's wife put an arm around him, and for a moment, he pretended she was his ma. She smelled of rosewater, and her thick glasses magnified her round eyes.

*"Another family?"*

*"While we do our best to make sure that children are sent to loving homes, we do make mistakes from time to time."* The reverend's wife had dabbed at her eyes.

*"Please don't cry, ma'am."*

*"We are sorry that you had to live with the Reddings. Will you please forgive us?"*

Malachi had shrugged. *"Sure, I forgive you."*

The reverend's wife had hugged him closer, and he'd wanted to stay there in the safety of her arms forever. He'd wanted to ask if they could adopt him, but he was afraid of what they might say. He'd once again boarded a train. This time, when they stopped in another town, an elderly couple stepped forward to adopt him.

For the next three months, Malachi resided with Mr. and Mrs. Kerr, a kindly childless couple, until all three of them took ill with typhoid fever. Malachi recovered. His new parents didn't. Sadly, the couple hadn't adopted Malachi, but he was grateful they allowed him to stay with them.

After time in the orphanage, he was sent to several more homes until he finally turned sixteen and set out on his own.

Ephraim's giggles when the hoop rolled down the hill to the garden below brought Malachi back to the present.

"Malachi? Are you all right?"

He blinked and turned to see Arrosa holding a sleeping Junior in her arms.

"Yes, I'm fine. I was just remembering something."

"From years ago?"

"Yes."

"Tell me about your childhood." The expectation in her eyes told him she would want to hear wonderful stories about a boy who lived a life as Ephraim did.

He cleared his throat. "I don't really have much to tell."

"Surely, you have some stories."

Thankfully, Adelia tugging on his arm interrupted the awkward moment. "Uncle Malachi, will you come play *Hoop and Stick* with us?"

"Reckon I can do that." He offered his best smile to Arrosa, hoping it hid the true feelings he'd stuffed deep inside about the childhood no boy would want.

# CHAPTER TWELVE

WORKING UP THE NERVE to ask her was no easy task. Why, he couldn't be sure. After all, he and Arrosa had spent a lot of time together and had become friends. He brushed off the front of his jeans, removed his hat, ran a hand through his hair, then flicked a piece of crusted dirt from the front of his shirt. Why couldn't he have taken the time to meander by the bunkhouse and clean up a bit? He probably smelled like manure.

His stomach growled. He'd have to stop by the kitchen and offer to round up some huckleberries for Cook once they were ripe in exchange for a late meal. Cook may present herself as cantankerous, but Malachi knew how to draw her out of her, at times, sour disposition.

Malachi traipsed up the steps and onto the porch. Was it too late to postpone his plans? He took a deep breath, and that's when he inhaled whatever it was Cook had fixed for supper. The sunset cast an orangey glow in the west. If he hoped to ask Arrosa *and* convince Cook he'd not last another day without one of her delicious meals, he best proceed.

He opened the door and stepped inside. Only the clanging of dishes in the kitchen sounded. The children were likely already in bed. Was Arrosa still awake? From what he knew, she wasn't an early-to-bed sort. The aroma engulfed him. Meatloaf? Potatoes? And was that...perhaps peach pie? He weighed his options.

Eat first, then ask Arrosa. Ask Arrosa first, then eat. Eat only and ask Arrosa another day. Ask Arrosa and skip eating, and likely die an early death. Should he pray about it again? Barnabas said God heard all prayers, big and small.

*Lord, can you please give me courage? And wisdom?*

"Malachi Callahan, what are you doing standing there all suspicious-like in the foyer?" Cook bustled toward him, a spoon in her hand.

"Hello, Cook. You're just the one I needed to talk to."

"Oh?" She twisted her mouth to one side. "What is it you want? It's half past eight, and I don't have time for your shenanigans."

"Not shenanigans, ma'am. I was actually hoping to barter for a meal."

Cook arched a gray eyebrow. "Barter for a meal? Did you not receive the telegram that supper is served promptly at six o'clock?"

"Yes, ma'am, I'm well aware of supper time. I just had some matters to handle before I was able to eat." That and he had spent an insane amount of time working up the nerve to ask Arrosa what was on his mind. The poor horses and cows in the barn had to listen to him earlier as he rehearsed the exact words.

"Harrumph. Well, be that as it may, I don't have time to be making supper at all hours of the night. You are old enough to ensure that you arrive at the supper table at a reasonable hour if you wish to eat. Mind you, this is not a restaurant."

"Yes, Cook, I fully agree with you. You are correct in stating that it is not a restaurant. Although if it were a restaurant, it would be highly rated and the best in all of Montana, if not the entire West."

Cook rested a plump hand to her heart. "Well, I'm not sure I could compete with a restaurant like the Bellerose in Missoula."

He'd never eaten at the Bellerose, however… "Yes, you could. You have a true gift for making delectable meals." He offered his broadest smile.

She narrowed her eyes at him, and as if she could read his mind, asked, "Have you ever eaten at the Bellerose?"

"Can't say as I have, but I sure have heard of its unsurpassed reputation. Unsurpassed, that is, until folks try your succulent meals." He'd spent far too much time listening to some of the womenfolk prattle on with their descriptive words a time or two at the mercantile. Although it might behoove him in this situation.

"You haven't eaten at the Bellerose Restaurant, yet you compare my food to the food served there?"

Malachi couldn't afford to lose this battle. He had maybe a moldy bread crust back at the bunkhouse, and that was it. If that. His stomach rumbled. "I also wanted to let you know that I found another place to pick huckleberries". Would Cook be wise to him and know he was avoiding her question? She was a smart woman.

"Oh, did you, now? And where might that be?"

He pretended to button his lip. "Can't divulge that kind of information, ma'am. However, I will say that if you were to allow me a plate of food, I will be sure to pick you all the huckleberries you could want once they ripen."

She fixed him with a pondering gaze and adjusted the little ruffled hat on her head with her free hand. "I do believe, Malachi Callahan, that you are a persuasive sort. All right. I'll fix you a plate, and you can pick me a generous bucket of huckleberries once they ripen."

He considered asking if she would keep it warm for him for a few minutes while he asked Arrosa the plaguing question on his mind, but then thought better of it. He didn't want to lose the opportunity to eat supper. "Thank you, Cook. I appreciate that."

"Yes, well, you're welcome." She turned around and headed back to the kitchen, her skirts and apron swishing as she did so.

Five minutes later, he said grace and thanked the Lord for the meatloaf, mashed potatoes, peach pie, and warm biscuits. When he finished, he delivered the plate to the kitchen. "That was delicious. Thank you."

Cook looked up from cutting celery. "You're welcome. Now off with you. It's nearly your bedtime."

"Yes, ma'am." He wondered if Cook ever had any children of her own. "I do have one question."

"Yes?"

"Do you know where Arrosa is?"

Cook's eyes widened. "Now I like that young lady, and I am quite protective of her. What is it you would need to speak with her about at this time of night?"

"I just have a quick question, and then I will be on my way."

It was Friday, and if he expected to take her on a buggy ride on Sunday, that left tonight and tomorrow as options to ask her. Tomorrow would be busier than today.

"Most recently, she was in the parlor."

"Thank you." He nodded and bolted from the kitchen. Was it too late to ask her? What did etiquette rules dictate?

When had he become concerned with etiquette rules? He meandered around the corner and stopped at the parlor doorway. Inside, Arrosa sat in one of the chairs, her head bent over a sheet of stationery, writing something on the paper. Should he interrupt her? He stood and watched as her head tilted from one side to the other as she scribbled the words on the page.

He, Malachi Callahan, had no business asking someone as lovely as Arrosa Chapman to go on a buggy ride. She was a member of high society, whether her family still owned their extravagant Missoula home or not. A woman who deserved to be respected and treated with utmost care. A woman deserving of someone far better than him. Who would want to be in the company of the son of an outlaw?

He rubbed his sweaty palms on the front of his pants. Should he hightail it out of there? If he did, she'd never even know he was here. He took a quiet step backward, edging from the doorway. His parched tongue cleaved to the roof of his mouth.

"Malachi? Is that you?"

Arrosa's soft, sweet-sounding voice caught his attention. "Hello, Arrosa."

She turned in the chair and faced him. Malachi froze. She was so pretty with her delicate smile. His heart beat erratically in his chest, likely loud enough for the neighbors to hear. When had he become so nervous around her?

*Even before you decided to ask her to accompany you on a buggy ride.*

*But we're friends. Have been friends since she moved here. Why the apprehension?*

Arguing with himself? He was daft for certain.

"What brings you to the parlor at this late hour?"

"I was eating supper, and thought I'd pay you a visit before I called it a night." He thought he sounded rather regal even in his own ears. Would Arrosa prefer a dignified man rather than one who mended fences, mucked stalls, drove cattle, and had nary a penny to his name? A man who stumbled all over himself like an oaf?

"Please, do come in." She gestured for him to enter, and Malachi strolled along the carpet to the maize-colored couch, facing her. Against one edge stood a piano. Against the other wall, a fireplace with a mirror above it and two portraits on either side. One of Thad and Mrs. Evanson, and the other of the entire family. A glass chandelier hung from the ceiling, and an ornate table with a frilly lace tablecloth was topped with books. Red drapes, matching the red ornamental carpet, hung from the windows, and several pictures of ships, mountain scenery, and one of an elderly couple surrounded a wall-to-ceiling bookcase.

He perched on the edge of the fancy couch, worrying that he might stain it. He leaned slightly to one side, at first resting his elbow on the rolled couch arm, then thinking better of it, and clasping his hands in front of him. He'd only been in the Evanson parlor one other time, and that was to deliver a message to Mrs. Evanson. The elegant room was far from what he was accustomed to and larger than two of the bunkhouses combined.

Arrosa set the stationery and the pencil on the table.

"Did I interrupt you?" he asked.

"Oh, no. Just writing a missive to Father."

One of the maids entered and set a pink-flowered teacup on the table. Arrosa thanked her before again redirecting her attention to Malachi.

He cleared his parched throat. "I was wondering if you would care to join me for a buggy ride after church on Sunday. I thought it might be a fitting time to take a tour of the countryside. We could stop and maybe have a picnic."

"I'd be delighted to do so, yes."

"You would?"

"Oh, yes, of course."

"Sunday it is, then."

"Sunday, it is."

He stood to leave, and as he retreated from the Evanson home, the thought smacked him upside the head.

He was falling in love with Arrosa Chapman.

She was falling in love with Malachi Callahan.

Arrosa watched as Malachi left the parlor. His broad shoulders stretched the brown shirt taut across his back, and his blond hair curled up on the ends against the collar. Her heart thumped wildly in her chest. Had he just asked her to join him for a buggy ride and a subsequent picnic?

But why should that be anything out of the ordinary? They were friends.

However, somewhere in the mundane hours of daily life, she'd stopped seeing him as only a friend. He'd become more to her. Someone she looked forward to seeing each day.

Malachi turned and caught her staring, and the warmth of a blush suffused her cheeks. She quickly averted her gaze to the stationery. Best she focus her attention on finishing her letter to Father rather than on the dapper man she'd spend time with after church on Sunday.

Arrosa anticipated the buggy ride. In the days before everything changed, she would have opened the door to her mahogany wardrobe and perused the numerous offerings of lovely dresses. It would take her considerable time to find just the perfect dress or evening gown.

Now, such was not the case. Her choices consisted of three options. But she was grateful for those three options, nonetheless. Arrosa opened the bureau and unfolded the green shirtwaist and deep rose-colored skirt that she typically saved for her Sunday best. If only she had the lavender perfume she used to wear for special occasions.

Arrosa settled on her green shirtwaist and dark pink skirt. Now, if only she could steady her erratic pulse at the thought of spending an entire afternoon with Malachi. How would she ever get through the next few days?

# CHAPTER THIRTEEN

THAD EVANSON HAD ALWAYS been a generous boss, so why then the apprehension as Malachi sought to ask him to borrow the buggy?

Could it be the reasoning behind it? Could it be that the thought of accompanying Arrosa gave him a bit of a pause?

"Thad?"

"Malachi, how are you today?"

"Fine, sir. Do you have a minute?"

"Sure do. What's on your mind?"

"Would it be acceptable to you if I borrowed the buggy on Sunday?"

"Sure."

He cleared his throat. "I was hoping to take Arrosa for a ride and a picnic."

"Yes, you can borrow it for as long as you need."

Was that a smirk on his boss's face? "Thank you, sir. I promise to take good care of it."

"I'm not concerned."

"All right, then. Thank you again."

Thad chuckled. "Glad to see you and Arrosa are getting along so well."

"Yes, sir, I am fond of her."

"As everyone on the ranch knows."

"They do?"

"Well, maybe not everyone, but most of us notice the way you look at her and all the time you've been spending with her."

"Yes, I do spend time with her." He kicked at the dirt. "I'm not sure how that would work, seeing as she's of high society." Malachi inwardly chastised himself. What was the saying about putting the cart before the horse?

"Not sure it matters if folks care for each other."

Malachi hoped that to be the case, but, nonetheless, he wasn't thinking about marriage at this juncture.

"Pete mentioned something the other day I wanted to ask your thoughts on."

"Oh?"

"He suggested we hold a men's Bible study each Wednesday morning before breakfast. Would you be agreeable to attending?"

"Yes, sure." Malachi missed the close camaraderie with Barnabas, where he could ask numerous questions about God, and Barnabas would do his best to answer those questions by thumbing through his well-worn Bible. While Malachi appreciated church, and Reverend Arkley preached a convicting sermon, there was something about being in a close-knit group with other men that appealed to him.

"It's a good way to grow in the Lord."

"Yes, and I'm always having questions about the Lord and such." He thought of one query that entered his mind throughout the day, nearly every day, and invaded his sleep at night. He looked askance at Thad. Should he ask? While Thad likely wasn't as well-versed in the Bible as Barnabas, might he know the answer to Malachi's question? Sweat trickled down his spine as he wrestled with asking or keeping his thoughts to himself.

Finally, the former consideration won. "Do you believe there is an answer to everything?"

Thad's eyebrows lifted. "I reckon there is. Care to elaborate?"

"There's been something that's been heavy on my mind for years." The sorrow of it tore at his heart. "I've prayed for guidance and for peace about it, but so far, the Lord hasn't seen fit to calm my trepidation. I have a lot of questions about this topic, but no answers. I know the Lord hears all our prayers, but I was hoping He'd provide me with an answer or two."

Malachi hoped Thad wouldn't ask him to explain his dilemma further. Talking about his ma and why she hadn't taken him with her was something Malachi didn't care to discuss with anyone.

"Reckon we all have questions. God is infinite, and He knows all. But I do believe there are some things we may never know the answers to or even understand this side of Heaven. Both with our own finite minds and because maybe there are some things our Heavenly Father doesn't reveal to us for one reason or another. Could be to protect us. Could be because it's not yet in His timing." Thad shoved his hands into his pockets. "I do know that He is sovereign and that whatever hurts we carry and whatever pain has knifed its way into our hearts—He can heal that."

It wasn't quite the answer Malachi had hoped for, and the disappointment sagged through him, but the truth, nonetheless. "I haven't prayed for healing from it. Maybe that should be my prayer."

Thad placed a hand on his shoulder. "God is the healer of all hurts."

Malachi blinked away the moisture that threatened. He'd never been one who expressed his emotion through tears, yet he wanted—needed—to know the answer about his mother. About why he wasn't important enough for her to try again to rescue him. About how his life would have turned out differently if *she'd* made other choices.

Thad waited, probably for Malachi to clarify, and several seconds ticked by until his employer spoke again. "Mind if I pray with you?"

"Thank you. I'd be much obliged for that."

Malachi bowed his head and clasped his hands as Thad spoke. "Dear Heavenly Father, we thank You for Your Son, and for the many blessings You bestow on us each day. For the way You invite us to come to You when something weighs on our hearts. I don't know the details of Malachi's concerns, but You do. Father, I pray that You would give him peace about the answers he is seeking, that You would calm his thoughts, and heal the hurts. Thank You for this day. May we do all we can to glorify You. In Jesus' name, amen."

His head felt heavy on his neck, and Malachi struggled to hold it upright again. How could so many emotions surge through him all at once? He worked through a sandy swallow, then spoke. "Thank you, sir."

"You're welcome. I'll continue to pray for you. As far as the buggy goes or anything else you'd like to borrow on occasion, including one of the automobiles..." a glint lit Thad's eyes.

The diversion of topic caused the tension in Malachi's shoulders to ease somewhat, and he laughed a wry chuckle. "Not going to be needing to borrow one of the automobiles, but thank you anyhow."

After Thad left, Malachi lifted his eyes to the brilliant blue sky and echoed Thad's prayer. "And, Lord, even if I never find the answer to my question, please let Your abiding peace settle within me."

Arrosa always appreciated Reverend Arkley's sermons, and as she sat with Mother on one side and McKenna on the other, Arrosa concluded that this sermon was no exception. Reverend Arkley spoke on Romans 8:28, using both Joseph in the Old Testament and Paul in the New Testament as examples of how God could take hardships, difficulties, and even bad choices and turn them to good according to His will when lives were surrendered to Him.

Mother squeezed her hand, and from Arrosa's side eye, she could see a tear sliding down Mother's cheek. She squeezed Mother's hand in return, then caught McKenna's gaze.

God *had* taken hardships and difficulties and Father's bad choices, and He was turning them to good. Arrosa's family was proof.

After the service, Arrosa spent time chatting with her family before exiting the church. Malachi wandered toward her and extended his arm. "My lady," he said, with a bow.

She giggled and placed her hand through his. Malachi assisted her into the buggy, then beckoned the horses.

They rode in comfortable silence before discussing the sermon. Malachi's gaze veered to her cane. "Have you always needed a cane?"

"No, not always." How much should she share? "I became ill with rheumatic fever, and with it came a sore throat, fatigue, weakness, chest pain, a rash, and painful and swollen joints. My wrists are all but healed, but there are some lingering issues. I'm still unsteady on my feet as well."

"I'm sorry to hear about the rheumatic fever."

"Thank you. It was a long road, and I'm grateful for the Lord's healing. Although…" she tried on numerous occasions not to give thought or worry to the future. For wasn't it all in God's hands? But the thought of cardiac trouble did linger in her mind often.

"Although?"

"There is a chance that I could have cardiac trouble in the future." She covertly allowed her gaze to settle on his face. Would that matter to him? Did her having a cane affect his opinion of her?

There was no sound other than the clopping of the horses' hooves and the breeze rushing past the sides of the buggy. Arrosa held her breath as she awaited his response.

"Maybe the doc who mentioned that is incorrect," he finally said.

"That's my prayer, but there is a chance."

"That will be my prayer, too."

"Thank you." She released the breath she'd been holding. Why she ever thought someone like her would have a chance with someone like Malachi Callahan was beyond her. As a ranch hand, he would need someone strong and capable. Not delicate and fragile with a cane and potential heart problems.

"And if the Lord does allow you to have cardiac problems, He'll be there for you as you go through that as well."

She nodded. "I know. I am just now learning how faithful He is. Still, I'd prefer not to have to suffer from that."

"I wouldn't want you to have to suffer either."

Malachi rounded the corner and up a hill. "I'm fixing to take you to the most incredible view you've ever seen. It's not far from the river where we can have our picnic."

Arrosa thought of the basket she'd meticulously packed with Cook's help. The woman divulged that pumpkin pie was

Malachi's favorite, and Arrosa had spent the last evening, after she'd finished caring for the children, assisting Cook with the preparations.

Just like she and McKenna had on occasion in Missoula when they were young girls.

Malachi turned left, and they rode through a more primitive area, the leaves of the aspen trees whispering in the wind. A woodpecker pecked at a towering poplar, and somewhere in the distance, a cow lowed. He stopped the buggy near a plateau high above the valley, and Arrosa sucked in a breath. "This is beautiful. It's as though we're on top of the world."

"I agree." An eagle soared on the breeze, and somewhere a prairie dog chirped. They sat in silence, admiring God's handiwork, until, after some time, Malachi turned the buggy around and parked so they could partake in their noonday meal.

He extended a hand and helped her from the buggy. She stood facing him, their faces so close.

A tingle of excitement wove its way from her wrist to her shoulder as he held her hand. It was as though time stood still. Finally, he reached into the buggy for the basket and again offered his arm. She took his elbow and leaned on her cane as they walked to a flat clearing. Not far beyond, the river, with its sparkling water, rushed over rocks, creating a soothing sound. Malachi released her and unfolded the quilt she'd brought for them to sit on.

Malachi blessed the food, and she withdrew first their sandwiches, then an apple for each of them, and finally, the pumpkin pie. Malachi's eyes enlarged. "I love pumpkin pie."

"Oh, yes, that's what a little birdie told me."

"Is the little birdie a somewhat cantankerous older woman with a good heart, and who wears a funny cap?"

"You described her perfectly."

Malachi chuckled. "She's a kindly sort, just can be terse at times."

"I agree, but you are correct in that she does have a kind heart. Really, everyone at the ranch is so nice and accommodating."

"That's true. I couldn't ask for a better employer." Malachi regarded her. "Did your family have hired hands and servants?"

"We did. Our cook was a lot like Cook. She ruled the kitchen and set up firm rules, but she was also warmhearted. We had three maids who resided on the topmost floor, where they shared a room. Cook, who was a widow, had her own room. My room at the Evansons reminds me a lot of our cook's room with its smaller size and the unpretentious furnishings."

"Do you miss those days?"

"I would be remiss if I said no. Our lives were happy, we never wanted for anything, and I will admit that McKenna and I were pampered. Our family has always been close-knit, but even more so after Father..." she swallowed the words. Malachi needn't know about the embezzlement.

"You mentioned your pa made some bad choices."

"He did. But the choices he made were for me."

"For you?"

She nodded as the indecision rose within her. "Have you ever known someone who made a decision that, while it wasn't conventional or even perhaps lawful, was done out of love?"

Malachi rubbed his jaw, and for a brief second, sadness flashed across his face. "Maybe."

"I was so very sick, and we were already in a lot of debt, but Father paid for high-priced cures for me. Cures that never worked."

"I'm sorry."

"Thank you. As such, we-he-Father made a poor decision...I shouldn't tell you this. I don't want you to think less of me."

"I could never think less of you."

"He just took some money that didn't belong to him, which wasn't right. He was trying to continue providing for us while managing our overblown debt, but his method was unlawful." Would Malachi put the pieces of her awkward statement together and figure that Father was in the jail in Bleakney? Would he care to spend time with someone whose father was a criminal?

"Your father now works in Bleakney?"

She was a terrible liar, and really, lying was unbecoming of the Lord. If only Arrosa hadn't allowed herself to share so much. "He had to do some jail time due to his choice of taking what wasn't his to pay for our debts and for me to have treatments." Her voice wavered, and she stared at her folded hands—hands folded so tightly that her knuckles had turned white. Dare she look at him? Would she see judgment in his countenance? Would he dismiss her as Wayne had when he'd seen Arrosa's cane?

"Arrosa..." he gently lifted her chin.

"Yes?" she whispered.

"Your pa sounds like the type of man who would do just about anything to help his child."

Emotion simmered just at the surface. "Yes. Yes, he is that type of man."

"You're blessed to have a father who cares about you and your ma and sister." An unreadable mask replaced the kindness in his eyes.

"Thank you. Yes, I think so too."

"I don't condone crime. Never have. And while he shouldn't have taken what wasn't his, he did it for a noble reason."

Noble reason in helping Arrosa with her treatments, yes. But not so noble when it pertained to paying off debt that he never should have accumulated in the first place, but Arrosa didn't mention as much. She was just grateful that Malachi hadn't judged her on the basis of her father's mistakes. "I was hesitant to tell you."

"I did wonder about a few things that day in Bleakney." The softness in his gaze returned. "I'm glad you told me." He dropped his hand from her chin.

"It's not been easy. That day in Bleakney, I visited him in jail. He's so gaunt now and looks so much older, although it hasn't been all that long."

"Trying times can do that to a person."

"When Reverend Arkley spoke about Romans 8:28 last Sunday, I was reminded of how bad the illness was and how awful it was to see Father taken away by the police. To see our house auctioned to the highest bidder. To hear the tongues wagging about our family from people who were once our friends." Her eyes prickled with shame. "No one, not even our friends, stood beside us. They distanced themselves and provided fodder for gossip. Even my aunt deserted us in our time of need until recently." The pain knifed her heart. "But in all of that, something good came of it."

Malachi smiled. "Just as Romans 8:28 promises."

She nodded. "None of us cared much about the Lord and His ways, nor did we understand the magnitude of what Jesus had done for us in the days before Father's arrest. Then, little by little, the Lord performed a miracle in all of us. The most profound difference is in Father. He's a changed man. He was always loving and caring, but now his priorities are in the proper order." A tear slithered down her cheek, and Malachi reached up and gently swiped it.

"Thank you for sharing that with me, Arrosa."

"Thank you for not walking away."

"Never. Not from you. I value our friendship."

"As do I. Now tell me about you. I know so little."

"How about some pumpkin pie?" Malachi cut them each a piece. "This is the best I've ever tasted."

She had to agree, although she had assisted Cook with the preparations. "Did you eat much pumpkin pie as a child?"

Malachi shook his head. "Not too often. Ma made it once that I recall, and then I ate it at the Kerrs' house."

"The Kerrs were friends of yours?"

"Yes."

"I know you mentioned that you and your mother were estranged. That must be difficult."

"It is. I have a lot of questions."

"Have you seen her recently?"

"No, not since I was a young'un."

Arrosa gasped. "A young'un? That was the last time?"

Malachi peered off into something in the distance. Had she been too nosy? Too forthright? "I'm sorry, I shouldn't have asked."

"No, it's all right. You told me about your father. My ma left when I was a little boy, and I haven't seen her since."

Arrosa covered her mouth with a hand. "Oh, Malachi." She couldn't imagine her life without Mother.

"I've always wondered why. Why she didn't come back for me."

The pain in his eyes stalled her heart. "I'm sorry," she whispered.

"But then Thad reminded me that we won't always know the answers to questions, and in those times, we pray for God's peace, and in my case, healing, because it was painful. And forgiveness."

They sat quietly for the next several minutes as Arrosa struggled with the words to say. Finally, she offered a promise. "I will pray for you." She sensed there was more that he didn't want to share, and she wouldn't press.

"Thank you. Now, let's talk about something more joyful, shall we?" A slow, sad smile shown on his face.

"Yes, let's do."

So instead, they discussed Ephraim's latest antics, Adelia's impressive reading, and Mamie's newfound love for sketching. And Junior, whom Arrosa could barely keep up with, since he now crawled so fast and was attempting to take steps.

All too soon, Malachi carried the basket to the buggy and assisted her to her feet as the sun began its descent, indicating that in several hours, nightfall would be upon them. "Thank you for the delightful afternoon."

"You're welcome." He grinned that crooked grin of his that endeared her to him, and they walked to the buggy. When they reached it, they both stopped and stood just at the side. What would it be like to have Malachi kiss her? To ask her to court him? To consider a future with him?

He lifted a finger and tucked a wayward stray hair behind her ear. His touch sent a zip of excitement rushing through her. Her heartbeat had taken on a mind of its own, thumping loudly in her chest, and she hoped he couldn't hear it too.

Arrosa couldn't be sure he felt the same way she was beginning to feel for him. The appreciation that he cared about what had happened with Father drew her all the more to this man who had all but claimed her heart.

But did he only see her as a friend? As merely the nanny for the Evanson children? Dare she believe that perhaps, someday, he would see her as more?

# CHAPTER FOURTEEN

"AND PLEASE DON'T FORGET to sign up for and note what you'll be bringing for the barn dance potluck at the Wier Ranch next Saturday," added Reverend Arkley after a fantastic sermon about the importance of prayer.

McKenna clutched Arrosa's arm. "It will be just like the days in Missoula. Remember the dances at Mother and Father's house?"

Arrosa did remember them as though they occurred just last week. The elegant homes, including their own, where the dances took place, the handsome and debonair potential suitors, including Wayne, who filled spots on dance cards, the orchestras, and the numerous types of dances. Oh, but to go back in time and relive those moments again. To appreciate every second more thoroughly.

"I only wish Father were here." McKenna nodded toward their mother, who had meandered across the aisle and was chatting with Mrs. Arkley and Mrs. Dell.

"As much as we miss him, I can't imagine how much more Mother must miss Father."

"Indeed. And our home and all of her friends in her social circle." McKenna laced her fingers across her abdomen.

Mother had been one of the most highly esteemed women in their society circle. She was also a gracious hostess, fashionable, and of good reputation. Until all of that had changed. Well, most of it. She was still all of those things, but now there was no need or ability to host fashionable events.

Arrosa allowed her gaze to settle on the woman who had so sacrificially given her time to benevolently assist her during her sickest days. While Arrosa had always respected her mother, that respect grew tenfold over the past year. She also respected her sister. She would never forget McKenna traveling to Hollow Creek to work in Aunt Julia Mathilda's boutique and sending money to Mother and Arrosa so they could survive. Arrosa blinked back tears. She knew she shouldn't complain about missing dances when she was so blessed.

"I daresay Mother has found many friends here in Hollow Creek in a short amount of time. And, she's doing quite well at the boutique. Erelong, I will be able to step back completely."

"Mother has always been assiduous."

"Indeed," agreed McKenna.

"Speaking of Mother and Father, I had a thought the other night. I have been praying for a job opening for Father once he is released from jail. Unfortunately, I've heard that the bank has no openings."

"Even if they did have an opening, I surmise it would be highly unlikely they would hire Father after what happened in Missoula."

Arrosa better steadied herself against the pew. For some reason, her joints hurt worse today. Not that she would disclose that to her family, for they would only fret. "I spoke with Emilie the other day, and she mentioned that perhaps we ought to inquire about a position at the new hotel."

"That sounds like a worthwhile idea. Once we have a better approximation of his release date, we should ask."

Arrosa watched as folks lined up at the tiny table in the back of the church to record what they would bring to the barn dance potluck. McKenna had linked arms with Mother as they stood in line. Obviously, nothing was keeping Arrosa from attending if she planned to partake as a spectator. However, she knew she'd never dance again.

Malachi finished speaking with the menfolk, then accompanied Arrosa to the buggy. As of late, Thad had allowed him to borrow the buggy whenever he wanted to do so, provided they didn't need the larger wagon to bring the children to church as well. Vera and Morris preferred the Model T, and Thad attended when he could, depending on how Mrs. Evanson fared.

That was one thing that Malachi noticed—the loving marriages between Thad and Mrs. Evanson and Morris and Vera. Yes, the marriages he witnessed between Mr. and Mrs. Kerr and the reverend and his wife, who were agents for the orphan train—were loving as well, but Malachi's witnessing of those marriages had been short-lived, and he'd been so young at the time. His own parents' marriage was not something he would ever emulate.

But Thad and Morris expressed their love to their wives on a continual basis. A love that was, from what Malachi could see, fully reciprocated. Marriage was not on his list of plans for his future, but if he did someday want to spend the rest of his life with someone, he hoped he would be the kind of husband Thad and Morris were.

Why had all these thoughts bombarded him?

"Thank you," Arrosa said as she settled into the buggy seat.

"You're welcome." Could be that spending time with Arrosa made him think of things he ordinarily wouldn't. No, he'd probably never marry, for who would want to wed a man few people cared about? One who'd been deemed unlovable? A man who was the son of a hardened criminal? Certainly not the lovely, smart, godly, funny, and compassionate Arrosa Chapman. He thought again about their pleasant buggy ride and picnic. His feelings for her had grown stronger, and he'd pondered more than once what it would be like to take her into his arms and kiss her. After properly asking her for her hand in courtship, of course.

Because Arrosa Chapman was a lady, he would treat her with utmost respect and consideration.

Courtship? He inwardly chastised himself. If marriage wasn't on his list of plans for his future, then why was he considering courtship, which most often led to an engagement?

Likely because the woman beside him was different from any other woman he'd ever met. And maybe, just maybe, he *could* see himself being married to someone like her.

If circumstances were different.

He beckoned the horses and waved at several of the other folks leaving the church. As long as no one discovered Boyd was his father, Malachi would likely always be welcome in Hollow Creek. That, and if he didn't make another mistake like he had when he'd taken matters into his own hands when a thief attempted to steal Barnabas's pocket watch. It had taken him weeks of constant nightmares to remind himself that one short stint in jail didn't make him the kind of man his father was.

Arrosa grew quiet on their way back to the ranch. She stared out the side of the buggy as the horses clopped along on the hardened earth. Was something wrong? Should he initiate conversation? Arrosa was far from what he would consider a chattering hen, but her usual blithe self was absent today and had been replaced with a hushed solemnity. Her shoulders slumped, and she'd sighed several times in the past minutes since leaving the church. Was something bothering her? He'd come to care deeply for her in recent days and wanted nothing to be amiss.

"Arrosa?"

She swung her gaze in his direction. "Yes?"

"Are you all right?"

"Thank you for asking. Yes, just contemplative."

Her sad smile didn't offer much reassurance. Should he prod? Malachi cleared his throat. "If you'd like to talk, I'm happy to listen."

This time, her smile reached her eyes. "I appreciate that so very much. You're a good friend, Malachi."

Something in his heart pinched. While he was honored to be her friend… Malachi shoved the thoughts aside. Wasn't he just thinking about how someone like her would never consider anything more than friendship with him? Yes, he was falling in love with her, but that would be something he'd keep to himself. "Reckon I'm grateful for your friendship, too." But his words sounded lackluster in his own ears.

A wistful sigh exited her lips. "I was just thinking about the barn dance."

"Ah, yes, the barn dance." Malachi had never been to a barn dance, nor did he ever care to attend such a festivity. He didn't even know how to dance. It was something he'd never aspired to. Being a man with two left feet left little room for gracefully moving across a barn floor.

"Have you ever been to a barn dance?"

"No. Can't say as I have."

"Nor have I. While I attended many a dance in Missoula, some of them hosted by my family, I wouldn't know what to expect at a barn dance."

Malachi shrugged. "May be that they're similar but with fewer stuffy folks." He caught his words too late. "I mean—" He sucked in a regretful breath. "I'm not saying you're stuffy." He averted his gaze to the road and left his attention there lest he see the disappointment in her face.

"Oh, no, I did not take that as such. Besides, you are correct. Some of the folks at the dances were stuffy. High society folks tend to be that way from time to time."

"Did you enjoy the dances you attended?"

"I did. Very much so. McKenna enjoyed them even more because she's far more sociable than I am, but yes, there was a thrill about entering the decorated room and hearing the orchestra play. Filling in your dance card and hoping that no cads wished to ask for your hand on the dance floor. Fond memories indeed."

He'd always known there were plenty of differences between them, and this confirmed that. He would no more be stuck in some fancy mansion associating with the wealthy while dancing with a plethora of women than work as a businessman. "Do you want to attend the barn dance?" he asked.

"No. It would hardly do to wobble around in an unladylike fashion while attempting the waltz."

"You could still attend and perhaps visit with friends instead of dancing." He hoped she could hear the sympathy in his voice. He wasn't attempting to minimize the hardship she faced.

"That sounds like something McKenna would say. I did give that consideration, but it just wouldn't be the same."

He pondered what he could say in response, but nothing came to mind. He cast another glance in Arrosa's direction. She laced her hands in her lap and stared straight ahead. Was she still wishing she could attend dances as she had in Missoula? Such a beautiful woman likely had her dance card filled within minutes. If she didn't need her cane, would she attend the barn dance?

A thought entered his mind, and he attempted to brush it aside, but it lingered.

*You're a nincompoop, Callahan, for even considering such a scheme.*

He had less than a week to implement it. But, honestly, was it even something he cared to consider?

But another glance in her direction confirmed his decision.

He'd do just about anything for Arrosa Chapman. Even this.

"Psst. Vera."

The older woman looked around her, but kept walking from the garden where she'd tended to Mrs. Evanson's flowers.

"Psst. Vera," he repeated.

She stopped again and finally looked behind her. "Oh, Malachi. Goodness, you gave me a fright. What is it you want?"

"Can I speak with you for a minute?" He wiped his dirty hands on the front of his jeans. The cattle, the stalls, and the fences were beckoning him, but he needed to ask before he lost the courage.

Courage. When Malachi thought of a man having courage, he thought about the battlefield. Or perhaps protecting his family from nefarious individuals. Or maybe even the courage to travel West and start a new life. But he wouldn't classify asking for dancing lessons as courageous.

Vera, thank goodness, was amenable to his idea. He'd spoken to her first because if she said no, there was really no sense in asking Morris.

"I will most certainly teach you how to dance. It's about time you learned how to do so, young man."

"Do you think Morris would be agreeable to playing the violin?"

"I think any excuse for Morris to unearth that dusty instrument of his would please him. But yes, do ask him. My question to you is, how will you get away with this without Arrosa knowing?"

"Arrosa?"

"Yes, I assume she's the reason why you are planning such an adventure."

"Adventure?"

"It will most definitely be an adventure to teach a man with two left feet—as you declared in your own words—how to dance."

"Do you think it would be futile for someone like me to learn how to dance?"

Vera patted him on the arm. "Absolutely not. I do not think you are too far gone to learn such an endeavor. However, Arrosa is an observant soul, and she might wonder why there is music in the barn and why she won't be seeing you for many nights after supper. You two do like to prattle on after dinner is served, correct?"

"We do." He scratched his head. "But how do you know this is for Arrosa?"

"It's as clear as a midnight sky lacking stars. You're fond of her, aren't you?"

"Well…"

She reminded him so much of Mrs. Kerr with her spunk and feisty personality. "Reckon you're the observant one, Vera. Yes, I am fond of her. But can we keep this between us?"

Vera buttoned her lip. "It will go no further. Now, you go ask Morris if he would be willing to play his violin, and I will refine some of my dance steps before this evening."

"This evening?

"You did mean to start posthaste, did you not? We have very little time before the barn dance."

"I guess, yes, tonight would be just as good as any." When he'd considered asking Vera on Monday after the noonday meal, he hadn't expected her to agree so quickly.

"Tonight it is then. Directly after supper at precisely seven o'clock. Don't be late."

Malachi stood there watching Vera as she ambled toward the house.

That evening, Malachi put on his best boots. Easy feat since he only owned two pairs. He wore this pair to church because it had fewer scuffs. If he were to be able to keep his balance and swing Vera around while dancing, he needed to give himself the best possible chance of success.

As usual, the meal was delicious, and he feared he'd eaten more than his fill. How could he learn the waltz or whatever other dances Vera had in mind if he was so full he'd need to be rolled around the barn floor?

"Would you care to meet outside on the porch after supper?" Arrosa asked.

Oh, he'd prefer it over dancing, all right. But, no. He'd made a promise both to himself and to Vera. And a man of character never went back on his word. "I'm sorry, Arrosa, but I have a prior engagement."

Her face fell, and he almost told her his reason. Almost.

"All right. Perhaps tomorrow night then."

It had become their custom, so it was no surprise that she'd consider another evening. "I'm sorry, Arrosa, but tomorrow won't work either."

"Oh. All right then."

Would she ask about Wednesday or Thursday night? Because he planned on having their special dance on Friday, and Thursday was his last night to practice with Vera. He reached for another biscuit and attempted to change the topic of discussion. "Biscuits sure are tasty."

"Yes, they are." He didn't miss the confusion in her eyes.

"Well, I best excuse myself. It was nice seeing you, Arrosa. Hope you have a nice evening and then a nice morning and a nice afternoon as well."

Malachi needed to exit the room before he made a complete fool of himself.

Arrosa watched Malachi leave the room. Disappointment and uncertainty cluttered her mind. She had enjoyed the times when she and Malachi had sat on the Evanson porch after supper and discussed their day. In her mind, it further secured their friendship. And while she had met several wonderful ladies at church and the Bible study, and while she chatted with Emilie, Sienna, and Roxanne, she considered Malachi her closest friend after Mother and McKenna.

Tonight, he'd worn his church boots. Yes, she'd noticed. He'd also seemed a bit nervous. While he had every right to do as he pleased with his evenings, she'd so hoped to continue the tradition of their talks on the porch.

She replayed the buggy ride in her mind. Something had shifted in her heart that day during their hours-long picnic. Yes, she'd already been falling in love with Malachi, but there was something else that weaseled its way into her scattered thoughts.

A future.

And not just any future, but a future she'd never anticipated. Dare she hope Malachi Callahan would be part of that future? Her entire life, she'd dreamed of marrying someone like Wayne Lingis. Of living in a mansion in Missoula, planning society balls and charities, and playing the part of a wealthy socialite wife to a much-revered dentist. To be a mother to several children, or, in her detailed planning, three girls and three boys. To visit with Mother and McKenna regularly as they met for tea. To walk again through the picturesque gardens, their own and Mother's and Father's as well.

But now, after her illness, after her family losing nearly everything, after Father's incarceration, after being burdened by using a cane for the rest of her life, after dealing with pain each day and the fears of future health problems, and after moving to Hollow Creek, things had changed.

For the better.

But how could that be? How could things change for the better when her lovely home was gone, she limped around and became easily fatigued, Mother worked in a boutique, and Father was in jail?

A glance at the Bible on the nightstand near her bed in her plain and unassuming room reminded her why things had changed for the better.

Because now, Arrosa was eternity-minded. Her newfound faith in the Lord was more important than any earthly valuables, dances, and even perfect health.

Still...Arrosa did struggle with what had been. What would never be again.

After assisting with preparing the children for their nightly Bible reading and time with their parents, Arrosa shuffled to her room. She rifled through the items she brought from Missoula amongst her valuables, withdrew the most recent dance card, and opened the silver holder. It had been a delightful evening, and her last dance before she fell ill. On the dance card, the order of the dances was listed, including the grand march, the waltz, the two-step, and the polka. There was then an intermission before six more dances. All of the lines had been filled, including four of them taken by Wayne. The yellow booklet boasted decorative swirls. The dance holder, with its attached pencil, had been a gift from Mother and Father for her birthday. She'd almost sold it twice when they needed the money. Mother, however, wouldn't allow it. *"You have so little left from our former lives."*

*"But if it means food for us."*

Mother had gently pushed her hand aside and tucked the silver dance card holder in a pile of worn linens. It was doubtful they would get what it was worth from it, and with its inscription, it meant far more to Arrosa, especially with its sentimental value, than it would mean to a stranger. She smoothed a finger over the top of the holder, noting a slight dent. It had become a treasured possession, and one she'd taken with her to each dance.

Would she ever attend another dance? Would she ever be able to dance again?

She no longer owned the floral folding fan with the lace edge that she once used so often. It was sold along with her exquisite dresses and bedroom furniture when the house was auctioned to the highest bidder. Given to one of the swirling vultures who'd deemed the Chapmans' loss their gain.

But the most important thing was that her family was healthy and safe. That Mother was now residing in Hollow Creek, and that Father would be released soon.

Silly notions like being unable to dance and no longer owning a well-loved folding fan were inconsequential in the scheme of a larger picture. Still, the niggling of disappointment wedged its way into her heart at the most inopportune times. Lest she forget to count her bountiful blessings, she could easily forget the Lord's mercy and grace through all the changes in her life.

# CHAPTER FIFTEEN

THE FOLLOWING MORNING, DOC Mangham arrived to check on Emilie. Arrosa prayed, debated, then prayed some more about whether she should ask Doc the question on her mind. He finished tending to Emilie and bid her goodbye. "Doc?"

"Miss Chapman, how are you today?"

"I'm well, thank you. I was hoping I could ask you a question."

"Certainly." He set his bag on the table and gave her his full attention.

"It's about my leg. Could you…"

"I'd be happy to check it for you."

She exhaled a sizable breath. "Thank you."

Arrosa thought about how she had contracted rheumatic fever and how there were times she hadn't been sure she would survive it. She'd been so ill. So weak.

"Rheumatic fever is a dreadful illness. It is now thought that it enters through the throat, although so much about this sickness is unknown."

"I still suffer from painful joints, and my doctor in Missoula mentioned I may have cardiac trouble in the future." She thought of how Father had tried every type of medicine and treatment, no matter what the cost, to heal her.

"I noticed you walk with a cane. Is that because of your knee?"

"It is. I've had some ankle throbbing, but it's mainly been my knee and the weakness I still struggle with in my legs. I've tried to stay off my feet as much as possible. But, as a nanny and as someone who isn't particularly fond of sitting all day, it's been a challenge."

"I understand," Doc said as he examined her knee.

"My physician in Missoula said it was likely I might always walk with a cane." Her voice wavered at the renewed realization that she may never dance again, walk up a mountainside, or do all the things she did before rheumatic fever.

Doc also listened to her heart. "While I would not dream of contesting your physician's diagnosis and counsel, I would tend to disagree somewhat."

Arrosa bit her lip. "You would tend to disagree?"

"What I mean to say is that I believe attempting to sit and rest as much as possible might not be the answer. It might do you better to strengthen your knee. To do so might obviate the use of your cane altogether at some juncture."

*Lord, might it be so?* "I may not need my cane?"

"I have no way of knowing for sure. However, I would encourage you to set your mind to doing gentle exercises and a stretch or two with your knee to strengthen it. Perhaps a short leisurely walk outside in the fresh air. Now, mind you, I don't want you to overdo it. We certainly do not wish for you to have a recrudescence of pain and experience more of an ache that you already have."

"But I might someday no longer need my cane?" Had she heard him correctly? "And I can strengthen my knee?" She already walked some when caring for the children.

Doc chuckled. "Yes, but as I mentioned, nothing is guaranteed. But if you are diligent and set your mind to it, along with plentiful prayer, I see no reason why it couldn't become a reality, or perhaps even a possibility that you would need your cane less than you do now. Do I think you should be running down the mountain or attempting to participate in one of those newfangled marathons? Absolutely not. But walking will do you good. I'm happy to check on you again in a month or so and see how you've improved."

"Yes, I plan to improve."

"Very well then, I best be on my way."

Arrosa held out two coins from her last pay. "I hope this will cover it, and thank you, Doc. You've given me hope."

"Yes, I have given you hope, for which I'm glad, but there's no need to pay me. I already needed to pay a visit to Emilie today, and we will just include your appointment with hers."

"Are you certain?

"Absolutely certain." He bid her goodbye, and for the first time, Arrosa held onto the hope that she would someday be able to discard her cane. While she was grateful for the Lord's healing, wouldn't it be something if He also saw fit to heal her knee and protect her from any future heart troubles?

She had to tell someone. Had to share the news. She wouldn't see Mother and McKenna until Sunday at church. Should she tell Malachi? But he'd been so distant as of late...

Arrosa didn't know Vera, Cook, or the maids well enough to share the news.

And the news truly was too good not to share. That she would not always need her cane? That she would be able to someday walk normally or almost normally? The children weren't yet awake, and if she wanted to share the news with Malachi, she would need to do so posthaste. Once the children were up and about, especially Junior, her day would be devoted to caring for them until evening.

Arrosa grasped her cane and carefully made her way down the porch stairs, which she'd found to be easier than the ramp Mr. Evanson had built. When she reached the bottom, she peered about her. Was Malachi in one of the distant fields? If so, she would have to wait until later to tell him. Could he possibly be in the barn? She hobbled in that direction, clutched the door's handle, and pulled it open.

Malachi was inside, hopping around on one leg.

What a puzzling sight.

"Malachi?"

He startled and whipped around to face her. "Arrosa, what are you doing here?" His voice came out terse and clipped as he clasped his hands behind his back and scanned the area behind her.

Something wasn't right.

Tears burned in her eyes. "What am I doing here? I just—I wanted to tell you something."

"Aunt Arrosa! Aunt Arrosa!"

She turned to see Adelia with her unique run and something in her hand. "I just losted another tooth! Can you believe it? That's two teeth in not a very long time."

Arrosa drew her attention away from Malachi and to Adelia. The little girl was still in her nightgown. "That's exciting, Adelia. Congratulations."

Adelia opened her hand to reveal the tiny white baby tooth. "I wanted to tell Mother, but she's sleeping. See? This is where it came from." Adelia pointed to her mouth, where she was now missing a bottom tooth and a top tooth. "Did you see this, Uncle Malachi?"

Malachi avoided Arrosa's eye and peered down at the tooth. "Good for you, Adelia. But what will you do when you have no more teeth?

"No more teeth?"

"I'm only joshing you. You'll grow new teeth to replace the ones you have lost."

"I know I will. And I can stick my tongue up there where that top tooth used to be. I've been trying to catch up with Ephraim and lose as many teeth as he has." She bowed her shoulders. "But Ephraim is older, so he got a head start." Her brow furrowed.

"What about Mamie? You two are near the same age."

"Yes, but Mamie is too frightened to lose her teeth. She says she wants to keep them forever and ever."

Sweet little Mamie. That sounded like the cautious girl.

"Come on, Aunt Arrosa. Let's go find Daddy and tell him before the others awake."

While Adelia once had a worse limp than she did now, nothing stopped her from bounding along. Arrosa, on the other hand, had to be sure to steady herself and walk much more slowly. She craned her neck for one last glance at Malachi, but he'd already disappeared in the opposite direction.

Something in her heart broke. She was so eager to tell him the good news, yet he'd acted like her intention had been an imposition. Thoughts of Wayne reentered her mind. While he had been gracious, it had been clear that he'd wanted nothing to do with her once he noticed she needed a cane. But that wouldn't make sense with Malachi. He'd always been kind to her. Had listened and offered compassion during their buggy ride when she shared about Father.

She attempted to shove the worry aside, but she regretted deeply her decision to wander out to the barn.

Thankfully, Arrosa and Adelia found Mr. Evanson nearby, and after Adelia shared her exciting news, she and Arrosa entered the house. Ephraim and Mamie were awake and sitting at the table, eating some of the scrumptious scrambled eggs and pancakes Cook had made. Usually, they all ate together, but Ephraim and Mamie had been especially tuckered out after a full day yesterday and therefore slept in.

Vera handed Junior to Arrosa, and when he saw her, he reached for her. "Roe-Roe? Roe-Roe?"

"Oh, you sweet baby." He smelled of sleep, and she nuzzled a kiss on his downy hair. Oh, but to someday be a mother. To snuggle her own child in those early morning hours. Emotion welled in her throat, and she set the fanciful dream aside.

Arrosa carried Junior into the kitchen and set him in his high chair. Vera piddled toward her. "Emilie would like to speak with you for a moment. I'll keep an eye on the children."

She gripped the railing and made the now-common journey up the stairs. Was it her imagination, or had her legs grown stronger since the last time she climbed the steps?

Arrosa found Emilie sitting up in bed. "Yes, ma'am?

"Please come in and have a seat."

Arrosa settled into the chair. "How did your appointment with Doc go?"

"I still have to stay in bed for the time being. Doc tactfully reminded me that I should take full advantage of being able to rest during the day because when the new baby arrives, the nights could be long if he or she is anything like Junior."

Arrosa smiled. "Junior didn't sleep well when he was a newborn?"

"To put it simply, Junior didn't sleep *at all* when he was a newborn. He's always been a very busy baby, and I was so thankful when he finally slept through the night. But, be that as it may, that's all part of motherhood."

While Arrosa didn't look fondly at not receiving much sleep at night, she might rejoice in it if it were someday the Lord's will that she be a wife and mother.

"How did your appointment with Doc go, Arrosa?"

"Thank you for allowing me to discuss my concern with him while he was here. It went well. Doc seems very knowledgeable."

"That he is, and he possesses a kindly bedside manner as well."

There was a lightness in her chest anew at Doc's news, and now someone to share it with as well! "He told me I will likely not always need my cane. That I may someday be able to walk well without it."

"Oh, Arrosa, that is wonderful!"

"I was always under the assumption I should rest and take it easy, but he says I should walk and do gentle exercises to strengthen my knee."

Emilie grasped her hand as if they were friends rather than employer and employee. No wonder McKenna spoke so highly of her. "I am so happy for you," she said.

"Thank you." Arrosa gazed out the window when she saw Malachi speaking with Sienna. The woman smiled at him, and Malachi threw his head back and laughed. The sting of envy wormed its way into her heart. A foreign emotion that she'd never felt before when it came to matters of the heart, although she'd experienced it a time or two with other concerns. Arrosa kept her attention on them as her ribs squeezed tight. They were obviously enjoying their conversation. She was reminded about how Malachi had been bothered when Arrosa had interrupted him in the barn. So unlike him. But then, she really didn't know him well, did she?

Malachi nodded at something Sienna said, then chuckled again before doing some sort of jig. Did he have feelings for Sienna? She was a beautiful young woman, a couple of years younger than Arrosa and Malachi. From what Arrosa knew, she was also sweet-tempered.

A peculiar emotion knifed its way into her heart. She and Malachi had only ever been friends, although he invaded her thoughts often, and she wished for more than friendship. Hadn't they shared much during the buggy ride? Her about Father, and he about his mother leaving when he was but a small boy? Sympathy for him flooded through her anew.

Malachi had finished his short-lived jig and placed a hand on the wood post, his attention captivated by something Sienna said. An odd comparison between Arrosa and Sienna filled her mind. She sighed. If Malachi did choose to cotton to Sienna, Arrosa would do her best to be happy for them.

"Arrosa?"

Arrosa reluctantly withdrew her attention from Malachi and Sienna. "Yes?" But her voice quivered.

"Is everything all right?"

"Yes, I just…" While Malachi had assisted her with the children, had taken her on the buggy ride and picnic, and had always been there to help her up the stairs or for whatever she may need aid with, she was not naïve enough to believe that he would be interested in someone like her.

Emilie craned her neck to see out the window where Arrosa had returned her attention. Malachi and Sienna were still laughing. Was it her imagination, or did Malachi look at the woman fondly? She attempted to ignore the tugging sensation in her stomach. She and Malachi were only friends, she reminded herself for the hundredth time in the past few minutes. If he and Sienna cottoned to each other, then that would be their business. They were both nice people and… A sudden longing to be sprightly entered her mind, but she'd never been vivacious and lively. Rather, Arrosa was more reserved. Subdued. Quiet and introspective. Dainty. While joyful and buoyant in personality, she'd never thrown her head back and giggled to her heart's content as she'd seen Mother and McKenna do. And now Sienna. Did Malachi find Arrosa to be dull?

"Arrosa?" Emilie repeated.

"And actually, why would he like someone like me?" The words tumbled from her mouth before she could give them scarcely a thought. "I walk with a cane, my father is in jail, my family has lost everything, and—" Tears blurred her vision. She'd been through rejection with Wayne. With her former friends. With friends of the family. This was nothing new. However, while Emilie may know some of her family's circumstances, Arrosa didn't need to share everything. She should have practiced forbearance, rather than blabbering on.

"How could he not like you?"

"I beg your pardon?"

"How could Malachi not like you? You're compassionate, godly, caring, and beautiful."

"I'm sorry. I hadn't meant to utter those ramblings aloud."

Emilie adjusted herself on the pile of pillows. "Arrosa, I know that I am your employer, but I also consider myself your friend. It is fine that you uttered those ramblings aloud. McKenna told me about what happened with your father and how his actions caused you to lose your family home. If a man is such a cad that he would dismiss you because of things that you have no control over, then you're better off without him. Likewise, if he has an issue with you walking with a cane, he is better off dismissed completely."

Emilie's words carried merit. "I'm so sorry. I'm not usually the jealous type, but when I went to tell Malachi about Doc's good news, he all but turned me away. It wasn't like him. We've been friends since I arrived, and I've valued that friendship. I've shared with him about Father and about my cane, and he has likewise shared about his mother. I'm not prone to envy, but after what happened with Wayne in Missoula, after he dismissed me once he discovered my limp, along with friends who now slight us and have nothing to do with our family, I guess I put myself into an unnecessary frenzy."

"Please don't apologize. I understand. I must say, however, that things aren't always as they seem." Emilie appeared to have experience with what she'd just mentioned, but Arrosa wouldn't pry. "Perhaps he has a rational reason for turning you away. In my experience, it's always best to give someone the benefit of the doubt."

She sighed. "Yes, you are correct." Arrosa prayed it was just a misunderstanding.

Malachi needed to apologize. He hadn't meant to be so abrupt when Arrosa came to the barn that morning. He'd just been horrified that she might discover he was in there practicing his dance steps. He hadn't much time to get them down, and if he wanted to impress her with his ability on Friday night, he needed to persevere and take full advantage of any time he had in the wide-open barn to gain more experience at something he never thought he would do. It would have been humorous had he not been concerned about what Arrosa might think of him.

And that she might guess what he was contemplating.

He sighed and rode his horse to the back pasture. He needed to drive cattle today, and unfortunately, such a task allowed him time to think. And think. And think some more.

He'd appreciated talking with Sienna. She promised she and Roxanne would tidy up the barn for him before the big event. He'd invited her and the others, and when he'd mentioned that Alejandro would be there, Sienna had changed her mind and agreed to attend. Also planning to attend were Jep, Pete, and, of course, Vera and Morris.

Malachi hadn't the opportunity to speak with Arrosa since the barn incident. Last night at supper had been awkward, and he'd wanted more than anything to take her aside and explain everything. Even if that meant divulging his plans.

What did Arrosa want to tell him? He recalled the smile on her face that morning.

Until he'd been the one responsible for dampening her joy.

He returned from the fields and met Jep and Alejandro by the coral. "Hattie will be so impressed," Jep was saying.

"Oh?"

"We've attended a lot of barn dances over the years, but Vera taught me some new steps. Reckon that will impress her."

Malachi laughed. The skinny, red-headed ranch hand and father of two talked often about his wife. It was clear he loved her.

"I've also convinced Hattie's sister to watch the children. We've made arrangements to attend the barn dance, but this will be fun too. A much quieter affair. Besides, I can't wait to see Arrosa's face."

"You and me both, Jep," said Alejandro. "You know, Malachi, she's probably wondering why you've taken to spending so much time in the barn instead of prattling on with her on the front porch after supper."

"Prattling on like a hen," Jep said, playfully slugging Malachi in the arm.

"How did you two..."

"Know that you two like to babble on in the evenings on the porch? We've known that since you two started your little tradition. Matter of fact, all the hands know. It's clear as the nose on your face that you're smitten with her."

"Smitten?"

The two men chuckled. "And here's Malachi gliding across the dance floor in a waltz." Alejandro provided an exaggerated example of Malachi attempting to dance.

"No, it's more like this." Jep alternated bringing one knee then the other to his chest, as his gangly self wheeled around the area.

"That's more like a hoedown," said Malachi.

Jep jumped around and settled again beside Malachi and Alejandro. "Either way, you're doing a good thing, my friend, by learning how to dance. Keeps the womenfolk happy when those barn dance invitations come along."

These two were such melodramatic pests, but Malachi wouldn't trade his newfound friendships with the ranch hands for anything. They'd been part of the group of people on the ranch and in the town who'd made him feel welcome.

Like he belonged.

For the first time.

That afternoon, he assisted Arrosa to the playroom, all the while contemplating his words and how he ought to phrase his apology. Adelia and Mamie brought a stack of books to Arrosa to read, Ephraim dashed to the corner to play with his train set, and Junior half-crawled, half-walked to his pile of blocks.

"Arrosa." But she didn't meet his eye. Made sense. He'd been harsh with her earlier, and now he needed to rectify that. Malachi rubbed the back of his neck. "I need to talk with you about yesterday."

"And then may you read to us, Aunt Arrosa?" Mamie asked.

"Yes. Why don't you two go see if there are any other books you'd like to add to your pile while I speak with Uncle Malachi?"

Adelia pushed Mamie's wheelchair to the bookcase, where they both perused the offerings.

Arrosa's eyes dropped to her hands in her lap. Junior, who had pulled himself up by hanging on to one of the chairs in the room, fell and hit his head on the floor. Arrosa scooped him up. "Oh, sweetie." She nuzzled him closer as Junior wailed.

Something in Malachi stirred. He didn't remember much of his ma, but he did recall a time when he'd fallen while running up the road to their house. She'd pulled him close and planted a kiss on his forehead. Then she'd tended to his scraped knees.

Emotion plummeted deep within him. He shoved the what-ifs aside and again prayed for God's peace and for His healing over the pain of never again seeing Ma. But he wished more than anything that he could have spent more time with her. That she had been there for him in his growing-up years.

But wishing for things had never gotten him anywhere, except stuck in a pit of melancholy.

Arrosa would make a caring ma someday, and her children would be blessed to have her for their mother. She sat in the rocking chair, rocking Junior gently while singing to him.

Had Malachi's mother sung to him? He couldn't recall that. "Is Junior all right?"

The baby peered up at him, tears in his eyes.

"He will be. He took quite the hard fall."

Arrosa looked at him but said nothing else. Malachi opened his mouth to speak, but the words wouldn't come. He slapped his hat onto his head. "I best get back to work." Before he could allow himself to think any more thoughts about his mother, about Arrosa, or about the childhood he'd missed out on, Malachi turned on his heel and fled.

# CHAPTER SIXTEEN

MALACHI ONLY HAD TWO more evenings to practice, and if Jep, Alejandro, and the other hands continued to interfere with Vera's lessons, Malachi would never learn how to successfully dance.

Before lessons, Vera and Morris "sashayed", as Vera referred to it, across the barn floor in each other's arms before the lesson. Morris always planted a kiss on Vera's cheek, and Vera always tittered about how dapper Morris was.

Tonight, as Morris pulled Vera close, Malachi stepped from the barn. It seemed as though he were intruding on this special moment between the two. As he turned to temporarily slither away, a thought struck him unannounced. He wanted a long-lasting love like that with Arrosa.

Wait, what?

A long-lasting love like that with Arrosa?

He was such a romantic fool.

He shook his head. Must be too many hours in the hot sun today messing with his brain. He'd never consider himself a romantic fool, yet there wasn't an hour that passed that Arrosa wasn't on his mind.

Malachi stood outside the barn and gazed toward the house. Was Arrosa sitting on the porch all alone? Would she forgive him for declining to spend the time with her once he presented her with his surprise? He honestly would rather be engaging in pleasant conversation than being reminded how uncoordinated he was.

"Malachi? Are we having a lesson tonight? The band is just about set up."

He turned to see Vera standing in the barn doorway. By the band, she meant Morris with this violin, one of the hands with a flute, and Pete, the foreman, with his banjo. "I just wanted to give you and Morris some time to dance before the lesson."

"Pshaw." She reached up and pinched his cheek. "You are such a sweet boy, Malachi. And you're really starting to dance well, too. You've come a long way in the last few days. Just imagine what an accomplished dancer you'll be by Friday night for Arrosa's surprise. Now, you come back inside. I see some of the men are arriving."

By some of the men, Vera meant the three additional hired hands who had shown up for yesterday's lessons and returned tonight. How had they heard about it? Between the "band" as Vera referred to it and the other hands, it was a regular hoedown in the Evanson barn.

Malachi returned to the barn, and the band started the first song.

"Good evening, ma'am, may I ask for this dance?" he asked Vera, just as she had instructed.

"Yes, you may."

He bowed, then took her hand in his as they began to dance. Vera was considerably shorter than his 6'2" height, but Arrosa didn't share Vera's lack of stature. As a matter of fact, her head would fit perfectly beneath his chin.

Thad poked his head in, chuckled, then left, and Malachi felt the heat climb his neck. What must his boss think?

It was then that the unfortunate incident occurred. Vera jerked away from him. "Ouch," she whispered.

"Vera?"

"Now, it will never do to step on a lady's toes." She released his hand and reached down to massage her foot.

"I'm so sorry." If he couldn't manage to dance properly with Vera, how would he ever achieve success at dancing the waltz with Arrosa?

"You need to be extra careful with Arrosa because she's not as robust as I am."

"Yes, ma'am."

But just as quickly as Vera offered him a crusty look, she smiled again. "Now, where were we?"

Just as Malachi was again feeling more confident about his steps, Alejandro tapped him on the shoulder. "Can I cut in?"

Friday began like any other day. Arrosa rose early and tended to the children. Thankfully, Junior was fine after his fall. Arrosa hadn't been able to speak to Malachi all morning; however, she did see him lurking about, ever watchful as he slunk into the barn and closed the door behind him.

Perhaps she should have been more gracious when he'd attempted to speak to her yesterday in the playroom before Junior fell.

Assisting Ephraim with tying his shoes pulled her away from her observations. She then stood and, with her free hand, placed it on her lower back and stretched. She cast her attention out the window when she noticed Malachi had at some point left the barn and was now again slithering back inside. Why was he being so secretive? He often mucked out the stalls or spent time in the barn. Why then would he be so watchful?

Besides witnessing his furtive lurking about, Arrosa hadn't seen Malachi all day. Lately, it was becoming commonplace not to see him as much, and she missed him.

Later that evening, she handed a squirming Junior to Vera and, after ensuring the older children were calming down after supper in preparation for their Bible reading time with their parents, followed them up the stairs. Morris deposited Mamie into her wheelchair, and she, Adelia, and Ephraim zipped into Adelia's room with the promise to be ready in fifteen minutes for Bible reading.

Arrosa hobbled into Emilie and Mr. Evanson's room just as Junior saw his mother and reached his arms to her. Emilie pulled her son close. "I've missed you, little one."

"Mama," he blabbered. For exactly three seconds, Junior allowed himself to be cuddled before the active and energetic child pointed to the floor. "Wa," he said.

"If you are all settled, I'll return to handling the evening chores." Vera's eyes darted about, and some sort of silent understanding passed between her and Emilie.

But Arrosa hadn't the time to allow her musings about Vera's suspicious nature to take root as Junior was skimming along the bed, standing on tiptoe, his fat little feet tottering along the floor while his hands clutched the bedding. "The way he has pulled himself up on the furniture has been astounding," she noted.

"I regret that I have missed so much of his latest achievements." Emilie's voice wavered, and she patted her swollen belly. "Not much longer, and I will be able to escape this room and once again tend to the children."

Arrosa didn't mention that it might be a bit longer than that since Emilie would be caring for her newborn. She rested a hand on her employer's arm. "Please don't worry about the children. They will be just fine. They miss you something dreadful, but the older ones understand, and Junior has many more triumphs and accomplishments ahead of him."

Emilie dabbed at a tear. "Thank you, Arrosa. You have been such a blessing. I don't know what I would have done without your assistance."

"You're welcome. And thank you for giving me the opportunity to work here. Your children are a delight."

At this, Emilie laughed. "They are a delight, but I am sure you have by now realized some of the shenanigans they are capable of."

"Well, when Adelia and Ephraim put their heads together, they do come up with some mischievous pranks. But all in all, they are well-behaved children, and I have seen Adelia's limp improve so much just in the time I have been here. And I believe Mamie is starting to feel more included."

"That is so good to hear on both counts. Yes, when we first adopted Adelia, her limp was quite profound. But, as we know, God has a way of taking our infirmities and assisting us through them. I think Adelia will always have the limp, but she's compensated for it and..." Emilie lowered her voice. "I daresay she can run almost as fast as Ephraim, although we won't breathe a word of that information to him."

Arrosa pretended to button her lip. Junior continued practicing his mobility alongside the bed. "Wa," he repeated with a giggle.

"He's going to walk any day now," said Arrosa.

Junior let go and held on with one hand for a few seconds before falling on his backside, then rising again.

"I would love to be the first spectator of such an event." Emilie smiled at her son. "You'll soon be keeping up with your brother and sisters."

Junior grinned as drool drizzled down his chin.

"While you're here, Arrosa, I have a surprise for you, "said Emilie.

"For me?"

"Yes. It's on the ottoman." Emilie pointed to the overstuffed paisley piece of furniture directly in front of the matching chair. Arrosa grasped her cane and walked to the square Queen Anne ottoman. A piece of fabric—a dress, perhaps?—was folded neatly atop it.

"This?"

"Yes."

Arrosa carefully unfolded the piece of clothing and gasped. "It's lovely."

"I would like for you to have it."

"But I couldn't. You may wish to wear it again after the baby is born."

"It's doubtful. Besides, I'd like to gift it to you. It would go well with your beautiful complexion."

Arrosa reached a hand to her cheek. She had a beautiful complexion? Truth be told, she'd always thought of herself as somewhat plain. "I—are you certain?"

"I am absolutely certain. Do you like it?"

"I love it." She hadn't beheld such a stylish ensemble since before Father's embezzlement. "But surely it is too costly to give away."

Emilie shrugged. "If I should miss it at some juncture, I can easily locate another one at Miss Julia Mathilda's."

Arrosa ran her hand along the sophisticated red dress with its lace collar, ruffled gathers, and black belt at the waist. Oh, but to wear something so refined once again! She held it to her chest as the tears swam in her eyes. But where would she wear it? Was it too fancy for church? Several of the ranchers' wives wore elegant dresses to church. Perhaps she could, too. It would seem a waste not to have an occasion to don it. "Thank you so much. I do hope it will fit."

"I believe it will fit quite nicely. And if it doesn't, Vera is handy with a needle."

Arrosa and Emilie were likely the same size before Emilie's pregnancy. "Thank you, Emilie. Thank you so much!" Before she could stop herself, she kneeled at Emilie's bedside and offered a quick hug.

"You are most welcome. I'm glad you like it."

Junior rubbed a slobbery hand against Arrosa's arm, a look of concern in his blue eyes. "Roe-Roe?"

"I'm fine, Junior. Just so incredibly grateful."

Emilie smiled and glanced at the clock on the mantle above the fireplace. "Now then, you must try it on posthaste. I'll call for one of the maids to tend to Junior."

Arrosa went downstairs and changed into the dress. It was even more lovely than she imagined! The smooth material and the color—she performed an awkward twirl. It was almost as though she were back in Missoula.

"Arrosa?"

She startled at the knock on the door. Cautiously, she opened it. Roxanne, one of the maids, stood there. "Oh, but you look beautiful."

"Thank you."

"You really should show Emilie. She will be ecstatic that it fits you so well."

Arrosa had never been one to make a spectacle of herself, but because Emilie couldn't very well leave her room, it was only polite to show her that the dress did, indeed, fit perfectly.

Hitching up one side of it, she maneuvered her cane, the railing, and the dress, and again ascended the steps back to Emilie's room. When she entered, her employer clasped her hands together. "That dress was meant for you."

"Thank you again."

"Would you mind terribly rounding up the older children for our Bible reading? Thad should be here soon."

Arrosa did as requested, then for the umpteenth time, descended down the stairs and toward her room when Roxanne found her in the hallway. "There seems to be a concern on the porch."

"The porch?"

What could be the matter? Should she fetch Vera? Or Cook? Or perhaps even Sienna? But when she looked around, she saw no one. Was there an emergency? Should someone fetch Doc? What was Roxanne referring to when she mentioned there was a concern? She turned around to ask for clarification, but Roxanne was gone. Should she notify Emilie? But no, she wouldn't want to alarm her employer if it was unnecessary. Arrosa made her way to the porch and stepped outside. Then she remembered she still wore the fancy dress that Emilie had given her. But there was no time to change. Not if the situation could be serious.

She surveyed both the porch and the surrounding area. All was calm. Extremely calm. Not even an owl hooted, and no wind whistled through the trees. A sliver of worry snaked through her. If there was a concern on the porch, where was that concern? Had Roxanne been mistaken? She was about to return to the house and seek clarification when she noticed Malachi in the distance, striding toward her. Perhaps he would know about the pending issue.

"Malachi?"

He waved and hastened his pace. When he drew nearer, she observed that he'd donned garments more akin to his Sunday best. And he was wearing his new boots. Usually, he wore a cowboy hat, but tonight, such was not the case. He'd combed his blond hair, had shaved, and as he drew closer, she inhaled the scent of clean soap.

Malachi Callahan looked utterly dapper. She attempted not to stare, but such a feat was nearly impossible. At the society functions she'd attended in Missoula, she had seen her fair share of handsome menfolk. But Malachi far surpassed them all. He smiled that crooked smile that she had grown so fond of. The crooked smile she'd missed in days of late because of his aloofness. She sucked in a breath as heat flamed her face. She ought not stare as it wasn't becoming, but...

"Good evening, Arrosa."

"It is? Oh, yes, it is a good evening. Yes, good evening to you, Malachi." She really needed to ask him if he knew anything about the concern of which Roxanne spoke, but for some reason, her words lodged deep in her throat.

"You look beautiful."

"I—oh!" She held a hand to her throat. "I, well, thank you." She was about to explain how Emilie had gifted her the dress when Malachi reached into his trouser pocket and withdrew a piece of paper. Her gaze settled on it, curiosity besting her.

"Arrosa Chapman, would you do me the honor of attending the Evanson barn dance with me?

"The Evanson barn dance?" How could she not have known about such an event? Further, how could she attend such an event when she needed a cane to even walk, let alone dance?

He pointed to the barn in the distance. "Yes, the orchestra has already arrived."

"Orchestra? Here?"

He nodded and handed her the piece of paper. "It's the best I could do on such short notice."

She unfolded the stationery, which boasted a colorful design on the front, and opened it to see a listing on the left-hand side with the word *waltz* written several times. On the right was the word *engagements*. Under that column were eleven lines. Malachi had written his name on the first line.

"A dance card?"

Malachi shrugged. "I hear it's only proper etiquette to provide a dance card for a dance."

"I thought you didn't dance."

"I do now."

She wondered if he might explain, but instead, he reached for her hand and pressed a kiss to the back of it before taking a slight bow. "Would you do me the honor of dancing the first dance with me?"

Their gazes connected. "But I can't dance with my knee."

A smile tugged at his lips. "You can if I help you."

A tangle of emotions swirled through her belly along with the rapid increase of her heartbeat. "Yes, if you help me, I can."

His hand clasped around hers, and he placed it through the crook of his elbow. A pleasant tingle zipped up her arm as he patted her hand with his, and for a moment, she forgot to breathe.

"I'll put the dance card in my pocket."

"Yes, thank you." A sudden thought struck her. "I should probably check on Junior first."

"No need. Roxanne is tending to him, and after that, Thad will be in from the fields to assist with the children."

"Oh." It was all she could say, for it sounded so preplanned. Could it be that he had organized everything to fall into place?

They ambled to the barn, and Malachi swung open the door. The second that happened, the music started. At the front of the barn on a makeshift platform, Morris played his violin, Pete strummed his banjo, and one of the hands, whose name Arrosa didn't know, played a flute. Music echoed throughout the building, a pleasing and rich melody in perfect harmony that lifted Arrosa's spirits all the more. Pink and purple crepe paper waved in the breeze from its place, streamed across from one side of the barn to the other. A table in the corner with two chairs and a tablecloth boasted a plate of tarts and another with small iced cakes. The scent of hay rivaled that of the baked goods, and the ambiance proved far better than any dance she'd ever attended in Missoula.

Her jaw dropped. It was almost too much to comprehend.

Malachi bowed again. "May I have this dance?

A soft giggle erupted in her throat before she nodded. "Yes, you may."

He set the cane aside, and for the briefest of moments, Arrosa panicked. How would she manage without it? But as he gently placed her arm over his right shoulder and clasped her hand with his left hand, any remaining apprehension drifted away.

The strains of "The Blue Danube" floated on the air. She and Malachi moved slowly, and although she felt clumsy and awkward, it was quickly remedied with Malachi's smooth movements. His face was close to hers, so close that she could see the green specks in his lake-blue eyes. He stepped in perfect timing with the music.

"I thought you said you had two left feet."

He only grinned, and her heart leapt in her chest. Had he been practicing?

The next song, "Tales from the Vienna Woods", started, and this time, Morris and Vera sashayed beside them, joined by Alejandro and Sienna.

The night couldn't be more perfect.

# CHAPTER SEVENTEEN

MALACHI COULDN'T TAKE HIS eyes off her. Not that Arrosa wasn't always beautiful, but tonight, her face radiated with joy.

He wasn't a romantic sort. Not in the least. But when he'd held her in his arms during the dances, steadying her, enjoying every moment with her, he'd suddenly become sappy.

Two hours and far too many tarts and cakes later, Malachi walked her to the front porch. "How is your knee?"

"It's fine."

He ascertained that the overuse had put a strain on her muscles, especially by the way she'd leaned into him as they navigated the distance between the barn and the house. But he also knew that Arrosa was a proud woman and wouldn't let anything stop what she'd put her mind to. Oh, but if he could have captured forever the pure joy that lit her face when she'd first entered the barn. The way she'd peered up at him made his heart surge as warmth filled his chest.

He loved her. There was no two ways about it.

They reached the top of the stairs. Everyone else had long ago journeyed to their respective homes or, in the case of Vera, Morris, and Sienna, the Evanson home. The early summer evening air lent a crispness to the night. Somewhere in the distance, an owl hooted, and a light flickered in the house. He didn't want this night to end and was about to offer her a seat on the bench on the porch when he instead stared into her eyes.

So pretty. So delicate. So dainty. So perfect for him. But did she feel for him the way he felt for her? He took a step toward her, and she took a step toward him, both of them in unison. He captured her in his arms, and she rested her head against his chest. She felt so perfect in his arms. He kissed the top of her head and held her tightly. What would it be like to court her? To kiss her? To consider a future with her?

A stream of uncertainties filled his mind. How could someone like Arrosa ever feel for him the way he felt for her? He'd been told so often that he was unlovable. Thankfully, because of Barnabas's patient instruction on matters of the Lord, along with Reverend Arkley's teachings confirming such, Malachi knew the Lord loved him. Loved him in a way no person ever could because He'd sent His own Son to die for him.

But could a woman like Arrosa ever love him? The question had plagued him ever since he'd begun to see her as more than an acquaintance. Then, as more than a friend. And now?

He closed his eyes and rested his chin on her head. *Lord, should I ask her to court me?*

If he could stay here forever, holding her, it wouldn't be long enough.

But what of her knee? She'd been on her feet all night. Surely she needed rest. Malachi reluctantly took a step backward. "Should we sit?"

She nodded, and they took their places on the bench on the porch, just like they had those nights before he'd become preoccupied with learning the waltz.

"Thank you for tonight."

"You're welcome." He wanted to reach for her hand.

"Am I to understand correctly that you've been practicing with Vera and Morris?"

"Yes, along with Jep, Alejandro, and a couple of the other hands." In the glow of the moonlight, he thought he saw tears brimming on her eyelashes.

"And you did that for me?"

"When you were disappointed that you couldn't go to the barn dance in town, an idea struck me about maybe bringing the barn dance to you. Not that we can't still go to the barn dance tomorrow night if you're amenable to that."

She blinked. "I appreciate you doing this for me more than you know. I never thought I would be able to dance again."

"You mentioned it was important to you and that you missed the dances you'd attended in Missoula. I know this isn't like the grand rooms in the mansions where you once danced, but…"

"It was better than the grand rooms in the mansions where I once danced. Until recently, I never could fathom even living somewhere besides a city, and now, I'm finding I like Hollow Creek much better. And as for the barn dance, the charming atmosphere and the outstanding company notwithstanding, it was everything a dance should be."

"Reckon that's a good thing." This time, he did reach for her hand and held it, his fingers intertwined with hers. And for the next several minutes, the only sound in the still night was a cow lowing in the distance and some nearby crickets.

"I'm impressed how you learned to dance so quickly. When did you have time to practice?"

"Suppose I should apologize about that. All those nights when we were to have met on the porch for our evening talks, I was in the barn practicing."

"That's where you were?"

"That's where I was.

Arrosa's brow furrowed. "I had no idea."

"Good. I was hoping it would be a surprise." He turned to face her. "I do need to apologize. I was harsh with you when you entered the barn the other day and caught me unaware. I was practicing dancing and was horrified that you may have seen my awkward movements."

A soft giggle gurgled in her throat. "You were?"

"I was. It's not easy learning something new in such a short amount of time, but I wanted tonight to be perfect for you. But in my desire for that, my words were more clipped than they ought to have been. Honestly, I missed meeting you on the porch after supper. Can you forgive me for being terse?"

"Yes, I forgive you, and I missed you as well." She smiled. "It seems, however, that everyone knew about this but me."

"That is true. From Vera teaching me to dance to Morris and Pete playing their instruments, to Sienna and Roxanne helping decorate, and Roxanne tending to Junior, and finally, Mrs. Evanson visiting with you while we finished preparing, and Thad offering the use of the barn, yes, you could say just about everyone was involved."

She reached her free hand to her mouth and closed her eyes briefly before reopening them. "Thank you, Malachi. Thank you so much." Her voice trembled.

"You're welcome. And like I said, if you want to go to the barn dance tomorrow night, we can do that as well."

"Do you think there will be other dances?

"I'm not sure. I would assume so since there've been several in the past, especially the harvest dance in October."

"I will probably rest my knee tomorrow, but I would like to attend another one in the future." She brightened, her jubilant countenance shining in the glow of the moonlight and lights from inside the house. "Oh! I almost forgot to tell you."

"Yes?"

"Doc said I someday may no longer need my cane."

"He did?"

"He did, and not only that, but I no longer need to continually rest and refrain from walking whenever possible. Doc encouraged me to walk a little more each day and engage in some knee exercises and stretches."

"This is fantastic news. Praise God."

"Indeed. It was something I never would have expected, and something that my physician in Missoula said he would doubt would ever happen. My dream, besides someday dancing again, is to be able to walk on that path where we had the treasure hunt without the use of my cane. Wouldn't that be something?"

"I have confidence that you will someday achieve that goal. And I'll be praying the Lord sees fit to make your leg stronger."

"Thank you. I try not to worry about such things like that and the potential for heart issues as I age, but at times, I find myself entrenched in trepidation, even though I know the Lord will carry me through whatever I may face."

"Yes, He will. We serve a faithful God."

She rested her head against his shoulder, and they sat for several more minutes in comfortable silence, and he inhaled the subtle scent of rosewater.

If he did ask her to court him, would she say yes? He offered a prayer heavenward, then mustered the courage. "Arrosa?"

"Yes?"

"Arrosa Chapman?"

This time, she lifted her head from his shoulder. "Yes?"

"Would you court me?"

"I would be honored to court you, Malachi Callahan."

All of the anxiety about her rejecting his offer melted from him. He inched closer to her, staring into her expressive hazel eyes. "And might I steal a kiss?"

"Yes, you may," she whispered.

Malachi cradled her head in his hand and tenderly kissed her waiting lips. If this were a dream, he didn't want to wake up.

Sleep was difficult to come by that night. Arrosa snuggled beneath the quilt in her room and stared at the ceiling. The dance, planned by Malachi and involving nearly everyone on the ranch, had been such a delightful surprise.

But nothing had compared to their moments on the porch. Malachi asking her to court him and then the subsequent kiss.

Never in her wildest dreams had Arrosa ever imagined such a romantic proposal. And she had all but given up on the thought of being married. Not that courtship always preceded nuptials, but...

She closed her eyes and clasped her hands. "Lord, thank You for this magnificent night. Thank You for the ability to dance when I thought it was all but impossible with my knee and weakness. Thank You for Malachi's proposal. Lord, I beseech You that if it is Your good and perfect will, that we would someday marry. In Jesus' name, amen."

Arrosa rolled to one side. It had really happened tonight, hadn't it? He had really asked her, right?

Yes, on both accounts, she reassured herself. And as she rolled over to the opposite side, Arrosa knew there would be no sleeping tonight.

# CHAPTER EIGHTEEN

THE FOLLOWING WEEK, MALACHI was walking down the boardwalk when he passed Wulf's Saloon. A man bolted from the swinging doors. "Sir? Could you help us a minute? We got ourselves an emergency."

"Would you like me to fetch Doc?"

"If you could just step inside and help us, we'd be much obliged."

Malachi had never been in any saloon, let alone Wulf's in Hollow Creek. But if someone needed help, how could he deny them? He followed the man inside. Several men playing poker at an oversized round table turned to face him when he entered. A saloon girl, with her off-key singing, belted a tune from a makeshift stage, and the thick stench of smoke and liquor assaulted his nostrils.

"It's right upstairs this way."

"Are you sure you don't want me to fetch Doc?"

The man kept running up the long, narrow stairs, and Malachi followed him. They stopped at a door upstairs. "He's right in here."

"Who?" But instead, another man, whom Malachi recognized from seeing around town, jerked Malachi into the room and slammed the door behind him.

"It's about time I got to see my boy again."

Malachi's jaw dropped as his muscles went numb. "Boyd?"

"Boyd? Is that any way to address your father? What about calling me Pa?"

Malachi attempted to shake off the shock. This wasn't happening. This *couldn't* be happening. "I haven't called you pa in almost two decades. What do you want?"

"What do I want? Well, to see my boy, of course. It's been a long time." Boyd slugged him hard in the upper arm, and the other man chortled.

"You ain't kidding when you said he was going to be surprised to see you."

"Malachi, you know Rantz, don't you?"

Rantz stuck a hand toward Malachi, and Malachi reluctantly shook it before returning his attention to Boyd. "I got nothing to say to you, Boyd."

"Well, now ain't that funny, 'cause I got a whole lot to say to you." Boyd fisted a wad of Malachi's shirt in his hand and twisted. "First thing I gotta say to you is I ain't never forgotten what you done that day when you turned me in to that teacher."

That was what this was about? "I didn't turn you in. Besides, maybe you shouldn't have been committing crimes." He voiced the words, not really contemplating the possible consequences.

Boyd inclined closer, their noses nearly touching. "You listen to me, boy. You ain't got no right to talk to me that way. You're just lucky I didn't kill you before now."

"Kill your own son?"

Rantz shook his head. "Sometimes things like that need to be done."

"That's right, they do, especially when your boy turns you in."

Malachi snatched Boyd's hand. "Let go of me."

Boyd did as he requested and swiftly squeezed Malachi's neck, constricting his airway. "I have no problem killing you for what you done. No man turns me in and lives to tell the tale."

"I took the gold nuggets from your heist to school. I had no idea you'd stolen them at the time," Malachi wheezed, struggling to draw adequate breath.

Boyd tightened his grip, digging his fingers into Malachi's flesh. "It wasn't easy being on the run all these years. But there's never been a lawman who could catch Bad Dog Goshorn." He released his hold, and Malachi doubled over, sputtering as he attempted to catch his breath.

"That's what you deserve." Boyd puffed out his chest. Malachi lifted his head and stared into the eyes of a man who looked much the same as Malachi remembered. Brown hair, gray eyes, full mustache and beard, but much older. Gray peppered his temples, and he'd gained weight on his already massive build, especially around his middle. A life of crime had aged him significantly, as his weathered face gave evidence to his ruthless lifestyle.

"Imagine all the things we could have done if you'd just stuck around. Just us, father and son, making our way in this world."

"I'm nothing like you. I don't commit crimes."

Boyd raised his hand and slapped Malachi hard across the face. It stung, and Malachi gritted his teeth to avoid wincing. He wouldn't allow this man to see any weakness.

"How did you find me?"

"Wasn't hard. Was sitting down having a meal at this restaurant in Butte, and a man beside me has a newspaper. He gets up and leaves it, and I help myself to some reading material. Lo and behold, there's my boy, my own offspring, helping the law find some stolen horses. I'd like to say it made a man proud, but it don't. Would have made me prouder if you'd been the one who'd stolen them horses, especially the prized stallion." Boyd's face reddened, and the nostrils on his hawk nose flared. "Ain't you just a hero?" He sneered. "There on the front page is something or other about some man named Malachi Callahan. Saddens me to think my boy, who I done gave my name to, changed it from Goshorn to Callahan. Who is Callahan, anyway?" His eyes darkened. "And why didn't you keep my name?" Spittle flew from his mouth and landed on Malachi's cheek, and he swiped it away with his hand.

"I thought to myself, that boy's always been a little dumb in the head. He should be helping me steal horses, not helping the law find missing horses. Figured I needed to have me a talk with this Malachi Callahan. See if he was really my boy. Turns out, I see you walking down the street one day, and shore as I've ever been, I know that's my kid. Rantz here helps me find a dimwit foolish enough to take a bribe to get you in here. Gave him some money, and he did a right fine job convincing you there was an emergency of sorts up here."

Boyd's orchestrated plan made his stomach churn. Hadn't he thought he was free of Boyd forever? "I need to leave."

"You ain't going nowhere until I said my piece."

"I want nothing to do with you."

A vein pulsed in Boyd's jaw. "You sure got a mouth on you, don'tcha?"

Malachi's pulse quickened. Boyd was volatile, and he needed to watch his tongue, but it was a challenge. There was so much he wanted to say to Boyd. So much he *needed* to say. Sweat dampened his forehead, and a stare down commenced between him and Boyd.

"Why am I here?"

"Well, it's like this. I figure you owe me."

"I don't owe you anything."

"Oh, yes, you do. If you hadn't been snitching about them gold nuggets, I wouldn't have had to leave Indiana."

It was no use arguing with Boyd. He would never admit that it was his own wrongdoing that got him into trouble with the law, not an innocent little boy who took gold nuggets to school to show his friends. It caught his teacher's attention because no eight-year-old boy should have nuggets at his disposal, especially when that same boy lived in poverty in a shack by the river.

"Now this is what you're going to do. You're going to help Rantz and me rob the bank in a few days."

"No."

This time, Boyd shoved Malachi so hard he fell backward against a chair. He stumbled to his feet, hands raised for both defense and protection.

"As I was saying, you're gonna help Rantz and me rob the bank. We're still getting our plans together, but I hear that for this being a small town, that bank carries a lot of cash and some silver too."

"It does," agreed Rantz.

"You have to find someone else to help you, because it won't be me." When had he gotten so brave? He'd always feared his father. A father who could snuff out his life and no one would know...or care.

He thought of Arrosa. They'd just started courting. If Boyd killed him—no, he wouldn't hurt her that way. He had to keep his wits about him—and his temper in check—no matter what.

Boyd reached over and again put his hands on Malachi's neck, this time to shake him. "You will do what I say, boy, you got it?"

Boyd's eyes bulged. If he thought Malachi would stand there and allow him to strangle him, he was sorely mistaken. Malachi kneed his father in the groin, and Boyd toppled backward. Rantz pulled his gun, and Malachi punched Boyd in the nose, causing him to double over. "Just shoot him," he groaned.

"But then we wouldn't have the help we need," said Rantz. "And remember, he'll be the one who takes the fall for this, not us. You willing to help him meet his demise so we have to take the blame for the robbery?"

Boyd straightened up once more, his face flushed and contorted.

"Look, just let me leave. You go your way, I'll go mine." Malachi started toward the door, but Rantz backed up and blocked it. Malachi eyed the window.

"Unless you're fixing to jump out the window and break your legs, I wouldn't advise it." Rantz kept his place blocking the door.

Boyd swiped a hand across the chair, causing it to fall. "Now, you'll do as I say to atone for the gold nuggets."

"I was a child."

"A child who could have made something of himself instead of...what did I hear you're doing with your life? Working as a ranch hand?"

"It's good, honest work."

Boyd shrugged. "Don't make half of what you could make robbing trains, banks, and the like."

"I want nothing to do with you." The words escaped his mouth before he could stop them.

Boyd slugged him hard in the stomach, ignoring how Malachi doubled over in pain. "When did you get so brazen? You weren't that bold back when you was a young'un." He threw his head back and chortled. "Matter of fact, you'd cower in the corner, so afraid of getting smacked again. You was a coward if there ever was one."

The memories flooded Malachi's mind, and the pain seared his heart.

"Now. Let's talk about that girl with the cane that you're so fond of."

"You leave her alone."

"Ah, now we got him concerned. And now we know for sure you're fond of her." Boyd and Rantz carried on with raucous chuckling, sneering, and a few choice words before Boyd continued. "You could do much better. Why cotton to a cripple?"

"Actually, she is a pretty thing if I do say so myself," said Rantz.

"You two leave Arrosa alone!" The anger rose so forcefully inside of Malachi that he wasn't sure he'd be able to contain it. They could do what they wanted to him, but if they lay a finger on Arrosa…

"There we go, she's got a name. Arrosa. Now, ain't that a purdy name?" Boyd poked Malachi hard in the chest. "If you don't help us rob the bank or if you mention a word of this to anyone, Arrosa meets an untimely demise. Matter of fact, she won't be hobbling around much longer." That led to more uncouth words and guffaws from the two men before Boyd continued. "And don't think that if you tell the sheriff and they arrest us, that nothing's going to happen. If you think that, you're sorely mistaken. We got all kinds of friends in this town, especially Rantz. This ain't the nice little family town some folks think it is. Something will still happen to your Arrosa. And then you'll have no one to blame but yourself." He paused before enunciating his next words loudly and clearly. "Be ready to go with me and Rantz in a few days." Boyd again shoved him hard. "Now get out of here. I'm sick of seeing your sorry mug."

Rantz opened the door and bowed as he gestured for Malachi to leave. "Better make sure you keep this between us," he hissed. "Your pa has killed more men than he can count on two hands, some women too. And I ain't afraid to help him, after spending some time with Arrosa beforehand. If you get my meaning."

Malachi opened his mouth to retort, but then thought better of it. He stumbled from the room, memories combined with what had just happened clouding his mind. Once again, he was that little boy crouching in the corner, afraid of what his father would do. The little boy who feared what might happen to him or his ma. He swallowed the pain and gripped the railing, bile singeing his throat.

Nothing could happen to Arrosa. Nothing. He would protect her with his life.

Downstairs, in the saloon, men drank to their hearts' content, gambling and flirting with the saloon girls. He wanted none of it. He wanted none of the type of life he had been born into.

He couldn't. Wouldn't. Shouldn't help his pa and Rantz rob the bank. But if he didn't—

Malachi had come to a decision. He'd do whatever it took to keep Arrosa safe.

# CHAPTER NINETEEN

IT WAS JUST LIKE old times in Missoula. Arrosa, Mother, and McKenna sat around a table at Olga's Café. "Have whatever you'd like," said McKenna. "Aunt Julia Mathilda sent us some money for a special lunch to celebrate her newest employee."

Mother smiled. "That was very sweet of her."

"Indeed," agreed McKenna. "She has certainly changed as of late."

Arrosa hadn't really ever known Aunt Julia Mathilda well. She inhaled the scrumptious smell of bread and some sort of dessert. Coconut pie, perhaps?

McKenna perused her menu. "Olga's has added to their menu options. I noticed that when Clayton and I paid a visit here recently with his mother and Hal."

"Everything does look delectable." Arrosa ran her finger along the words of the plain and unpretentious menu. At the Bellerose and other fine dining establishments in Missoula, the menus were adorned with decorations and engraved embellishments. Such wasn't the case in Hollow Creek, and Arrosa oddly found that she preferred the less elaborate ways of her new town.

The waitress arrived to take their orders. "Are you certain we can have whatever we'd like?" Arrosa asked. She'd always taken those moments for granted when money was of no consequence.

"Aunt Julia Mathilda said to spare no expense since this is a special day of not only celebrating Mother as the new employee, but also celebrating her move to Hollow Creek."

"In that case, I'll have mutton broth, boiled turkey, and cauliflower au gratin," Arrosa told the waitress.

"And for you?" The waitress asked Mother.

"I'll have the mutton broth as well and boiled sweet potatoes with ribs of beef."

McKenna ordered the same as Mother, and the three of them engaged in pleasant conversation. "Have you been apprised of Father's release date?" Arrosa asked Mother.

"I received a missive just this morning. If all goes well, your father will be released in September."

"Praise God!" said McKenna. "I was just praying about that this morning. Clayton and I were discussing the new hotel, and he suggested that—with yours and Father's permission, of course—that he might inquire as to whether they are hiring a manager."

"Would anyone hire Father after—" Arrosa's words remained suspended midair.

"By Clayton's way of thinking, if he were to put in a good word for Father, it would make all the difference, as it would be better coming from a sheriff than family members regarding Father's upstanding character."

"Clayton does have a point." Mother lifted an eyebrow. "Of course, any position—not to mention a more affluent managerial one—will be more daunting for your father to obtain until we establish his stellar character."

"Indeed, however, by my way of thinking, once he proves himself, it should be no problem at all." But Arrosa's words sounded more confident than she felt. She attempted not to worry about Father struggling to obtain a job. Yet who would hire a man who had been convicted of embezzlement from one of the largest, most prestigious banks in Missoula? All one would have to do would be to write and inquire as to whether the bank owners would vouch for Father before he'd misappropriated the bank's funds. The way things had gone in Missoula, Arrosa doubted any of the managers would do so.

"Something to pray about for certain, although I know we've all been lifting this concern to the Lord heretofore." Mother rested her hands in her lap. "I have learned so much more about the Lord and His faithfulness through this trial. While your father may not be able to obtain the hotel position, I do know the Lord does have plans for him. He is the God of second chances."

Arrosa agreed. She'd seen the Lord's providence time and again. "Mother, how are things at the boutique?"

"I'm finally understanding some of the intricacies of the business. As one who formerly only frequented such shops as a customer, it has been an experience, to say the least. I do like it there, and I have been blessed to meet many of the respectable women in this town. And what about you, Arrosa? How is your employment at present?"

"I am still enjoying it even more than I ever thought I would. The children are growing and learning so much, and Junior is starting to walk. I was so grateful I was able to take the day off today to spend some time with you two."

Mother grasped her hand. "What an answer to prayer that McKenna found you the perfect job."

"And did I hear from a little birdie that someone has entered into a courtship with Malachi Callahan?" McKenna offered a pointed look at Arrosa.

Mother held a hand to her heart. "And you didn't tell us?"

"He only asked me Friday evening, and I meant to tell you both at church on Sunday, but there wasn't time."

"Pshaw." Mother waved away her excuse.

In truth, Arrosa wanted to wait to share the news until they had sufficient time to discuss it, rather than a hurried moment while she was assisting Vera and Morris with rounding up the children and returning them to the ranch. It hadn't helped that those from the Evanson Ranch, including Arrosa, had nearly been late for services. "He has written a letter to Father seeking his permission."

McKenna nodded. "Father will say yes. How could he not?"

"He doesn't know Malachi," Arrosa pointed out. Such an unorthodox way to seek someone's daughter's hand in courtship, but Clayton had traveled to the jail when he sought to court McKenna. Malachi would do the same were it not that they were entering into a busy time on the ranch.

"Well, I'm thrilled for you," said Mother. "From what I've seen and heard, Malachi seems to be a perfect gentleman."

"Indeed. Godly, kind, thoughtful, and generous. Handsome, too," added Arrosa as the heat crept up her face.

"And, of course, we are praising the Lord for the news that Arrosa will walk someday without her cane and that the pain, swelling, and weakness are not permanent," added Mother.

"Yes, and I've already noticed my legs getting stronger and my knee hurting less."

Mother reached over and wrapped an arm around her. "God is so very good."

Tears smarted her eyes. "Yes, He is. My goal is to be able to walk the path where the children had their treasure hunt without my cane."

"No doubt with the Lord's help and your tenacity, it will become a reality. And, McKenna, dear, what is new with you?" Mother asked, although Arrosa ventured that Mother and McKenna saw each other nearly every day.

"I have started decorating the baby's room, although I know I still have time, I just couldn't help myself. What with the prices of things, I've had to procure a little here and a little there."

Pleasant conversation continued, and after they ate, Arrosa bid Mother and McKenna goodbye and walked down the boardwalk to meet Malachi at the implement store. Visiting with her family had done her heart good.

God was so faithful.

When she thought of where they'd been last year and how the Lord had taken care of them, even in some of their darkest moments, unshed tears burned her eyes, and emotion welled in her throat. *Thank You, Lord.*

"Excuse me, miss?"

The voice interrupted her gratitude, and Arrosa stopped just as an older man sidled up alongside her. She stopped just outside the bank. "Yes?"

"Miss Chapman, isn't it?"

Who was this man, and why was he inquiring about her name? "Yes."

He removed his hat, revealing a mass of wiry gray hair. "Excuse me for interrupting your…" his gaze traveled over her and settled on her cane. "Your walk." He fisted the brim of his hat. "Just thought it was necessary to give you a fair warning."

*Fair warning?*

"I beg your pardon?"

"Malachi Callahan. He's a friend of yours, ain't he?"

"He is." Why was this man asking so many questions? Arrosa scanned the boardwalk. Folks chatted nearby, and in the street, someone in an automobile tooted the horn.

"That's what I thought."

"And who might you be?"

The man lowered his voice but failed to answer her inquiry. "One of my jobs is to ensure justice is served. To protect the people."

"Are you a lawman?" The man could possibly be one of her brother-in-law's deputies, but she'd never seen him before, and why wouldn't he just say he was a deputy instead of being evasive?

"A covert one, you could say."

"Covert?"

"Yes, ma'am." He leaned closer, and the odor of stale cigars assaulted her nostrils.

She inclined away, and he veered toward her, invading her space. "What did you say your name was?"

"Just think of me as a concerned citizen."

Arrosa was about to continue on her way when the man spoke again, his whisper coming out as more of a hiss. "You best be mindful of Callahan. He ain't who he purports to be."

"I'm not sure I understand."

The man stared at his worn boots, shook his head, closed his eyes for a few seconds, then caught her gaze. "Don't know that I should go into details."

Part of her wanted to know what he had to say, but a larger part wanted to scurry past him, find Malachi, and return to the ranch. "I best be on my way."

He exhaled sharply, flooding the air around her with his fetid breath. "Reckon I should say something. Don't think I could live with myself if I didn't."

"What is it you mean to tell me?"

"Did you know Callahan frequents the saloon? Has a drinking and a gambling problem. Owes a lot of money."

"He doesn't imbibe. That much I know to be true. Nor does he gamble." At least, she didn't think he did. Why was this man telling her just the opposite?

"On the contrary, I saw him in Wulf's Saloon just a little bit ago. He's mixed up with some bad people."

Malachi in the saloon? Mixed up with bad people? "Surely you are mistaken."

"No, ma'am, afraid not. He's got a sordid past. Just be careful. That's all I'm saying." He slapped his hat back on his head and pivoted in the opposite direction.

There was no way Arrosa would believe what the stranger had said about Malachi. He was a godly man of honor, wouldn't step foot in Wulf's Saloon, didn't gamble, and didn't consort with bad people, nor did he have a sordid past. While he didn't share much about his life before coming to Hollow Creek, Arrosa knew his former life wasn't anything like what the man mentioned.

*Right?* Why did a flicker of doubt threaten to invade her mind?

She stiffened her shoulders and started toward the implement. Malachi was at the counter paying for some items.

"Thank you, Callahan. Pleasure doing business with you."

"Hello," she said, greeting him as he stepped onto the boardwalk. She noticed some redness on his left cheek. Arrosa was about to inquire about it when Malachi spoke.

"Are you ready to return to the ranch?"

"I am."

But Malachi was not the happy sort he'd been when they'd first arrived in town and had gone their separate ways, him to the livery and implement, and her to partake in lunch with Mother and McKenna. Instead, wariness etched his handsome features.

He assisted her into the wagon when she caught the whiff of stale cigar smoke. Her throat tightened as the worry gnawed at her. She inhaled again, expecting the scent of soap, or perhaps hay. Anything but something that reminded her of a saloon.

Wulf's Saloon, where the man said Malachi frequented.

No. That couldn't be. She'd never smelled such a distasteful odor when she'd been around him before, and she'd been around him plenty.

What then?

Could it be that someone was smoking in the implement? Or the livery? Or wherever Malachi had tended to errands, and the stench had permeated through his clothing and skin?

She glanced at his profile. His jaw clenched, and his face was an unreadable mask. "Malachi?"

"Yes?"

His answer was short and clipped. But she'd learned her lesson last time when she'd assumed things before the special dance he'd arranged for her in the Evansons' barn.

They drove in silence until they rounded the final corner, and Arrosa asked, "Is everything all right, Malachi?"

Something indiscernible flashed across his face. "Yes. Why do you ask?"

"You're just...different this afternoon. Did it go well at the livery and the implement?"

"Yes."

Usually, he would ask how her time with Mother and McKenna went. But instead, he returned his focus to the road ahead. As though if he didn't watch it closely, he'd miss the turn to the ranch.

Even though she ventured that he'd been on this road countless times.

"The noonday meal went well at Olga's," she offered.

"That's good."

But he didn't look at her. Didn't inquire further. Nor did he say anything more until they arrived at the ranch. Malachi parked the wagon, then assisted her from it.

"Will you be in for supper?"

"Plan to be."

"All right. Thank you for delivering me back to the ranch. I'll see you then."

But she wasn't sure he'd even heard her as he was halfway to the barn.

# CHAPTER TWENTY

HE KNEW HE WAS being distant. Yet, he couldn't exactly tell Arrosa why. The trepidation about meeting Boyd and Rantz at the saloon had needled him since it happened. He'd barely been able to pay the implement owner much mind. Malachi was perturbed at himself not only for not standing up to Boyd and Rantz, but also for causing Arrosa to worry. He'd seen the concern in her face. As a matter of fact, he'd barely been able to even look at her as they rode to the ranch. She didn't deserve to be put into danger because of him. She'd done nothing wrong, yet Boyd would take out his fury on an innocent woman.

Heat flushed through him. He couldn't tell anyone, yet he couldn't *not* do anything. On the way home, he'd considered every possible scenario. Maybe he could anonymously turn Boyd into the law. But Boyd was evasive. He was slippery and experienced at avoiding the law. That's how he'd done it for all of these years, all the while continuing to commit crimes. Besides, even if Malachi did convince the law that he'd tracked down a wanted man, Rantz would still be loose, and from what he knew of the man, revenge was no stranger to him. And no doubt Boyd would return to exact his own vengeance.

He couldn't tell Thad and endanger the Evansons. Nor could he tell Sheriff Beringer, who was out of town. Malachi didn't know the deputies, and if he tried to warn the bank, that would only cause more questions and issues. Warning another town's sheriff wouldn't help due to jurisdiction and the inevitable fact that Boyd would find out.

And if he turned in his father, folks would know he was related to a wanted murderer and thief.

His only option boiled down to the fact that he would have to meet them when demanded and do his best to act like he was robbing the bank to appease them, while also making sure he stayed on the right side of the law. That was the only way to protect Arrosa.

And Malachi would pray mightily for the Lord to safeguard the woman he loved.

Malachi didn't dare look at her, for if he did, he'd be even angrier at himself than he already was. Especially angry for hurting her. He'd seen the sadness in her eyes when he'd provided his clipped answers. He wanted to ask how the noonday meal went with her mother and sister. Wanted to hear all about her day. But he couldn't distract his mind from the fear of losing her at the hands of Boyd and Rantz and their nefarious schemes.

Boyd would accomplish whatever he set out to do. Murder and thievery meant nothing to him other than a way to achieve whatever twisted goals he'd set for himself.

When Malachi arrived at the Evanson ranch, he noticed a horse tethered to the post in front of the house. He helped Arrosa out of the wagon, and she hobbled quickly toward the house without looking back. He unhitched the horses. Likely, whoever was visiting was inside the house. His mind kept drifting back to the conversation with Boyd and Rantz. How Boyd had found him was nothing short of a miraculous coincidence. If Malachi even believed in coincidences—which he didn't.

Hadn't he thought, after all these years, that he would be safe from his father? Of course, the newspaper had to print the story with him being so helpful with the missing horse. He didn't need the notoriety. It really wasn't as big a deal as they had claimed, at least not for him. And now, knowing how Boyd had found him, invited a flood of emotions into his heart.

He had never wanted to see Boyd again. Had never wanted to conjure up those feelings of abuse, neglect, and turmoil. He'd lived a new life all these years, and by the grace of God, hadn't become anything like his father, but now, all was in jeopardy. If he agreed to rob the bank to keep Arrosa safe, he would be just like Boyd.

He was in a predicament. Tell someone and risk Arrosa being injured or worse. Go along with the plan and risk being arrested, thrown into jail, or worse. And being accused of being just like Boyd.

Malachi's protectiveness couldn't allow the first. His pride couldn't allow the latter.

He left the barn and headed toward the back corral. That's when he noticed Thad talking with a familiar person. Rantz.

What was that ne'er-do-well doing on the ranch? Malachi clenched his teeth. He had every mind to tell Thad what Rantz had done in town earlier today. But then he reminded himself of all the reasons why he couldn't breathe a word about the meeting at the saloon.

He reversed direction. He had other chores to tend to and had no care to see Rantz again. But Rantz's words, carried on the breeze, stopped him in his tracks. He slid behind the tack room, out of sight of the two men.

"Just warning you, Evanson, that's all. Man ain't who he proclaims to be. He's got a sordid past, that one."

Malachi was about to launch from the side of the building and give Rantz a talking to for attempting to dishonor his character.

But by God's grace, his feet remained firmly rooted. He held his breath, waiting to hear Thad's response.

"All I'm sayin' is that you're well-known around these parts. You got yourself a good reputation. Are you willing to throw that all away by hiring some no-good ranch hand? He's a rapscallion, Evanson. Likely steal from you when your back is turned."

"If Callahan was considering stealing from me, why hasn't he done it already? Today is not his first day in my employ."

Rantz shrugged. "You know I've dealt with scoundrels like him when I was a lawman years ago, before Beringer got voted in. Maybe Callahan is just taking his time. Doesn't want you to get suspicious and all."

"If he is a man of poor character, then why did he help me get my horse back?"

"I didn't know I was going to have to suffer through an interrogation. I'm just trying to help you out. I can tell from your responses that it's a waste of my time. Won't be long before I'm saying I told you so. Besides, Callahan ain't even his real name."

Malachi's pulse quickened as weakness settled in his legs. If Rantz told Thad who his father was, Malachi would no longer have a job on the Evanson Ranch. He couldn't let that happen. Not after all this time. Not after having to reinvent who he was. His neck muscles tensed. *Lord, please guide me.*

Suddenly, as though a wayward train losing control on the tracks, Malachi's thoughts spiraled. If Rantz spoke the truth about who Malachi *really* was, if Thad removed Malachi from his employ—the air whooshed from his lungs. He would lose his job, and he would lose Arrosa.

He cautiously peered around the building, wanting both to hear Thad's response but also dreading it.

"Rantz, I don't know why you're here trying to stir up trouble. As long as Callahan has been working for me, he has been nothing but honorable and forthright."

"Suit yourself, but you're a fool."

"One thing I can tell you is that Malachi Callahan is a godly young man. He's loyal and a hard worker. If he had another name or even another life before the one he has now, that's his business. As long as he continues to prove himself a capable and dependable employee, he'll remain at the Evanson Ranch unless he decides otherwise. Good day, Rantz."

"But—"

"Good day, Rantz. I trust you can see yourself back to your horse."

Rantz uttered a stream of curse words as he kicked up the dust with the toe of his boot. "Ain't heard the last of this, Evanson. You'll see."

Thad waved a hand, gesturing for Rantz to move along.

And for the first time in several minutes, Malachi's breathing returned to normal. He ducked inside the tack room until Rantz passed, climbed onto his horse, and sped away.

Not many people, aside from Barnabas, had defended Malachi. Yet, Thad had. Malachi was determined to work even harder to prove that his boss's assessment of him was correct. Now, to just figure out what he was going to do about having to help rob a bank.

Malachi awoke the next morning, not sure of what the day would bring. Would this be the day Boyd and Rantz would solicit his assistance in committing a crime?

Malachi stretched, pulled on his clothes and boots, then stepped out onto the bunkhouse porch. He hadn't slept well last night. Thoughts of Arrosa being injured or worse had kept him awake. Once he'd turned that over to the Lord as best as he could, worries of the law believing he truly did want to rob the bank and arresting him took over. Spending time behind prison walls.

Becoming just like his father.

Becoming just like Miss Becht's wayward cousin.

He'd prayed, turned over onto his other side, prayed some more, then lay there staring at the ceiling. Finally, sometime before sunrise, God had granted him the peace that allowed him to fall asleep.

Yet, here he was again, worried about Arrosa and his future.

What was it Barnabas would have said about such dilemmas? He scratched his head and searched his memory. A Psalm came to mind: *"Deliver me from mine enemies, O my God: defend me from them that rise up against me."*

"Lord, please deliver me from Boyd and Rantz. Defend me from them, and let there be a way out of this dilemma. In Jesus' name I pray, amen."

Yes, the Lord would resolve this according to His will. There was nothing that surprised Him and nothing that would go unnoticed. There was nothing He couldn't handle. But what if the answer to God's will was Arrosa being hurt or Malachi living the rest of his life in prison?

Malachi focused his gaze heavenward. "I just need to trust You, Lord. Trust Your faithfulness even in times like this, as I muddle through this predicament. Forgive me, Lord, and help me to trust."

Inhaling a breath of the fresh mountain air, Malachi determined, with the help of the Holy Spirit, not to dwell on anything beyond his control. Yet, even before he reached the barn, the thoughts consumed him again.

"Malachi? Do you have a minute?"

He turned to see Thad standing near the barn, and for a moment, Malachi's heart dropped to his boots. Would Thad release him from his duties on the ranch due to what Rantz said yesterday?

"Hello, sir."

"I wanted to talk to you about a serious matter."

Worry snaked through him. Surely, Thad didn't regret defending him yesterday. Surely, he would keep Malachi as a ranch hand. Surely, the Lord's will was that Thad would give Malachi the benefit of the doubt.

"A serious matter?' His breath shook as his stomach knotted.

"Yes. Now, feel free to disagree."

Disagree? Suddenly, Malachi's appetite for some of Cook's pancakes and bacon left him. "All right."

"As you know, there is a substantial amount to be done on the ranch, and I need ranch hands who are dependable, trustworthy, and honorable."

Should he just come right out and apologize for being the son of Boyd Goshorn? Apologize for landing himself in the Hollow Creek jail after the drunk attempted to steal Barnabas's pocket watch that night in town? Share that the only reason he'd even consider robbing a bank was to protect Arrosa? Just offer to pack up his bags and leave?

Sweat beaded on his brow. *Lord, please give me wisdom.* "Yes, sir, I do know that."

"And, as you know, the hours on a ranch are long and at times never-ending. The management of employees is not easy. Sometimes you have to let them go even if you don't want to."

Was that Thad's plan for him? Should he ask? His mouth grew dry. "I understand."

"It's obviously not something we would want to do, but it is necessary at times. Evanson Ranch has a stellar reputation, and we want to keep it that way."

Malachi noticed Arrosa gripping the handrail with one hand, arm around Junior with the other as she ambled down the stairs. Of all the things he would miss about the ranch, he would miss her the most. "Thad, I know Rantz paid you a visit yesterday." Although his voice didn't sound like his own, he figured getting what he had to say out in the open was better than continuing to stuff the fear inside.

"Rantz?"

"Yes. I returned from town and overheard some of your conversation."

Thad brushed his comment aside. "Oh, yes, Rantz." He pursed his lips. "That man should find something to do with himself rather than causing trouble."

Malachi gulped a hard swallow. "What you need to discuss doesn't have anything to do with that conversation?"

"No, it doesn't. I don't know how much you heard, but for what it's worth, I'm not fond of Rantz, and I don't really care about what he has to say. Especially when he comes here attempting to destroy the reputation of one of my best hands."

"One of your best hands?

"He mentioned you had a sordid past and to beware of you." Thad directed his gaze at Malachi, and for a second, Malachi thought the man could see clear through his soul.

"Besides stealing a pencil in school when I was a kid and having to deal with the man who stole my pocket watch, I've always been law-abiding."

"I had no thought that you would be anything else."

"That isn't what this is about?"

Thad shook his head. "No, I wanted to discuss with you the fact that we're losing Pete."

"Is everything all right?"

"Yes, he and his wife, Anne, are moving to be closer to the children and grandchildren. As such, I'm losing my foreman. Emilie and I have prayed long and hard about who we would choose to replace Pete. Your name kept coming to mind. As I mentioned earlier, feel free to decline the offer. But we would be grateful if you would accept and become our new foreman. It would be longer hours, and you would oversee the ranch hands. It's not an easy task. Sometimes the hiring and the firing can be more than a chore."

Malachi's jaw dropped. "Me? Your new foreman? What about Jep?"

"Jep's a good man. But he doesn't have the leadership skills. I believe you do. Take some time to pray about it and think about it. We do have about a month or so before Pete and his wife leave. If you do decide to take the position, you will have a pay increase, and you will be able to reside in the house Pete and Anne currently live in, which was my former home before Emilie and I married."

"I-I-I don't know what to say. Yes, I'll pray about it. Thank you, sir. Thank you very much."

Thad grinned. "You're welcome. You're diligent and reliable, and I believe you'd do a quality job, but again, seek the Lord's guidance before you give us a definitive answer." He pivoted and gazed at the house. "Reckon you should get inside and get some grub before Cook cleans the kitchen and there'll be no more to be had until the noonday meal."

An unexpected release of the pent-up tension rolled off of Malachi's shoulders. "I will do that. Thank you again. I will let you know."

Thad nodded. "Keep up the good work, Malachi. This ranch wouldn't run nearly as smoothly without your help. And I also want to thank you again for the wagon you purchased for Mamie. That meant a lot to her that she was able to join the others on their treasure hunt. Thank you also for the table you built for her so she could do her schoolwork more easily. It's things like that that make me know that the words Rantz spoke about you were untrue, and further, it makes me realize how I want to do whatever I can to keep you as an employee."

# CHAPTER TWENTY-ONE

ARROSA LEFT THE LADIES' Bible study at the church feeling refreshed and rejuvenated. The more she dug into God's Word, the hungrier she became to know more.

Grasping the cane with one hand and her Bible in the other, she shuffled along the boardwalk, grateful for a day off from work, but missing the children at the same time.

Malachi would be in town shortly to retrieve her. She appreciated that even when he had other matters to tend to, he was able to return her to the ranch.

She crossed the alleyway when she heard a sound. Upon closer examination, she noticed a kitten mewing by some discarded crates. She pivoted and limped toward the animal. Was it hungry? Perhaps she could find it a home.

"Hello, there, little one." She clutched the Bible under her arm and gingerly stooped down. The orange-and-white cat purred and peered up at her with blue eyes.

She was about to lift the cat and carry it to safety when a hand clamped over her mouth and an arm snaked around her and pinned her own arms to her sides. The Bible fell, and her assailant kicked her cane aside. "You won't be needing those where you're going," he hissed.

Fear gnawed at her insides. Who was this man? Why was he intent on harming her? Where was he taking her?

Her heels skidded in the dirt. Pain radiated up her leg as he proceeded to drag her backward away from the street and from anyone who could intervene.

*Lord, please help me!*

She struggled to move her arms, but she was no match for the man. He responded by tightening his hold until suddenly he stopped moving. Arrosa heard the sound of footsteps. Had someone come to rescue her? She attempted to say something, but her words were muffled against his hand.

"Hold her still," another male voice said.

There were two of them?

Her body went cold with dread. Why were they doing this? And why did one man's voice sound familiar?

Arrosa's back was to both of them, and one was tying her wrists with what felt like rope. The man who'd dragged her down the alleyway gripped the back of her neck. "If you so much as make one sound, I'll shoot."

The other man, one who looked vaguely familiar with his cowboy hat lowered over a good portion of his forehead, stuffed a gag in her mouth.

"Let's go."

They were taking her somewhere?

She scanned the area, but there was no one from what she could see with her limited view of the alley. Surely someone would see what was happening and assist her.

Surely!

She wriggled and raised her stronger leg to stomp on the man's foot. The cold barrel of a gun jammed into her ribs. "Did you not hear me? I will shoot if you don't stop moving."

Nausea roiled in her belly as a shiver of fear gripped her throat.

They lifted her onto a horse, and the first man climbed on behind her and jabbed the gun harder into her side. Her body trembled, and tears flooded her eyes. What was happening?

The familiar man sidled up alongside one of the buildings and peered around the corner. "Wait." He then angled himself from sight before taking another gander around the edge of the building. "All right, let's go."

The man behind her commanded the horse forward, and they exited the narrow space between the two buildings and into a remote area behind Main Street. Only tall weeds and a tree or two, but no people.

Where was everyone?

The horse's speed increased, and they crossed a bridge before leaving town. She strained to observe her surroundings as they passed houses and fields. Nothing was familiar as they traveled in a direction she'd not yet been during her time in Hollow Creek.

She lost track of time. The further they were from the town, the less the chance someone would come for her.

*Lord, please, please help me. Let someone have noticed.*

The questions pummeled through her mind. Why would they take her? She didn't even know them. Was it a random kidnapping? Had she somehow done something to offend them? But what? That didn't make sense. She spent most of her days at the ranch.

Where were they taking her?

The latter question was answered when they dragged her inside a musty cabin that boasted one chair, a rickety table, and three buckets. After seeing the one man without his cowboy hat, Arrosa now recognized him. He was the one who'd told her that Malachi was in the saloon and warned her of his sordid past.

The familiar man bound her ankles so tight she could barely move her feet, and Arrosa's arms tingled from being held in one place for so long. The gag tasted something akin to dirt mixed with lutefisk. She'd unfortunately tasted that once at a restaurant when her family visited Norway. The taste repulsed her then as it did now. Was this a nightmare from which she'd soon awaken? What would they do with her now that they had her trapped in this hideous abode? Had anyone seen them ride off with her? Would anyone question why her Bible was left in the alleyway? Would Malachi wonder why she wasn't at the mercantile when he came to retrieve her?

The questions buzzed through her mind even as the fear clamped so forcefully she struggled to breathe. If no one had seen them ride off with her, then no one knew she was here. If no one knew she was here…

*Lord, please protect me. Let someone find me. Keep me safe from the harm these men could inflict on me.*

The man who'd dragged her down the alleyway shuffled across the splintered floor and stood in front of her. "Well, well. So this is the woman my son is fond of."

This man claimed to be Malachi's father? But that didn't make sense. Hadn't Malachi mentioned that his father had passed?

She attempted to speak, and the man released the gag.

"Say your piece, then I'm replacing the handkerchief."

"Why are you doing this?"

He chortled and slapped his leg before just as quickly sobering. His face contorted into an evil scowl, and his lip curled. "You're about the only thing that's gonna make Malachi do what we want him to do."

"Malachi? What?"

"Enough." He re-tied the handkerchief, and a flurry of curse words escaped his lips. "We ready to go get that no-good scoundrel of a son of mine?"

"Yes, we are." The familiar man leaned into Arrosa's face. "Now, don't you go and do nothing stupid while we're gone."

The men left, and Arrosa attempted to remove the ropes from her wrists to no avail. When would they return? What did he mean when he said they were going to make Malachi do something?

If only she could warn him.

She leaned forward, wishing her hands were at least bound in front of her instead of behind her. The chair teetered, and she nearly crashed to the floor before righting herself. Panic fueled her, and she attempted several more times to break free of her bindings before sliding the chair forward, but she didn't get far before she heard the rumbling of a wagon outside.

The offer of being a foreman for the Evanson Ranch claimed Malachi's attention for the next few days. As he hitched up the horses to retrieve Arrosa from the Bible study, he pondered telling her the news. Dare he hope he'd somehow be able to accept the offer and live a normal life after dealing with Boyd's robbery plans?

The answer came when he arrived in town and went to the mercantile, only to be told Arrosa never arrived. Could she still be at the church? The sight of a familiar cane lying discarded in the alleyway warned otherwise.

A heavy hand landed on his shoulder. "It's time," Boyd hissed. "If you want your woman to live, come with us."

Both numb and seething with anger, Malachi stumbled back to the wagon, aware of Boyd watching his every move. No one else paid him any mind, and as he followed Boyd's and Rantz's horses, Malachi attempted to concoct a plan—to no avail.

They eventually stopped in front of a dilapidated cabin south of Hollow Creek. Malachi parked Thad's wagon beside two trees, and Boyd and Rantz tethered their horses.

At one time, it may have been a respectable place with its small porch boasting a turned newel post railing and shutters on the front-facing window. But whatever the house had formerly been was in the past. Now, the railing needed fresh paint, the logs on the front needed to be repaired, and the broken window replaced. Would the decrepit, listing porch even hold their weight?

"Is this your hideout?" he half-asked, half-mocked. Leave it to Boyd to hole up in a house that was about to topple. He'd spent so much of his life running from the law when he could have settled down and made a life for himself...and his son.

A rush of fury washed over him anew as he disembarked from the back of the wagon. Boyd slunk up behind him and hit him hard in the left shoulder. Malachi stumbled, then righted himself.

"Never thought I'd see the day when my boy helped me make a living."

"Make a living? Robbing a bank isn't making a living. It's stealing from others."

Boyd's lip curled. "What are you? The morality deputy? You talk like some preacher man. Well, I ain't having it. You ain't a Christian. You the same as you always was." Boyd shoved him hard, and this time, Malachi lost his footing. He scurried back upright before Boyd could have the upper hand.

"That's right. You stand up, boy." Boyd spat to one side. "You know how I know there ain't a God?"

Rantz tucked his fingers through his suspenders and huffed. "We gonna talk about religion right now? Time's a wastin'."

Boyd ignored Rantz. "I know there ain't a God because iffen there was, He wouldn't have given me a sorry, worthless excuse for a son like you."

The words jabbed him in the heart so forcefully that it was almost Malachi's undoing. He gritted his teeth and willed that his shoulders wouldn't shake.

*"I know you ain't had a good earthly pa, son, but you got a Heavenly Father who loves you and gave His life for you. In the midst of sorrow, thinking about Boyd Goshorn and all he done, don't stop thinkin' about the Good Lord and all* He *done."* Barnabas's words filtered through Malachi's mind. He stood straighter and peered at the man in front of him.

Thinning brown hair, gray eyes, a mustache, and a beard. While tall, he had short legs and an expanding paunch. Malachi looked nothing like him.

*"And just remember, you, with the Lord's help, will make choices in this life. Choices to be like your pa or choices to be just the opposite."* Barnabas's words again rang through his mind. But here Malachi was, preparing to conspire with Boyd and Rantz to rob the Hollow Creek Bank. Was there really a difference?

Arrosa's lovely face flashed through his mind. To save her, he'd do whatever was necessary, whether that be robbing a bank or traveling to the ends of the earth.

"You two gonna stand around all day, or are we gonna tend to some business?" Rantz's gaze bounced from Malachi to Boyd.

"Little impatient, ain't ya?"

"A whole lotta impatient. Besides, should we check on the woman?"

"You think she'd escape?"

"What woman?" Malachi's heart fell to his boots.

He'd hoped and prayed they hadn't truly abducted Arrosa, but Boyd and Rantz chortled, their evil voices carrying through the otherwise still surroundings. "Let's take him inside. That'll answer his question better than anything else." Rantz nudged Malachi in the upper arm. "Don't take it so hard, Callahan. If you do what we say, she'll be just fine. Maybe."

Malachi shoved past both of them and up seven crumbling steps to the cabin's porch. He flung open the door and bolted inside. Arrosa sat in a chair in the filthy room, bound and gagged. "Arrosa!"

He scrambled to her and lowered himself to his knees, his fingers fumbling to remove the ropes around her wrists and ankles and the handkerchief from her mouth.

The cold barrel of a gun to his temple paused his frantic movements. "Stand up and back away from her. Now."

Anger surged through him, but he did as Boyd demanded. Not that he had a choice. If Boyd shot him, where would that leave Arrosa? The expression in her eyes haunted him. While he couldn't articulate all of the details, he knew this was his fault.

"Now, back slowly away from her."

Malachi reluctantly did so, even as the gun remained on him. Finally, Boyd lowered his revolver and tucked it into its holster.

A myriad of thoughts came to mind, some unrealistic, such as striving to overtake the two men. Others, more pragmatic, such as attempting to negotiate for Arrosa's release. But the thought that surged to the forefront was that of prayer. *Lord, please don't let them hurt her. Please.*

Desperation consumed him. His pulse quickened, and he clenched his fists at his sides. "What have you done to her?"

"Nothing. Yet." Boyd's evil laugh was joined by Rantz's snickering.

"If you want her to live," said Rantz in a calm voice, as if he were discussing an everyday event, "you'll do exactly as we say."

"I'll do whatever you want me to do, just let her go. It's me you want."

Rantz's eye twitched. "But if we hurt her, that's punishment to you."

The tears that streamed down Arrosa's face devastated him. He had to help her. His body froze for a moment, and he inhaled a shaky breath. But as quickly as those brief emotions that nothing could be done entered his mind, the opposite emerged even stronger and more forcefully. A flush of heat rose up his neck, and he pivoted to face Boyd. "You need to let her go, and then I will do whatever you want me to do."

"Did you hear that, Rantz? If we let her go, then Malachi will do whatever we want him to do."

Rantz slapped his leg and emitted a false chortle before he sobered. His dark eyes narrowed, and the multitude of wrinkles and scars covering his face became more prominent. "He'll do whatever we want if we let her go? I don't think so. You'll do whatever we want *first,* and if you do, then her chances of survival just increased." Rantz intertwined his hands behind his back and sauntered to Arrosa. He unlaced his fingers and ran a thumb down her cheek. Arrosa flinched.

Malachi bolted into action. He gripped Rantz's shoulder, spun him around, and shoved him so hard that Rantz fell backward against the wall. "You will leave her alone!" He towered over the older man sprawled on the floor, and for the briefest of moments, thought he saw fear in his adversary's eyes.

A gunshot rang out, and Malachi jolted. He swallowed the burn of bile in his throat and cautiously turned around.

"If you so much as utter a word we don't like, the next bullet I use will not be aimed at the wall," Boyd snarled.

The air in Malachi's lungs evaporated. *Thank You, Lord.* Arrosa was still all right. Trembling and sobbing, but alive.

Rantz stood to his feet and whacked Malachi hard upside the head. "You ever try shoving me again, and I will kill you."

"Why do you need my help anyway? You two are experienced. You can pull off the bank heist without me."

"We could. But we ain't gonna. My reasons for wanting your help are twofold." Boyd again replaced the revolver in its holster and paced the room in front of Arrosa. She watched his movements and shrank back the closer he got to her. "First, it was always supposed to be you and me working alongside each other. Pa and son stealing, maiming, killing, making a name for ourselves. The second reason," he said, his glare boring into Malachi, "is that I will do whatever it takes to make you regret the day you told the teacher about those gold nuggets."

"I told you I didn't tell him anything. He surmised it all because not every kid takes gold nuggets to school."

"And you should have known not to do that." Boyd slugged him hard in the ribs, and Malachi doubled over from the gut punch. And lest he be tempted to fight back, Rantz pulled his gun and aimed it at Malachi's head. Pain pinched his ribs, and Malachi fought for a breath.

"I will make a man out of you yet. No son of mine is going to be a sissy." Boyd smiled disparagingly, a piece of brown food rooted between his two front teeth. "Do you ever wonder what happened to that teacher who turned me in to the law?"

Of all the people Malachi had been concerned about over the years who had succumbed to his father's evilness, the teacher had not been one of them. But he wouldn't give this vile man the satisfaction of asking the question.

Boyd slapped him hard across the face. "I asked you a question, and you best answer it."

The sting hurt worse than the one at the saloon, and Malachi held back the wince. "What happened to that teacher? What happened to him?" Malachi thought of the kindly male teacher who had done all he could to assist a boy who struggled with learning the printed word. Who'd been the first one to plant the seeds of a love for reading in a boy who later escaped into all the books he could get his hands on at the orphanage.

Boyd threw back his head, and the roar of his amusement sounded. His Adam's apple bobbed in his throat. "He died." Boyd shrugged. Don't worry, he didn't suffer. It was a quick death. But I will say he didn't leave this earth not knowing what he done. Had I not needed to hightail it out of town, I would have taken care of the reverend and his wife as well." Boyd clenched his fists so forcefully that his arms trembled. "They put you on that train, and I never found you again until I saw you in that newspaper. All them wasted years."

"As much as I'd love to continue listening to this pathetic rant, we have better things to do." Rantz stomped the floor with his boot as if throwing a tantrum. "If we are going to be successful with this bank robbery, we need to sit down and make the appropriate plans."

"When did you get so antsy, Rantz? Or should I call you 'antsy Rantzy'?"

Rantz and Boyd now stood face to face. Maybe this was the answer to prayer. If they turned against each other, Malachi would have a chance to free Arrosa, and they could both escape.

But lest he contemplate any more plans, the two men reconciled. Malachi's gaze connected with Arrosa's. He hoped he could communicate to her that everything would be fine. That he would do whatever he could to rescue her. That she meant more to him than anyone ever had. That he loved her.

She blinked, and he thought he saw unshed tears. "Arrosa..."

"Hey! There'll be no talking to her. Now get your sorry self over here and help us plan." Boyd gripped Malachi's arm so forcefully that it cut off the circulation. "It's time to make our plans for the robbery." His face contorted as he sneered.

Malachi cast one last glance at Arrosa before begrudgingly following Boyd to a makeshift table in the corner of the room. Buckets had been overturned and used as chairs. Would anyone come looking for Arrosa? He knew Mrs. Evanson had given her the day off to attend a Bible study with her ma, sister, and some of the church ladies. Had Arrosa already attended the meeting or had they apprehended her before she'd had a chance to do so?

He was to have brought her home afterward.

The troubling thing was that no one would miss either of them until this evening.

And now there seemed no way out of this predicament. Would they release her once he acquiesced to their demands? Would she be freed before they robbed the bank, or have to wait until after tomorrow?

The thought of her being held captive in the cabin infuriated him in a way nothing ever had before. "Can you unbind her?"

"Now, why would we do that? What do you think we are? Half-wits?" Boyd shook his head. "You sure don't got much for brains in that head of yours."

"It's not like she's going to escape, what with that bum leg." Rantz shrugged. "What's the harm in loosening the ropes and the gag? If she wanders off, we can easily catch her." He snickered. "She's a cripple, remember?"

Malachi's neck and shoulders tensed. He was about to rebuke them for their hateful words when he thought better of it.

"All right. Go ahead." Boyd gestured toward Arrosa. "You can have the honors, Rantz."

"Don't mind if I do." He swaggered to Arrosa, and Malachi prepared to stand and defend her should the need arise.

Boyd placed a hand on the butt of his revolver. "Don't you try nothing, boy. Got it?"

Malachi said nothing. He wouldn't make any promises. Yet, if he gave in to brashness, there would be consequences.

Rantz leaned close to Arrosa. "You're a pretty gal. Too bad you got that limp."

"Rantz..." The word was out of his mouth before he could stop it.

The man ignored him and took his time untying the ropes around Arrosa's wrists and ankles. He then removed the handkerchief, and Arrosa gagged and choked.

"Don't she got some kind of family money or something? Maybe we could hold her for ransom," suggested Boyd.

"Could be, but the only thing that matters to me is robbing that bank tomorrow. Besides, if her family has money, why is she a maid for the Evansons?" Rantz trailed a finger across her upper arm and leaned closer to her, his lips nearly brushing her cheek. Arrosa flinched and squeezed her eyes shut. "Maybe you and I could make a deal."

Malachi jumped to his feet and stormed over to Rantz. "Leave her be."

"Or what?" Rantz stood nose to nose with Malachi. "You can shoot me, but your pa will return the favor. Either way, you lose."

"Just leave her alone. She has nothing to do with this."

"Oh, but she does."

"I'm going to help you, but you need to leave her be."

Rantz's long, yellowed fingernail jabbed Malachi in the chest. "Aww, ain't that special. A man defending his woman's honor."

A low, guttural growl rose in Rantz's throat. "Thing is that I don't care one little bit if you are defending your woman's honor. You're nothing but a fool, Malachi Goshorn."

"It's Malachi Callahan. Not Malachi Goshorn."

Rantz released a stream of curse words. "You can call yourself what you like, but you are Malachi Goshorn, ain't that the truth, Boyd?"

"Yeah, that's the truth. You'll always be my boy, no matter what. You can't change that."

Rantz stomped away and again took his seat on the bucket. "Now this is how it will be tomorrow. I overheard there's $18,000 in the safe due to a new shipment. That don't count everything else. They know and respect you, Callahan, so you'll go in first." He proceeded to explain the elaborate details, having obviously been scheming this for some time. Rantz periodically kept an eye on Arrosa, but she remained in the chair watching them. "If anyone gets in our way, we'll shoot 'em. Hopefully, that Beringer keeps his nose out of things. About had enough of his interference," he snarled. "We'll ride to that cave in the hills between here and Cullman."

Boyd extracted some whiskey from a nearby crate. "Ain't had nothing to eat in hours. But at least we got ourselves some moonshine." Rantz continued to outline the plan while Boyd downed more whiskey. "Good ideas, all of them. Sounds like we got ourselves a plan that calls for some celebration." He slurred his words, took several more hasty swigs, causing much of the whiskey to drizzle down his chin. Minutes passed, and a memory clouded Malachi's mind.

His pa had drunk far too much that night. First at the saloon, then at home. His violent temper took hold. Malachi hadn't meant to ask him a question about something he'd learned in school.

Poor timing on his part. Boyd reached up and shoved Malachi so hard, he flew through the air. Malachi wasn't sure what happened next, other than he awoke in his bed with his ma sponging a cloth on his head. Obviously, Boyd hadn't given up his penchant for liquor.

His ma...that was one thing he'd never ask Boyd about.

Boyd continued slurping his drink and emptying it as Rantz joined him before passing the whiskey to Malachi.

"No, thank you."

"No, thank you? What, are you some polite man of high society? No, thank you? Drink up, boy."

"I don't imbibe."

"Since when?"

"Since never."

Boyd started on his second flask.

In all of the ruckus, they didn't realize that Arrosa had left her perch and was quietly making her way to the front door.

"Get her!" shouted Boyd.

Rantz jerked up so rapidly, his leg kicked over the bucket, and it fell to the floor with a crash. Arrosa turned the doorknob and slid through the door. Rantz dashed in her direction, Malachi running after him. He had to reach Arrosa first.

Boyd shot several shots in the air, wavering as he did so on unsteady legs in his inebriated state.

Rantz grabbed Arrosa and flung her back inside as though she were only a rag doll. She toppled over into a heap on the floor. Malachi punched Rantz square in the jaw, then extended a hand to Arrosa. As he did so, Rantz smacked him over the head with a bottle, and Malachi crumbled to the floor. The world around him spun, and he attempted to sit up as the dizziness overcame him.

Arrosa screamed as Rantz gripped her arm again.

In an act that could only have been orchestrated by the Lord, Malachi fought through the blurred vision and stood. His head pounded. He swung and allowed the punches to fly as they connected with Rantz's face and torso. They wrestled each other onto the floor, Malachi gaining the upper hand. "Go, Arrosa, go!" he shouted.

"But…"

"Go!" He gestured to the door before landing another hit. Rantz retaliated with a hit of his own, landing squarely on Malachi's jaw. Something popped, and Malachi reached up to massage his jaw just as Rantz planted his hands around Malachi's neck. "Go after her, Boyd!" Rantz shouted.

Malachi struggled to breathe, his airflow severely hampered. He scratched, clawed, and shoved. Rantz was a smaller and older man. There was no reason for him to be able to gain the advantage.

*Lord, please help me. Please help Arrosa. Keep her safe.*

"Where did she go?" asked Boyd, still slurring his words.

"You idiot, she's outside. Probably halfway to town by now."

Malachi took the opportunity of Rantz's distraction to chop at Rantz's neck and shove him to the ground. Rantz's arms fell to his sides as he crumpled in a daze. Malachi's breath came in gasps, but time was not something he had the privilege of having. He spun around and jumped to his feet, the room spinning around him as he started after Boyd, who staggered after Arrosa.

Rantz stood and charged him once again. Malachi delivered a hit to his nose.

Boyd sneered. "Don't worry about this, Rantz. He won't win." Boyd aimed at Malachi and raised his revolver.

The sound of gunfire filled the cabin.

# CHAPTER TWENTY-TWO

ARROSA PAUSED WHEN SHE heard the gunshot. What had happened? Was Malachi all right? *Lord, please protect him!*

She stumbled to the side of the cabin and peeked inside through a broken window. Malachi lay on the floor, blood staining his arm.

Arrosa held a hand to her heart as her shoulders quaked. "No," she whispered, not daring to speak louder, lest the men hear her.

The voices clamored, and she slunk back behind the side of the house to avoid being seen.

"Come on, we gotta get out of here!"

"But what about the woman?"

"Don't care about the woman, we gotta get out of here now."

"But what about the bank?

"You talk too much, Boyd. We can rob another bank."

Arrosa peered around the corner of the house as the men climbed onto the two horses and rode away. When she could no longer see them, Arrosa ascended the steps, attempting to maintain her balance as pain and exhaustion surged through her entire body.

She tripped and collapsed on the porch. Arrosa lay on the filthy wood as the hot tears slid down her face. But no, she couldn't remain here. Couldn't recline on the deteriorating stoop while Malachi fought for his life. If only she weren't so feeble.

Arrosa pushed herself up onto her knees, then stretched an arm to the splintered railing. It shook as she attempted to pull herself to her feet. She lost her grip and fell into a prone position. *Lord, I can't do this without Your help.*

This was not the time to bemoan her frailty. With a boost of determination, she again extended a hand to the railing and shakily rose to her feet. If only she had her cane.

Arrosa bemoaned her lethargic pace as she entered the house. The sight of Malachi brought the emotion to the forefront as the sobs wracked her body. *Lord, please let him be all right. Please!* With effort, fearing she may not be able to stand again when the situation necessitated it, Arrosa slowly crouched by his side. "Malachi!" She grabbed his calloused hand and clutched it in her own. Crimson saturated his shirt.

He stirred, his eyes briefly opening. He raised a hand to her face and stroked her jaw. "I love you, Arrosa. I love you so much," he rasped.

"Malachi, please stay with me. I'm going to fetch help." There was so much blood. Would he survive by the time she fetched help?

Fetch help? What was she thinking? She could no more walk to town than fight the men who caused this.

"You have to-you have to-to get away. From Boyd and from-from Rantz," he stuttered.

"Please don't try to talk."

How would she manage to seek assistance? Thad's wagon was outside, but she'd never driven a wagon before. And how would she load him into it? She sent multiple prayers heavenward once again. "Malachi, we have to leave."

"Can't move. Hurts."

Adrenaline surged through her as she yanked the grimy curtain from the window and rolled him onto it. Then she tugged it, but the material didn't budge. Arrosa floundered, losing her balance before finally dragging him to the door, then the porch, and down the steps. But it didn't solve the problem of getting him into the back of the wagon.

"I can...I can stand."

"You can?"

He nodded, and somehow rose to his knees. She flung his uninjured arm over her shoulder. Her wrists ached from being bound, and pain shot up her leg. Malachi's full weight nearly toppled her, and she leaned him against the back of the wagon, thanking God there was no back panel. He fell face forward into the wagon, and she lifted each leg, attempting to hoist the rest of him into the back.

"Malachi?"

But he'd lost consciousness. "Malachi, please. Stay with me." His legs hung over the back as he was nearly bent in half, and she feared that if she hit a bump while driving, he'd fall out. She gently pushed him as far as she could into the wagon, but couldn't obtain the required leverage.

How would she be able to climb into the back of the wagon and get him fully onto the wagon bed? She gripped the side and forced her foot onto the wheel before heaving herself up and into the back.

"Arrosa?"

"Please don't try to talk." Mindful of his injury, she managed to roll him over before tugging on his uninjured arm and shoulder to drag the rest of him into the wagon.

"I-I need you to know about-about Boyd."

"What about him?"

"He-he is my pa. When I said my pa was dead, I meant—"

She smoothed his hair against his damp forehead. "It's all right, please don't try to talk."

"You need to know. He is my pa, but Barnabas adopted me. I-I took his last name." Malachi's voice was so soft that she nearly missed it.

Arrosa pressed a kiss to his forehead. "I will get us to town. Please just stay with me."

She crawled to the buckboard and pulled herself onto the seat. Tears streamed down her face. What if she couldn't determine how to properly drive a team of horses? She blinked and glanced up at the cloud-filled sky above. *Lord, please go before me.*

Then, ignoring her churning stomach, she fingered the reins. "Giddyup," she said. One of the horses did nothing while the other tossed its head.

"Giddyup," she said again.

"The-the brake."

"The brake?"

She released it, and the wagon lurched forward. Finally! But as the horses' hooves clop-clopped on the packed dirt, she realized something. They were going in the wrong direction. Somehow, she had to steer them the other way and into town. "Malachi?"

No answer.

"Malachi?"

She craned her neck. He was lying still. So very still.

*Lord, please, please keep him alive.*

Arrosa veered the wagon and beckoned the horses forward. How far was town? She was still ill-acquainted with Hollow Creek. Searching her memory from—had it been mere hours ago when the men had abducted her and brought her to the cabin? She struggled to recall the way that led to Hollow Creek. Or at least a house where someone could assist her. Desolate for as far as the eye could see, then finally, a grove of willow trees and a corral on the right-hand side.

But there were no houses in the immediate vicinity.

The horses proceeded at a decent clip. Arrosa shivered when a brisk breeze blew. What time was it? Would anyone notice she and Malachi hadn't yet returned to the Evanson Ranch?

The road was barely visible through some overgrown weeds, and Arrosa feared she'd gotten them lost. Should it take this much time to return to town? She clutched the reins so tightly, her fingers throbbed. Tension settled in her neck, and she attempted to adjust her posture on the buckboard. Arrosa again peered behind her at Malachi. Still no movement. They hit a bump, and the wagon jerked.

A mangy coyote prowled through the trees, and a vulture staked out a lookout in a tall, wispy tree, its guttural murmurings a sharp contrast to the meadowlark's buoyant melody sounding from the aspen to the left.

Time passed slowly. Too slowly. Finally, as she advanced around a curve, she thought she saw some buildings ahead. Hollow Creek?

She drove the wagon over a bridge. Yes, she was close. Two houses came into view, then the population sign. Tears stung her eyes. *Thank You, Lord!*

The second she entered town, Arrosa sounded the alarm. "Fetch Doc! Someone fetch Doc!"

Reverend Arkley looked her way before running down the boardwalk. Arrosa slowed the horses and parked just outside Doc's office.

Clayton ran alongside the wagon. "Arrosa? Is everything all right?"

"Please fetch Doc. It's Malachi. He's been shot."

Without another second of hesitation, Clayton flung open the door of Doc's office and ran into the physician as he was exiting. Together, they, with Reverend Arkley, unloaded Malachi and transported him to the doctor's office.

Mr. Dell from the mercantile arrived and assisted Arrosa from the wagon. Clayton met her just as she limped to the boardwalk. "Is he going to be all right?"

"Not sure yet. He's still breathing."

She wobbled, and Clayton steadied her. "Let me help you inside. I'll also need to know all of the details about who shot him."

Arrosa leaned against her brother-in-law, and he accompanied her into the physician's office, where she took a seat in one of the three chairs in the foyer. Trepidation gripped her in a stronghold. Would Malachi survive the wounds? Was she too late? Had she taken too long to drive the distance to town?

Mrs. Mangham, Doc's wife, stepped beside her. Compassion lit her eyes as she answered Arrosa's unspoken question. "Doc is doing all he can. We'll let you know as soon as there's a change."

"Thank you."

"In the meantime, how are you doing? Were you injured?"

Arrosa instinctively rubbed her wrists. The indentations from where the ropes had bound her tightly had left red marks on both her wrists and ankles. But other than that, she was fine. "No, not really."

"All right, well, please let me know if there's anything you need." Mrs. Mangham rushed back inside the room where Doc tended to Malachi.

Malachi. The man she had grown to love. The man with whom she'd hoped to have a future. Would the Lord see fit to bring him through this tragedy?

She wouldn't, couldn't allow herself to think otherwise.

Arrosa thanked the Lord for sustaining Malachi. For guiding her in driving the wagon to town. For protecting her when things could have gone so completely awry. She involuntarily shivered when she thought of what Rantz and Boyd could have done to her.

Clayton took a seat beside her. "I know it's been an eventful afternoon, but I need to know as much as you can tell me about who shot Malachi and what happened."

She described the events of the day, beginning with the kidnapping in the alleyway. "I saw them head north from the deserted cabin where they were holding me. They're planning to rob the bank tomorrow morning."

"I know who Rantz is, but I'm not sure who this Boyd fellow is. Do you have a first name for him?"

She shook her head. "That might be his first name. I don't know much about him..." She thought of how the man mentioned he was Malachi's father and how Malachi confirmed it. Surely someone so vile would have no relation to the man she loved. Arrosa described Boyd, then added, "I don't know anything else about him, but I would imagine he's probably a wanted criminal."

"I'll form a posse, and we will catch them."

"Please be careful. You've only just returned to town, and if..." Arrosa thought of her sister.

"You needn't worry, Arrosa. I have a wife and a baby on the way, and I'm not going to let anything happen." He left the building, and Arrosa offered a prayer for the Lord's protection over her brother-in-law.

Reverend Arkley settled into one of the chairs. "They're doing all they can to stop the bleeding and keep him from hemorrhaging. They'll need to remove the bullet." He paused and settled a hand on her arm. "Let's pray."

Arrosa closed her eyes and agreed in prayer with the words the reverend spoke. When they finished, she struggled to catch her breath. It was as though the air was too thick to breathe. "I just-I just want him to be all right."

"I know. Me too. Malachi is a fine man."

"What if he doesn't make it?"

"We have to keep praying that it's the Lord's will he does."

Her voice quivered. "I'm trying not to worry, but it's so hard."

"Yes, it is, but the Lord wants us to rely on Him. To lift those concerns and those moments of doubt and fear to Him."

"Malachi was trying to protect me. To keep them from coming after me."

Compassion and concern filled Reverend Arkley's green eyes. "That sounds like something our Malachi would do."

"When will we know how he fares?"

"Mrs. Mangham will give us a report as soon as she's able."

"He lost so much blood."

Reverend Arkley prayed again with her, then, with the promise to fetch Ma and McKenna and the plan to organize a prayer vigil, hastened out the door.

If she thought the drive to town in the wagon took forever, the wait for news on Malachi's condition was just shy of eternity.

The door squeaked, and in rushed Mother and McKenna. "Arrosa?" Mother took a seat on her right-hand side, and McKenna took the left. They both embraced her, and Arrosa let down her resolve and wept. The tightness in her shoulders eased, releasing the profound tension she'd carried throughout the day.

"Oh, Arrosa, we are so grateful you are all right."

"So, so grateful," added McKenna.

Mother patted her hair and planted a kiss on her forehead. "They're forming a prayer vigil outside. Let's go join them."

Mrs. Mangham appeared in the doorway between the foyer and the patient room. "Go ahead. I'll fetch you if anything changes."

"There has been no change?" Her voice broke, and McKenna squeezed her shoulder.

"Not yet, but these things take time. Malachi is a strong one, and we've been praying for the Lord to guide Doc's hands."

Mother and McKenna assisted Arrosa to her feet, and the three of them stepped out onto the boardwalk. "What happened to your cane?" asked Mother.

"I'm assuming it's been discarded somewhere, perhaps in the alleyway." She sandwiched herself between Mother and McKenna, leaning on them for support.

A crowd had gathered, and candles illuminated in the twilight. Reverend Arkley took his place on the boardwalk in front of the crowd. "Ladies and gentlemen, thank you for joining us for the prayer vigil for Malachi Callahan. He was shot earlier today and is fighting for his life. We are grateful he is in Doc's capable hands, and I hope you will join me in praying for him."

Everyone bowed their heads as the reverend prayed. "Dear Heavenly Father, we are grateful for this beautiful day you have given us. Thank you for protecting Arrosa and Malachi from those who were bent on harming them. Please guide Doc's hands and give him wisdom as he tends to Malachi. Please strengthen Malachi, enabling him to valiantly cling to life. Heal him completely. We thank You that Arrosa courageously drove him into town, even though she'd never driven a wagon before. We owe the fact that she was successful to You. We also pray that you would return Sheriff Beringer, his deputies, and his posse safely to Hollow Creek, and that the outlaws would be apprehended. We thank You for Your tender loving care that You bestow on us each and every day and for the millions of ways You care for and protect us. In Jesus' name, amen."

After the vigil, Mother and McKenna accompanied Arrosa back to Doc's office. Mrs. Arkley delivered some food from Olga's Café, but Arrosa lacked an appetite.

An hour later, Clayton and the rest of the lawmen and posse returned, Mr. Evanson included. McKenna sprang from her chair and embraced her husband.

One prayer answered. Arrosa breathed a prayer of gratitude.

Clayton wrapped an arm around his wife. "God protected us. These were some dangerous men." He took a step toward Arrosa. "You should know that both Rantz and Boyd lost their lives in a shootout. They'll never harm anyone ever again."

Arrosa released a stifled breath. "That is a relief."

"It is. Boyd Goshorn was wanted in several states for a lengthy list of crimes, including murder. Rantz has been suspected of participating in some nefarious activities prior to your abduction." Worry knotted his brow. "Have we heard anything more about Malachi?"

"Not yet."

Clayton nodded. "God made him strong. I'll keep praying for healing."

"Thank you."

McKenna walked her husband to the door before returning to her seat beside Arrosa. Weariness overcame Arrosa, but there was no way she could even entertain the thought of closing her eyes and getting some rest. Not when Malachi's life hung in the balance.

Finally, Mrs. Mangham emerged from Doc's office. "He's going to make it."

The crowd that had remained gathered on the boardwalk for the vigil cheered, and with the help of Mother and McKenna, Arrosa stumbled into the office and lowered herself into the chair beside Malachi's bed.

"He's not awake yet, but you're welcome to stay with him for as long as you'd like," said Doc.

"Mother and I will be just outside the room if you need us."

Arrosa nodded as her family returned to their seats. She reached over and rested a hand on Malachi's arm. His face was so bruised, and his arm, torso, and head were bandaged. She tugged the quilt to his chin. Was he cold?

"Malachi," she whispered, knowing he may not be able to hear her, but hoping that if he could, her voice would comfort him.

He didn't respond, but she saw the gentle rising and falling of his chest. "I was so worried about you, Malachi. Praise God, you're going to be all right."

She gently touched the bruising on his face. So much pain and horror at the hands of his own father. A sob choked in her throat. She could never understand how someone could be so vicious and so hateful to their own child. Arrosa lifted her eyes heavenward. "It is only by Your grace, Lord, that Malachi is the man he is today, despite his rearing. I don't know the details, Jesus, but You do, and I humbly thank You for keeping Malachi safe and for making him a man who is so vastly different from his father." She bent over and rested her head on Malachi's chest. "I love you, Malachi Callahan."

When he awoke, he wasn't sure if he'd been dreaming. Why else would he be in a bed with pain radiating through his entire body? He opened one eye first, then the other to see...Arrosa?

He blinked, willing his vision to cooperate. Arrosa was sitting in the chair beside his bed, head lolled to one side, sleeping. He could barely hear her soft snores above voices somewhere else in the building. Why did every part of him hurt? What had happened?

And then he remembered how Boyd and Rantz kidnapped Arrosa and forced Malachi to assist them with a bank robbery. He recalled worrying about the harm they would inflict on Arrosa. It hurt to turn his head, but he could see her clearly if he slightly tipped his head to the right. She'd somehow escaped them. And somehow he'd ended up here. In a bed in Doc's office.

He kept his gaze on her. She was so beautiful sleeping. His memory was fuzzy, but bit by bit, flashbacks of earlier events infiltrated his mind. Emotion welled within him, and while his thoughts were jumbled, he knew without a doubt that because of the Lord's mercy, the woman he loved had survived.

# EPILOGUE
## EARLY OCTOBER, 1913

ARROSA PLACED HER HAND through Father's elbow as they walked up the aisle at the church, her heart thrumming wildly in her chest.

In just a few short minutes, she would be Malachi's wife, and they would start a new life together.

He stood at the front of the church looking utterly handsome in his suit, with his hair combed and his face clean-shaven. The affection glowed in his blue eyes.

Father patted her hand and whispered, "I love you, Arrosa," before leaving to sit in the front pew with Mother, McKenna, and Clayton.

The entire town was in attendance, and Adelia and Mamie waved at her from their places in the second pew beside Ephraim. Emilie held hers and Mr. Evanson's newest addition—a tiny baby girl. Vera's smile covered her entire face, and Morris wasn't even looking toward the front of the church, but at Vera. Perhaps he was remembering the day when he'd exchanged vows with his own bride.

While there were times that she still struggled with weakness in her legs and painful joints—and particularly in her knee—Arrosa was determined to stand at the altar with her soon-to-be husband without the help of her cane. She tottered slightly, but quickly righted herself as Reverend Arkley spoke the words that would unite her and Malachi in matrimony and finished it with, "I now pronounce you man and wife. You may kiss your bride."

Malachi took a step toward her, embraced her in his strong arms, and she raised her chin to meet the kiss that stole her breath. He took a step back and caressed her cheek before reaching for her hand. They hurried, well, as best as Arrosa could, down the aisle as cheers erupted from family and friends.

Outside, he assisted her into the wagon, which was decorated with strings attached to cans on the back. He settled into his seat, and they started toward their new home. "I considered learning how to drive the automobile for our special occasion."

"Oh?"

"Figured I'd ask Thad about borrowing the Model T sometime and we'd make an adventure out of it."

She laughed. "I was once given the opportunity to drive Father's automobile in Missoula, not that anyone but McKenna, myself, and our former chauffeur knew about such an exploit."

"How far did you go?"

"To the end of the driveway before Father arrived. It was one of those few things McKenna and I kept from our parents. Even if you never drive the automobile, I'll be content in the buggy or the wagon. And someday, I'd like to learn how to ride a horse, although such a thought does give me some serious trepidation. I'm not sure I could achieve such a feat."

"You could if I helped you." His smile caused her heart to skitter. "And we have our whole lives ahead of us for all of those goals."

"And walking down the path."

"And walking down the path," he confirmed.

They passed a small white house on the edge of town with a porch and green shutters. "It will be delightful for Mother and

Father to own their own home again," she mused as they passed by.

"It's within walking distance from the hotel as well," added Malachi.

"Indeed." It would still be some time before her parents raised the funds for the down payment and secured the loan from the bank, but it was just another dream about to come true.

"How is your pa taking to his new job at the hotel?"

"He is perfect for the position, and a huge thanks to Clayton for vouching for him."

And in just a few months, Arrosa would be an aunt. She couldn't wait.

The drive to their new home was littered with canopies of brilliant red, yellow, and orange leaves on the trees, revealing a perfect autumn day. Malachi drove the buggy to the front of his—their—new home on the ranch, formerly Mr. Evanson's home before he married Emilie. Although it was far too large for just two people. Someday, if it was the Lord's will, several children would run about, playing in the front yard, assisting Arrosa with the garden she planned to have, or assisting their father on the Evanson Ranch.

And chickens. Yes, they would need chickens too, and Malachi mentioned he'd like to have a dog.

Malachi set the brake and hastened to Arrosa's side of the buggy. Lifting her in his arms, he brushed a gentle kiss on her forehead before opening the door with one hand and entering their new home. He set her on the floor, and she fell into his arms. His kiss began as gently as an autumn breeze before passionately sealing the vows they'd just made moments before. Her stomach fluttered as she returned his kiss.

Oh, how she loved this man!

It wasn't long ago that Arrosa wondered if it was in the Lord's plan that she would someday marry. Now more than ever, she knew that everything happened in His perfect timing.

# A Promise to Keep

## Preview

SHE NEVER SHOULD HAVE asked the question.

Selah's husband narrowed his dark eyes and plunked the crate of provisions on the table. "Don't matter none where the money came from, only that we have what we need."

It mattered to her, but she'd not insinuate as much. Selah unloaded the items and put them on the shelves while Dale took a seat in one of the chairs at the table.

"Gonna be gone tomorrow, but I should be back the day after."

At least Dale had the courtesy to let her know when he left town. To do what, she had no idea. She wanted to ask, but before she could, her husband offered an explanation. "I'm gonna be starting to work on the new railroad spur."

Dale flitted from job opportunity to job opportunity, hence the reason they moved to Briggman's Gap several months ago. The man was adept at finding employment but particular on what he spent his hard-earned wages on.

Selah shuffled toward the shelf and added the flour, sugar, two cans of coffee, three cans of pickles, and a can of baking powder to the robust supply of other dry goods. Being married to Dale offered a shortage of love, affection, and compassion, but never of food. The man, although wiry thin, loved to eat.

"Make some polka gingerbread after supper." More of a demand than a request, and without awaiting an answer, Dale stalked outside to the barn where he spent the majority of his time. Not milking the cow, for that was her job. Not collecting eggs, for that chore beckoned her each morning. And not mucking the stalls. That was something she tended to every Saturday. Selah wasn't quite sure what Dale did in the barn, but she dared not ask. While the man had never laid a hand on her, he wouldn't take kindly to any inquiries regarding how he spent his days.

Selah sat for a moment and placed her hand on her swollen belly. Exhaustion overwhelmed her along with the almost-always-present nausea. The Lord had blessed her with a new little life growing inside of her. Selah only wished she could have chosen a better father for the child.

But things were what they were. Dale provided a home for her—a marriage of convenience—and that was what she'd needed when suddenly left homeless.

If you want to be among the first to hear about Penny's
latest book projects, sign up for her newsletter
at www.pennyzeller.com. You will receive book and
writing updates, encouragement, notification of current
giveaways, occasional freebies, and special offers.

If you enjoyed this glimpse into the lives of Arrosa and Malachi, please consider leaving a review on your social media, Amazon, Goodreads, Barnes and Noble, or BookBub. Reviews are critical to authors, and those stars you give us are such an encouragement.

# Author's Note

Dear Reader,

Thank you for taking a trip to Hollow Creek with me. For some of you, this may be your first trip, while for others, it's a return visit, having previously enjoyed *Love in Disguise* and *Love in Store.*

I knew from the second I created Arrosa in *Love in Store* that she needed her own touching and heartwarming story. Malachi's character has been percolating around in my mind since *Love in Disguise*, and I was thrilled to give him his own story as well.

Writing historicals is always an adventure. Pretty soon, we authors begin speaking like the words we pen. For instance, I've been using some reckons, partakes, and daresays lately. Speaking of words, there are some that surprised me as having been used for centuries. Below are some of the most profound ones that I had no clue until recently, were used even in "olden days" vernacular.

Riffraff – 15$^{th}$ century

Stickler – 1799

Daddy – 1523

Stellar – 1656

Leadership – 1765

Proximity – 15$^{th}$ century

Jiffy – 1779

Relocate – 1829

Snobbery – 1843

Chaotic – 1688

Bungle – 1530

Head start – 1859

Which one(s) surprised you the most? For me, it was head start, jiffy, and stellar.

Clothing choices for historical characters are always interesting as well. Did you know that jeans made their first appearance in the 1870s? As for the women of that era, the Edwardian fashions were so elegant and feminine. As one who personally loves cute clothes, I would have loved to wear some of the early 1900s styles.

Graces and hoop and stick were both real games played in that era, with Graces being particularly popular with girls. The game of restaurant came from my own childhood when my siblings, cousins, and I would play as though we had our own restaurant and serve meals, i.e., crackers and snacks, from the porch of the playhouse my dad had won for us in a contest.

Dance cards were a real thing, and recently, my oldest daughter and I visited a museum and were able to see the cards from the woman who once resided in the turn-of-the-century home. Silver holders were also real.

The Lightning Express wagon was based on the real toy made by Sheffield Manufacturing and sold for 75 cents to $2.

As always, we authors do take fictional liberties in our books. I did so with some of the wheelchair aspects.

There is a possibility of a fourth book in the series starring Ophie as the main character. You'll likely remember her from *Love in Store.* As I have for over a decade now, I've lifted every aspect of my writing and books, including the continuation of this series, up to the Lord in prayer. I'm excited to see where He leads me. I do know that while I thoroughly enjoy writing suspense and rom-coms, I'll never be able to stray from historical for too long. There's just something sweet and wholesome about the days of yesteryear. Not perfect by any means, as we know some suffered mightily in the late 1800s-early 1900s, but it was a different time for sure.

Thank you, as always, for being a loyal reader. Until next time, happy reading!

Blessings,

Penny

# Acknowledgments

The writing of this book would not be possible without the help of so many.

Thank you, as always, to my family. A huge thank you to my oldest daughter for assisting me with acting out the suspenseful scenes. I'm not sure what I would do without your help in securing legitimate escape routes for my characters.

Thank you to Josh Wageman, PhD, DPT, MPAS, who helped me with diagnosing Arrosa's rheumatic fever and assisting with the symptoms, care, and rehabilitation both in *Love in Store* and in *Love in Time*.

Thank you to my beta readers for being the first ones to read my books and offer invaluable suggestions.

Thank you to my Penny's Peeps, who are amazing in helping me spread the word about my books. You are always awesome, but especially this year when you've assisted me with several books in a short span of time.

To my readers. May God bless and guide you as you grow in your walk with Him.

And, most importantly, thank you to my Lord and Savior, Jesus Christ. It is my deepest desire to glorify You with my writing and help bring others to a knowledge of Your saving grace.

# About the Author

Penny Zeller is known for her heartfelt stories of faith-filled happily ever afters and her passion to impact lives for Christ through fiction. Her books feature tender romance, steady doses of humor, and memorable characters that stay with you long after the last page.

While she has had a love for writing since childhood, Penny began her adult writing career penning articles for national and regional publications on a wide variety of topics. Today Penny is a multi-published author of over three dozen books and is also a fitness instructor, loves the outdoors, and is a flower gardening addict. In her spare time, she enjoys camping, hiking, kayaking, biking, birdwatching, reading, running, and playing volleyball.

Penny resides with her husband and two daughters in small-town America and loves to connect with her readers at her website at www.pennyzeller.com, her blog, www.pennyzeller.wordpress.com, and her Facebook page at www.facebook.com/pennyzellerbooks where she posts faith, funnies, writing updates, and encouragement. All of her socials can be found at https://linktr.ee/pennyzeller.

# HOLLOW CREEK

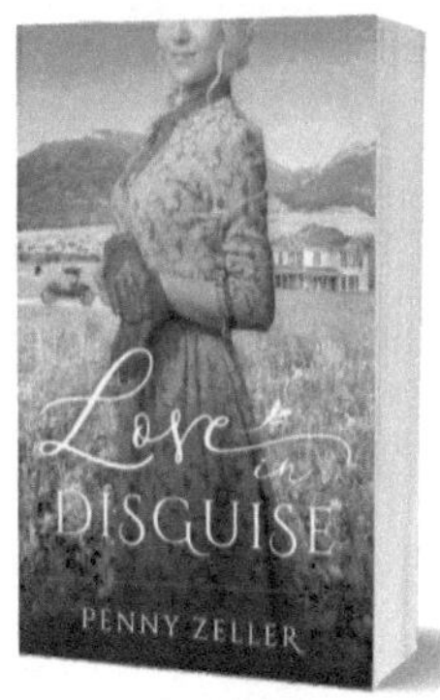

# WYOMING SUNRISE

# HORIZON SERIES

255

# HILLTOP SERIES

# CHRISTIAN ROMANTIC SUSPENSE

## MOUNTAIN JUSTICE SERIES

# small town shenanigans

# CONTEMPORARY ROMANCES

STANDALONE

CHOKECHERRY HEIGHTS SERIES